ROBERT KARJEL

# MY NAME IS N

Translated from the Swedish by
NANCY PICK & ROBERT KARJEL

HarperCollins*Publishers*

HarperCollins*Publishers*
1 London Bridge Street
London SE1 9GF

www.harpercollins.co.uk

Published by HarperCollins*Publishers* 2015
1

Originally published in 2010 by Wahlström & Widstrand, Sweden, as *De redan döda*

A catalogue record for this book
is available from the British Library

ISBN: 978-0-00-758601-1

Text design by William Ruoto

Printed and bound in Great Britain by
Clays Ltd, St Ives plc

MIX
Paper from
responsible sources
FSC
www.fsc.org
FSC™ C007454

FSC™ is a non-profit international organisation established to promote
the responsible management of the world's forests. Products carrying the
FSC label are independently certified to assure consumers that they come
from forests that are managed to meet the social, economic and
ecological needs of present and future generations,
and other controlled sources.

Find out more about HarperCollins and the environment at
**www.harpercollins.co.uk/green**

To the memory of Hugh Swaney, homicide detective.

# CHAPTER 1

New York, May 17, 2008

THE SWEDE'S BREATHING SLOWED. HE could actually analyze it, how he grew calm. How the adrenaline drained away
when he squatted down and rinsed his hands in the water. The
gravel crunched under the soles of his shoes. Most of the blood
was on his hands, as if he'd dipped them in it. Blood had splashed
his jacket, his face. He rinsed and scrubbed, took his time. But he
had no mirror. He was maybe a half mile north of the Williamsburg Bridge, with the East River and Manhattan's whole skyline
splayed before him. It was a still-life of light and dark, without visible movement. He heard no sirens, only the murmur of Brooklyn
traffic and nightlife. He pressed his lips together one last time to
avoid getting the river's filth and oil in his mouth. Then he stood,
snorted, and shook the water from his hands. He could still feel the
man struggling beneath him like an eel being squeezed to death.
He looked at his hands, spread his fingers apart, turned them over.
Hands that had done more than defend.

Clean enough.

He pulled a plastic bag of clothes from under some bushes in the
vacant lot. Removed the ones he was wearing and threw them in a

pile, even his shoes. He didn't feel the night chill. Between the dark buildings, he could see the Brooklyn clock tower. He switched old clothes for new, tied up the bag of bloody laundry, and hacked holes in the plastic with an awl from his pocket.

With one clean throw the tool sailed far out into the river, followed by the sack. The current bubbled and gurgled as the sack slowly sank. He stood rooted to the ground, legs apart with his hands in his pockets, a solitary silhouette on a spur of land near the electrical plant.

Only then did the shaking come, his whole body racked with the trembling of exhaustion, of adrenaline ebbing away. It was the aftermath. The man had thrashed with all his strength. But the Swede had overpowered him, nailed the bastard's face in an iron grip.

In the Wyckoff Street emergency room a man lay screaming. The truck driver, a petty thief released on bail, had promised to testify. Except that he'd gotten himself involved in something bigger than he could handle. Even among the nurses who thought they'd seen it all, there were some who had to look away. He would survive, but with empty eye sockets. He would never be able to pick out anyone in a lineup, never recognize anyone again, never talk about who he'd seen where, or when.

The Swede by the river could breathe.

# CHAPTER 2

*Three weeks earlier*

US Federal Building, 26 Federal Plaza, New York City

S HE FLIPPED THE COIN THROUGH her fingers, moving it
back and forth while absentmindedly sorting papers with
her other hand. She was expecting a call, passing the time
with files, newspapers, and photographs. *Kansas City Star*: "Topeka Murderers to Be Executed Next Month," a front-page story.
She picked up a photo of a haggard, overweight man in an orange prison jumpsuit, set it aside. The coin wavered between her
thumb and index finger, then started moving again. Next to the
press clippings lay a stack of witness statements labeled "Murder with robbery, Central Park. Unsolved." And next to those,
a black-and-white photocopied picture of a woman who'd been
dead for several years. A few art books, and a receipt from a bar
in Toronto.

The phone rang.

As if the coin had been waiting for the signal, it ran swiftly over
to her little finger and back. She caught it in her hand. Answered,
then hummed in response while someone else talked.

3

"So it's settled then," she said after a while, and leaned back with the picture of a stone sculpture in her hand.

"What name did you get?" She nodded. White marble. The sculpture in the picture was human, neither woman nor man. An outstretched bare body lustfully asking for more.

"Grip," she repeated. "Ernst Grip. Good. No, that's not necessary. I'll send people to meet him at the airport."

## CHAPTER 3

### Flight SK901 from Arlanda, Stockholm

A S THE AIRPLANE CLIMBED, ERNST Grip gazed blankly at the dirty gray landscape out his window. A copy of *Expressen*, the Stockholm evening tabloid, lay on his lap; he stuffed it into the seat pocket in front of him. He tried to get comfortable—never enough room for his knees in the misery of economy class—and looked forward to his first drink and snacks. Needing something for his hands to fiddle with.

Eight hours to New York.

The American seated beside him grilled the flight attendant about the alcohol selection.

Grip said, "Whisky, any kind," and got two small bottles without further comment. They slid down with the sad bag of nuts.

Flat chicken with bland red wine—even though he'd left at the last minute, someone had still managed to find him an economy-class ticket. He had the petty Swedish bureaucrats to thank for it. On the electronic map across the cabin, an airplane symbol crept along the coast of Norway. Then came coffee, and, rare for him, a cognac. Felt the liquor spread comfortably. He switched back and forth between movies on the seatback's video screen. Fell asleep.

Grip was dark, with the easy, familiar sort of face you think you've seen before. Looked older in a suit, younger out of one. The passport he carried said thirty-seven. If pressed, he could have stretched ten years in either direction. Agreeably broad-shouldered, he got good treatment from flight attendants, both female and male, who'd stop their carts to exchange a few extra words.

The day before, the Boss had called to tell Grip he'd be going to New York. Now and then, his old chief at the security police still summoned him in. Tugged on the old leash—and his new boss would get a phone call: "Grip will be away." Nothing he needed to worry about himself. His role was simply to execute: when Grip entered the room, he was handed a plane ticket and a credit card.

"Just keep a summary of your expenses" was the Boss's only admonition. This was the shorthand of a hardened security officer, no mere bureaucrat but a shrewd old operator with his own accounts. Perfect, for those who preferred not to know the details.

"And . . . ," said Grip, wondering about more than covering his eating and sleeping.

The Boss made a few notes on his pad. "The Foreign Ministry wants you to go see the Americans."

"About?"

"The ministry doesn't know. The Americans want to ask you some questions."

"You mean all three hundred million of them?"

The Boss snorted. "No, just the Justice Department. Their people will meet you in Newark."

"And they want me in particular."

"I guess you're one of the 'knowns' in the ministry offices. You were there when we turned over the Egyptians to the CIA at Bromma Airport. The Foreign Ministry's mess, we did the job—

they remember—what do I know? They asked for you, and I said yes."

"What a fucking setup."

"Pack a comfortable suit." The Boss smiled with sagging cheeks. "Answer a few questions, eat a few decent meals, come back home."

"You have no idea what this is about?"

The Boss tore off a slip of paper from his notepad and extended it between two fingers.

Grip read it out loud. "Topeka."

"The Americans want to know what we know about Topeka. City in the middle of nowhere."

"No instructions from the Foreign Ministry?"

" 'Send Grip over' is all they said. They just want this taken care of, whatever it is."

"So I'm the Foreign Ministry's errand boy."

"But I'm the only one you talk to." The shrewd silverback still ruled from his hilltop in the jungle.

"A week at most?" Grip prodded.

"Whatever it takes."

"Visa?"

"Don't bother. Enter as a tourist."


Grip woke up when his neighbor started fumbling for something down by his feet. He apologized, kept searching. Impossible for Grip to fall back to sleep. Then he squeezed salve from a tube and smeared it on his nostrils.

"Vaseline," said the American, "for dry air. Want some?" Grip shook his head. The man beside him kept talking. He'd been visiting his newlywed daughter, who'd met a Swede on vacation. Now they were living in Sundbyberg, a district within Stockholm. The man laughed as he said it—"Soond-bee-berg"—and launched into a full-blown description of the park next door. As if it were the most exotic place on earth, a place Grip could never imagine. Sure, he liked the birch trees, but he worried about the world his grandchildren would grow up in.

"You know," he said, "given the way the situation looks now." He was still upset that he'd had to surrender a full can of shaving cream and his nail scissors at the airport. "But you have to put up with it, don't you?"

The man lived in lower Manhattan. He had stood on his balcony that morning and watched the Twin Towers collapse. He'd seen the clouds of dust and all the hollow-eyed people come running out.

"Then this," he said, slapping the front page of the *New York Times*. It was something about Iraq, a picture of an incinerated car and people running. "It's everywhere, it's terrible." He looked at Grip uncertainly, the thin ice Americans knew they were on, the please-don't-hate-me-personally air they wore when abroad. "So many dead, I don't know. It's complicated."

"Did you vote for Bush?"

"Me?" A feeble shake of the head. "Not the second time."

The flight attendant went by, holding a catalog and chanting a monotonous "Duty-free . . . duty-free."

"My neighbor lost his grandson," the man said as she passed. "In Iraq. Just an ordinary driver in the army. Awful."

Grip said nothing.

"Well, everyone does his part," the man continued. "My old man fought against the Germans in the Ardennes, the Battle of the Bulge. 'Fucking cold,' that was the only thing he ever said about the war—'fucking cold.'" The man looked straight ahead and laughed in the same expressionless way as when he'd said "Sundbyberg."

He fell silent. Perhaps a minute passed.

"But that was a different kind of war," he said.

A re you an American citizen?" asked the flight attendant.

Grip shook his head. Soon he'd written his passport number so many times in the forms she handed him that he knew it by heart. Checked no in all the boxes, swore that he was not entering the United States to engage in prostitution or terrorism and had not engaged in exterminating Jews during World War II. Last, he checked himself off as a tourist and gave a Hilton near Central Park as his address. He'd found the hotel in an ad in the airline magazine.

Sorting through his wallet, he found the slip of paper the Boss had given him.

"Topeka," he said to his neighbor. "What state is that in?"

"Kansas," the man answered. "Are you going there?"

"No." He had already crumpled up the paper and put it in the seatback pocket.

"So where are you going then?"

"New York, just for a few days."

"Is this your first time?"

Grip shrugged.

"You're going to love it."

E rnst Grip waited for the aisle to clear, then put his unread *Expressen* in his shoulder bag and exited the airplane. What stopped him next was the labyrinthine line in front of immigration. Passengers from distant flights waited red-eyed, their half-asleep children sitting on luggage or right on the floor. A few women patrolled the winding queues, yelling out the forms all foreigners were supposed to have in hand. They wore simple uniforms, a spike of keys in one hand, a big communication radio in the other hand. Swaying gait, tough expression.

Grip had observed them over the years. Doing a job that used to be one step up from flipping burgers at McDonald's. Since the fall of the towers, they acted as if they had the whole Marine Corps at their backs. Raised their voices as soon as someone hesitated, or—God forbid—talked back. At the front of the line, near a passport stamp booth, he heard a commotion in several languages. Grip couldn't see, but thought someone was being led away.

Finally he was waved up to a booth. Two men sat behind the chest-high counter in bleached shirts and crew cuts. One glanced at Grip's form and flipped through his passport. He stopped, with an impassive expression, on a page.

"What were you doing in Egypt last year?" he asked.

The other one studied Grip. The interrogation gaze.

"Diving in the Red Sea," Grip answered. "Sharm el-Sheikh."

The officer leafed further, found another stamp of interest. "And South Africa?"

"A week of winter sun, down in Cape." That too a lie. He was not unaccustomed.

And then new stamps on a page and Mr. Grip, dark-haired but blue-eyed, just thirty-seven, was wished a nice day. He took his passport and said thank you.


At Newark arrivals, two men in suits held a small sign, looking more bored than hopeful. ERNEST GRIP, it said, in plain red letters. Even in a crowd of sign holders, the men seemed strangely out of place, as if they were wondering themselves what they were doing there.

"*Ernst* Grip," Grip corrected.

"Welcome," said the man with the sign. He didn't get the hint, seemed simply relieved. The other took charge of Grip's bag.

Two sunburned crew cuts—typical Feds. They offered him coffee in the car; otherwise they didn't say much. Grip had no reason to talk to them either as they rolled over the whining concrete expressway and dove into an orange-lit tunnel, surfacing in the middle of Manhattan.

"Is this the hotel?" Grip asked when they stopped in an underground garage.

"No, the office."

"I need to get something out of my suitcase."

The driver opened the trunk for him. Grip pulled out his suit jacket, buttoned his shirt at the top, and made a knot in the tie stashed in a side pocket.

"Got a gun on you?" asked the driver.

"A gun?" said Grip. "You just picked me up at the airport."

The man shrugged his shoulders.

They took an escalator up to a marble grotto; office palms stood in obligatory islands. The entryway echoed with their steps as they walked through arches of metal detectors. Grip's escorts showed their IDs, uncovered their weapons, and pointed to a note on a chart, which permitted Grip to enter.

On the twenty-third floor, they wound past cell blocks of conference rooms occupied by men with rolled-up shirtsleeves and baggy trousers, and signs with odd prohibitions. Plastic takeout boxes, greasy cartons, half-filled bottles—there seemed to be constant eating going on. People said hello while drinking or wiping their fingers on a handful of napkins. One of the men offered Grip coffee. He declined.

They led him through a glass door past a secretary, who looked up and nodded, and into a large office.

"Here. She'll be with you in a moment," whispered one of the men behind him, and then they disappeared.

Grip stood alone. She sat behind a desk, facing the window, talking on the phone—or rather listening. She was aware of his presence but hadn't given him a glance. The room was very quiet. Grip saw her in profile and evaluated the fact that she was a woman. Given the warren of little offices he'd seen on the way, the presence of a secretary outside, and the thick wall-to-wall carpeting indicated that he was with a boss. It was harder to determine her level. On his way in, he'd seen enough caps with FBI and DEA to understand the landscape. She looked about his age, something Asian about her features—her eyes, the delicate tone of her skin. She had smooth dark hair. No portraits, diplomas, or self-glorifying photographs on the walls. Only a huge tropical landscape, a reproduction, hanging behind her. A watercolor with sea-bleached wooden bungalows, a few figures lounging in shadows.

She said something inaudible, put down the receiver, and turned around. Hands on her armrests, she looked at him with interest, raised her eyebrows slightly, and said, "The Swede."

"Yes, the Swede," Grip answered. "Or Ernst Grip—as perhaps it says somewhere."

She glanced down at her desk. "Ernst, of course," she said, standing up to greet him. "From the Foreign Ministry?"

"From the security police."

"I see." She paused. And then, delicately: "Have you ever witnessed an execution?" Without waiting for a reply, she continued, "My name is Shauna, by the way. Shauna Friedman."

# CHAPTER 4

*Thailand, Boxing Day, 2004*

Fish swimming past a car, that was his first memory. He was standing in water up to his waist before the Wave began to recede. Fish, their brilliant colors, that was the first thing he remembered.

N. wasn't sure where he was going. He walked around slowly after the sea finally withdrew. He didn't see many other people; the few he encountered were wandering as aimlessly as himself. At one point, he heard screams. It could have been a human being, or an animal in trouble.

Then came the itching. Not that it was overwhelming in any way, but it was there, vaguely annoying. He waved his hands over his arms and legs, shooing away the flies that were drawn to his wounds. His mouth was dry, but he couldn't bring himself to drink from any of the hundreds of water bottles that had spilled from their crates, in the mess outside a shop.

Some villagers found N. and pulled him up onto a flatbed truck that took him away from the sea. Packed in close to other people, he sensed their fear. In the back of the truck, people talked too fast, calming down only after the tractor pulling them began to struggle into the hills beyond the village. Up there by the trees, lots of people had gathered. Someone gave him water; he drank and returned the bottle empty. A man, seeing his bloody arms and knees, led him to a paved spot where the wounded were being treated. Most were lying on the ground. A nurse came up to him. She looked concerned, but couldn't do much beyond wash out the deepest wounds with water. She apologized several times for not having brought more supplies from the infirmary in the village. Then N. sat down. Stayed put. Someone tried to make small talk, but he didn't answer. Another held up a pot of rice—he waved it away.

In the evening they heard the sound of a helicopter. People got excited and started shouting, but the noise faded. An evening breeze stirred the trees. The rumors died away.

Night fell among the groves on the mountain. N. moved from the pavement onto the bare ground, which felt less cold. He curled up but soon froze anyway, and the cuts on his knees began to ache. It was impossible to find a comfortable position, and in the end he sat leaning against a tree. There, he managed to nod off a few times, but in half-sleep he began to think of the fish again, their bright colors. Other images rose up as well. He saw the little girls, their faces, and a woman. Heard their voices. A woman and two children. He wasn't at all sure that they were his, but it had been morning and they had sat and eaten something. They had eaten together. . . . Then there was once again only the memory of the fish.

Someone crouched down next to N., he felt an arm hold him. He did not hear the sounds of his own moaning. People near him thought he was crying.

The sun went up and then down again. Yet another night spent on the mountain. The next morning he was seized with such thirst that he grabbed and emptied the bottle of water that stood near the little boy who slept next to him. On the third day, a group of soldiers in a jeep said that everyone could return to the village, the danger was past. N.'s wounds were swollen and festering, and the nurse washed them one last time and said that he must get to a hospital. Said he had a fever, he needed help. And so he joined the thin line of people returning down from the mountain.

At first he had trouble orienting himself in the village because of all the destruction and debris. The sun was torture. But then he recognized the car he'd been standing beside when he saw the fish, and the mess of water bottles in the street outside the shop. He opened one and drank. In the distance he saw the gable of a house he thought he recognized. Then he approached and wasn't sure. White walls stood without a roof, most of the building had collapsed. All signs of the small hotel were gone. There was no trace of the inner courtyard he remembered, only rubble: planks, piles of plaster, palm leaves. Pool chairs lay like wrecked boats on top of the mess. They had steel frames, with slats made of thick plastic strips in black and white. N. remembered how they always stuck to your skin, he remembered that not too long ago he had been sitting right there. Suddenly his heart began to pound and he felt that something terrible was at stake. He grabbed at whatever he could reach and threw the broken planks to the side. But the power flowed out of him almost immediately, and he grew clumsy when he tried to push himself farther. Unsteady on his legs, and seeing all the sharp pieces around him, he sat down. The sun burned intensely, his head throbbed. It wouldn't get better. He looked around, stood up with a moan, and tried again.

What he first thought was a branch turned out to be a blue arm sticking out of the mess. A hunk of fallen wall covered the body, but he saw a ruined face: too swollen to reveal anything. Gently, he covered it with a piece of foam. Then he looked again, this time with new eyes, and realized that he was surrounded by sticking-out limbs and bulging, half-naked bodies. He sank down exhausted and overcome, crying in despair.

N. wasn't quite clear on how he got there, but at the hospital, he was assigned to a bed. By that time the fever had overtaken him, and for a few days he mostly slept. The staff was very friendly, but they called him by a name he did not recognize and asked him about things he couldn't remember. Wounds were washed, scraped out, and sutured. It took a week before the fever went down.

One morning when N. returned from the bathroom, he discovered a cloth bag hanging at the foot of his bed. Green, with a worn-out shoulder strap, the kind tourists get from an army surplus store. He took it off the bed and looked around. The three people who shared the small room took no notice—apparently the bag did not belong to any of them. He opened the zipper and examined the interior. Sure enough, he found a few guidebooks, a dive log, and various travel receipts. In an inside pocket he found a fat envelope of dollars, and in an outside pocket he found a passport.

That must have been where the nurses got the name. There was some kind of mix-up, right? Could . . . He didn't know. Looking at the passport picture, N. paused at finding familiar features: the same irregular bangs he saw in the mirror, the same crease between forehead and nose. Most of all, the same gaze. He turned the bag over and found a jagged arc of salt stain. He couldn't tell if it had been left there by the sea, or by a sweaty back. He flipped through the passport stamps and returned to the picture. He could only sit there on the bed.

During the rounds, they called that name again.

"Yes," said N.

"The fever has broken," said a short doctor with beads of sweat on his forehead, "and the wounds seemed to heal fine." He cast an anxious glance toward the corridor.

"I understand," said N.

The doctor excused himself: "We need the bed. People keep pouring in."

"Of course." He looked down at his short hospital gown.

"We had to throw out your clothes," said the nurse. "Take this." She held out a plastic bag. N. saw a pair of faded but clean jeans, a short-sleeved shirt, and a pair of sandals.

"You'll have to look for someone who can remove the stitches," the doctor said, "in about a week or so. That shouldn't be a problem. "

"No."

"Where will you go now? "

"I need to look for someone."

The doctor nodded. Left the room to continue his rounds.

N. got dressed, slung the bag over his shoulder, and left.


The buses had begun to run again. The roads were clogged with trucks, bulldozers, and groups of men in every imaginable uniform. It took time, but he could still make it back to the village.

By the sea, all the old signs of devastation were still there, along with some new ones. The village was plastered with bad photocopies of missing people, taped up wherever there was space. Utility poles fluttered with white paper as high as a man could reach. In another world, they'd be for a political race with hundreds of candidates. Near a temple on the outskirts of the village, people wore thick gloves and masks over their noses and mouths. In other spots the authorities had set up small offices—often just a large tent— where people cried or barked senselessly at one another. N. was constantly harassed by people wanting to know if he had seen this one or that one. Disgusted, he withdrew.

He felt a strange sense of distance. The village he saw was not his, never had been. Only a few weeks before, he hadn't known a thing about it. He'd come there as a visitor—a tourist's random choice. He could have ended up on any beach, on any day, in any village, anywhere. It was just a roll of the dice.

He kept going. There was a place he had to get to. Then he saw that they'd cleaned up the shop where all the bottles had been scattered on the street. And N. remembered the fish again. And then the breakfast. That they had eaten fruit, and that the little girls had worn new bathing suits and squinted at the sun. So they were, they were his children. And that woman, who must have been his wife, she had smeared their arms with sunscreen while they ate. The silent memory, how they let her do it but whined between mouthfuls.

Then they stopped, the pictures.

Again, N. found the hotel's gable, but the garden and surroundings were gone. The few walls that remained formed a kind of whitewashed monument; the rest was only brownish-red sand and soil. The bulldozer had left no trace, not even a plant.

N. stopped, squatted down, and felt the damp earth with his hand. Smooth earth and deserted white walls. No trace. He felt that he ought to cry, but nothing came. He got up and walked away.

He took the white envelope filled with dollars from the bag, though he wasn't exactly sure the money was his, and paid for transport into town. They had told N. he must register; he had to go register at the consulate. To have something to do, that was the only reason he left. He arrived just as the sun went down, found a simple room for the night, and then went out on the streets again. It was strange to see all the lights, to see people relaxed and strolling, even to hear someone let out a laugh. The smell of food in the evening was overwhelming. No longer did he have to endure the silence of the beach village, with its paper faces staring down from billboards and utility poles. Here there were no hopeless pilgrims clutching at straws. For a time he was released from the torment of his own survival.

He bought small skewers with chicken and mango and headed late in the day toward the consulate—someone had said they were open all the time now. He found his way with the help of a guidebook from the bag. The row of consulates would be, according to the map, a little outside the town center. The crowds thinned out around him, and the lights as well. He had to stop beneath them, to read the map. A half-dozen police officers came walking toward him in a narrow street. They walked slowly, talking in pairs or smoking. All of them wore helmets with visors and carried long, thin sticks that swayed casually. The sticks drew his gaze, their worn ends suggesting that someone had just had a taste of them.

The police passed without noticing N. He reached the park where, at the far end, the consulates were supposed to be. The asphalt was wet; leaflets were floating in the puddles. He kept walking.

"Filthy pigs!" someone shouted from far away. The cry's echo died away between the houses. N. didn't see a soul. The park next door was dark and uninviting. He stayed on the sidewalk, but moved nearer to the street and the lights from the few windows on the other side. A block farther down, he passed a couple who looked Western. They were walking quickly.

"Wishing that even more people had died," the woman said indignantly as they passed.

"Idiots," replied the man. Their steps faded away.

N. heard someone yell: "Death to America!" It came from the direction he was heading.

He stopped for a moment, feeling watched. The park was quiet. When he heard a car, he started walking again, trying to figure out what was happening down the street. He saw lights and made out a group of figures on the move. The loud voices came from a demonstration outside one of the consulates, now over. He thought back to the police he'd passed in riot gear, and then a car came up the street. As it sped up, someone rolled down a window. An arm stuck out, and as the car passed N., out flew masses of leaflets. The car swerved across the wet pavement and disappeared up a side street. A leaflet fluttered past him, and N., sensing something vaguely familiar about it, followed a few steps. He caught it just as it landed upside down in a puddle. He shook off the drops, holding it by a corner, and then turned it over.

It was the photograph of a dead man that he'd seen before, without really looking. Now he looked. A corpse, surrounded by dirt and grass, a gaping mouth and sunken eyes. Arms twisted unnaturally along the body. There were several similar images along the leaflet's edge. "Thank God!" he read. The text that followed looked like a press release. He stumbled to grasp the context, but after a few lines, he understood. The leaflet was a copy of an Internet posting from the United States, reprinted by protesters. A group of religious fanatics in America had hailed the tsunami, seeing God's punishment in the sea's wrath. They found divine justice in the fact that thousands of people were rotting in unmarked graves. They described in rich detail how all the missing people would float away with bloated bellies and never be found. Their biblical quotes were carefully chosen. A picture of the minister they called "Beloved Father" smiled out at N. All the dead children particularly pleased him. God was sweeping the earth clean, punishing all sinners.

N. looked out at the street again, toward the lights, the figures. His gaze returned to the flyer, the pastor's world seen through his words: sodomites, bastards, and rapists. Everyone tainted by the devil's sex. The world crawled and swarmed with sinners.

The only memory N. had of anything was of his two girls. It was the only image he'd ever see, even if someone held a gun to his head. They were dead, and people were rejoicing?

N. stood looking at the minister's smile, trying to see something more than lips and teeth. Then he slowly crushed the flyer, as if he had lost all feeling in his hands.

It came rolling over him, and he screamed. The first strong feeling since the Wave hit—burning hatred.

# CHAPTER 5

"WHERE WILL I BE SLEEPING?" asked Grip after shaking Shauna Friedman's hand. "Have you—"

"No," she replied. "We haven't booked a hotel. It's not necessary, we won't be staying in New York. We'll leave"—she glanced at the clock—"as soon as we can."

Grip looked at her, questioning.

She gazed back for a moment. "We need to make sure certain people end up where they belong—that is, on death row." She lingered at some thought and added, "Yes, people who probably deserve it." She got up from her desk. "Have you eaten?"

"No."

"Good, then we'll pick up something on the way. I have a car waiting. I'll make sure your bags get loaded."

Grip followed Shauna Friedman out, where she handed her assistant a stack of papers. "For the final signatures," she said, and then gave instructions about the luggage.

"When will you—"

"Don't know," Friedman said, cutting her off.

The assistant arranged some papers on her desk, exposing for a moment a manila folder marked "Ernst Grip." The folder vanished again, but Grip had seen it. He wasn't sure if the assistant had made a mistake, or if she wanted to observe his reaction.

"The name is Grip," he said, reaching out his hand.

"Norah," replied the assistant uncomfortably.

"Please, sit down," said Grip, and continued: "I work for the Swedish security police. You must forgive me, Norah, but do you work for Ms. Friedman?" He released her hand.

"Of course." She was nervous, but Grip held her gaze.

"May I ask who you are employed by?"

"It's—"

"Justice Department," Friedman shot in, from somewhere just behind Grip.

He didn't move, still looking at the assistant. "Justice Department, in the general sense, or . . ."

"No need to be rude, Mr. Grip. I'm just doing my job."

"I don't want to be rude, Norah, but since I landed in Newark hours ago, I have been . . . pushed around."

"I'm sorry."

"Thank you. Maybe this isn't important, but a few days ago I received a note saying 'Topeka.' Beyond that, I have no clue. Maybe you can tell me whether we're headed to Topeka. Do you even know?"

Getting the expected reaction, Grip turned around with a "No, not again," as soon as Friedman tried to speak. She said nothing, but didn't look particularly disarmed.

"Mr. Grip," said the assistant acidly, "I know exactly where you're going. But I have no intention of telling you. *That* is Agent Friedman's job."

End of the road.

"Finally an honest answer." He smiled.

Saber-rattling. Grip didn't know if he had scored a point, or if his insolence had set him back.

"Can we go now?" said Friedman, walking away without waiting for his reply.

They rode the elevator down in silence, but by the time they reached the parking garage, Friedman seemed to have completely forgotten their little spat.

"What do you think?" she said, twisting and turning a car key. "I asked for a full-size."

"Sorry?" said Grip, who was waiting for another shot.

"What do you think we'll get?" she repeated, pointing at the row of cars in front of them. One squeaked, and some lights started flashing.

"White Cadillac, apparently."

She nodded at him. "A pimp car. I guess you get what you ask for. Do you have these too, in the security police? You said security police, right? Or do you just drive around in a Volvo?"

"That's the safest way."

"Safest way . . ." The trunk swung open when she pushed the key again. His bag was already there, next to the ones that were probably hers—two bags, both larger than his. "Believe it or not," she said, "there's more paper in them than clothes," and slammed the trunk.

They pulled out of the garage into the afternoon light. Again, rows of streets and highway ramps. The buildings shrank as they headed out of the city. Shauna Friedman snapped off her earrings and put them in her pocket, made a few attempts to find a radio station and eventually chose one playing solo guitar. Acoustic, old-fashioned, crackling—revealed by the announcer to be a recording of Django Reinhardt.

Friedman cleared her throat. "I know what you're thinking. We invite you here and treat you like this. Not the best way to make friends, right?" She glanced at Grip. He shrugged. Thought he'd played a part.

"It's my fault," she continued. "This thing was my idea."

"No kidding," he replied, making an effort to say something. He felt tired, his thoughts chased around among the melancholy guitar chords.

The song ended, a truck horn blasted somewhere nearby, and he felt a pang of annoyance at what she'd said.

"I could be wrong," he went on in a low voice, as if not expecting to be heard, "but I do think you should brief me, give me a clue about why I'm here. Of course"—the old record kept rasping—"if you prefer to treat me like something the cat dragged in, go ahead. I'd just like to take a shower and eat once in a while."

"How about we start with food?"

"If that's the agenda."

"Korean?"

Grip shrugged. She turned off at the next exit.

The fizz of the beer revived his brain. There were only a few tables in the cramped family restaurant, but Friedman seemed to know the place. Grip chose at random from the speckled menu, getting a couple of small pancakes with scallions, and what he hoped was some kind of beef with noodles. Friedman didn't even look at the menu, but ordered from memory. When the food arrived, she maneuvered her chopsticks quickly, pecking like a bird.

"My mother is from Hawaii," she said.

Grip didn't understand what that was intended to explain—her eyes, the chopsticks? "Hawaii," he repeated. Sure, he knew how to use chopsticks, but not the way she did.

"Where did you grow up?" she asked, while stirring a bowl with some sort of sauce.

Grip looked at her for a moment before replying: "In a small town."

"But now you live in?"

"Stockholm."

Friedman tore a bite from one of his pancakes, sitting on the platter between them.

"You've probably figured it out by now, but I'll say it anyway. I work for the FBI." She smiled professionally. "Maybe that doesn't tell you very much."

Grip didn't respond. He picked up something that looked like a little burned leaf and moved it to the side with the tips of his chopsticks.

"Yes, it's true that we asked you to come here. I need your help with something, but I didn't want you to be influenced until I asked the first question. It's just my way of avoiding preconceptions. So we can start with clean sheets, if you know what I mean?"

"I already know that your mother is from Hawaii," said Grip.

"She is. From the tiny island of Lanai. She lost the tip of her pinkie in a childhood accident, and she hates boat rides. But you still don't know what I'm working on, or why you're here."

"When do you plan to ask the first question?"

"In a couple of days."

"Is this about Topeka?"

"Our discussion of Topeka will come later."

"A couple days. What should I do in the meantime?"

"You said all you needed was to eat, sleep, and shower, right? First we'll pay for this, and then we'll fly to California."

# CHAPTER 6

ONE NIGHT, THAT WAS ALL N. meant to stay.

His life had been shattered, and the more he began to remember, the clearer it became that he'd reached the end. According to the authorities' lists, he was missing, and so he would remain. It was while passing through a nameless village that he'd seen the sign: WEE-JAY'S FAMILY HOTEL AND BAR. An arrow pointed the way. Under it, on a board hanging from strings, a hand-painted addition: WEEJAY SURVIVED—WE'RE OPEN. N. turned off the paved road and followed the arrow into the green forest, down toward the sea.

The sign said 200 meters, but after more than a kilometer, he still hadn't found the place. Impossible that he'd made a wrong turn, not with only one trail, a strip of patchy grass lined by two hard ruts. On either side rose towering trunks and impenetrable thickets. It was like a tunnel, and only when he looked straight up could he see the sky past the treetops. He walked on. The forest was silent. No birds singing, not even a breeze.

Eventually the red earth grew sandy under his feet, and he saw where the green tunnel suddenly ended. In the light, a striped umbrella.

And then the beach.

He made his way to a bar under a big palm-leaf roof and asked for the reception. The bartender instantly served up a tall glass of juice, indicating that it was on the house.

"You found the place okay?" asked the man. Hoping to make up for the lie about the distance. N. shrugged and drank, his thirst intense.

"Room?" asked the man.

N. saw keys in a drawer. He nodded.

"Your name?"

N. didn't even hesitate. He gave the name from the hospital, rooting in his bag until he found the passport to confirm it.

The bartender, hardly looking, scribbled something on paper and held out a key. "Just follow the trail," he said, pointing.

The hand-painted sign in the village, the tunnel through the rain forest, the lie about his name—all that had been more than a week ago. N. told himself that sleep had kept him there. He was surprised that he slept so well at Weejay's. As if nothing disrupted his thoughts. The dark night hours slipped by, dreamless. He passed the days in a pleasant haze, like the few other guests, under the shelter of the palm roof. Just sat in the shade and watched, a stone's throw away from the waves. Soon he stopped counting the days. The money in the canvas bag seemed never to run out. He could afford to wait.

Weejay's was built in a protected cove. "If the wave hits again, we're safe here. We always come out okay at Weejay's," said the boy who served him breakfast on the second morning. "Not even the cat drowned." A few days later the bartender suggested that he dive in, but N. pointed to the dirty bandages on his arms and around his knees, and the man apologized. Another day, a couple tried to get their daughter to swim. She screamed and fought when, laughing, they carried her into the water. N., unable to watch, walked until he couldn't hear the screams.

Still, it wasn't often that the dark thoughts came, that images of The Missing Ones washed over him. The two faces of his children. He tried to shut them out.

What did he have left to look back on? Not much. His girls, of course . . . But the common thread was lost. A hell of a lot of years seemed to have simply slipped away. What really matters in life? Good deeds? Wasn't there some act that made a difference? Anything?

There were images, but they seemed diffuse, or as if they belonged to somebody else: a summer cabin, dinners for two, a boat on a trailer. Like scenes from a promotional video for suburban life. He never fit in there, and frankly, he hated it. When do you start to live? Can you decide? What if you actually took an idea and ran with it, all the way to the end—had he ever done such a thing? He knew too little about himself, and it felt like he really didn't want to know. All he had was the memory of his girls. He longed only for them, and somehow he had to do them justice before his time was up. At Weejay's in the evening, he learned to kill the hour before bed with whisky, to the rim of his toothbrush glass.

The only world he knew now was the one under the palm-leaf roof. Here, with the sand floor and the scattered plastic chairs. The oversize bar, which doubled as reception desk and office, stood in one corner, a South Seas cliché of bamboo and mirrors. After sunset every night, long strings of LED lights flashed white, red, and green, as if a Christmas tree had crashed into the bottles and mirrors. Two blue-green insect lamps hissed, hanging like stoplights at either end of the bar. Beyond the palm-covered bar, Weejay's consisted of a dozen bungalows, a few sun-bleached wooden chairs, a palm grove with hammocks, and two pedal boats, chained. There was no other sign of civilization, anywhere.

Early in his stay, N. made an acquaintance, a tall Czech wearing large glasses with heavy black frames. They spent the afternoons together, had a few beers. In the morning, as N. came out of his bungalow for breakfast, he often found the Czech coming back from his beach run, dragging odds and ends: the hook from a rusty anchor, bleached animal bones, a diver's knife without a sheath, one blue flipper. Other times the Czech swam out in the sea until he became a dot and then returned, snorting, from the waves. When N. asked about his occupation, he said that he traveled. Every night before dinner the Czech stared at Weejay's laminated menu as if he'd never seen it before. He read, muttered in frustration, then ordered whatever N. told him to. He introduced himself as Vladislav Pilk.

One evening as they sat eating, Vladislav asked, "Were you there?"

N. tried to look uncomprehending.

"The wave, did you make it, in the tsunami?"

"Yes . . ." N. nodded.

"Me too." Vladislav emptied the beer glass and called for another one. "Damn stupid question, obviously you made it." He snorted. "Well, shit. I was on a bus heading north, packed with people. And then, you know . . . someone screamed and the whole thing was pushed over sideways and we were floating. Floating at

32

first, that is, but soon water started gushing in. There was one way out, through the open window, but everyone was fighting—bam, crash, pushing and pulling—total chaos. What to do? I grabbed my backpack and held myself down in the seat with my hands and feet. Then when the time came, three fast ones . . ." He breathed in and out quickly and took a deep breath. "Thinking it was the right thing, to sit there as long as possible. That I could take it. Until the water reached the top. It was black in there, with stuff floating around, and someone kicked me in the face. I mean, the ultimate. When you can't take it any longer, you know, Christ how your chest gets tight, you want to get that air." He laughed and bared his teeth. "Then I let go of my seat and found my way to the window, felt my way. Wall, wall, wall . . . and then a hole. I swam out and kept swimming until I reached the surface. Like a damn flash flood in springtime up there, not another soul. Only me. Backpack and glasses intact." He laughed again.

Then he grew serious and looked straight at N. "It was the most exciting thing I've ever experienced. Don't you agree? Incredible . . . unmatched." He snorted and drew his fists to his chest. "Couldn't sleep a wink for nights afterward, what a high." He exhaled. "Feels like you could take on everything, do anything. No?"

N. made a vague gesture.

"Another beer?" said Vladislav. "Or dessert?"


The next day N. watched Vladislav throwing pebbles at a palm tree. He stood more than fifty yards away, firing stone after stone. The hits sounded hollow. He didn't miss once.

In the same palm grove N. sometimes saw a leg dangling from a hammock. From his view at his table in the shade, he guessed it belonged to a woman. The rest of the body hidden by the fabric of the hammock. He thought he'd seen her around the place. Long black hair and smoky eyes. She kept to herself in the shade, reading. If you met her eye, she smiled.

When N. came down for dinner one evening, she had suddenly appeared at Vladislav's table. He looked around for another table when Vladislav called, "Come, come and sit down. This is . . ."

"Mary. Still Mary," she said, resigned.

"And here we have Mary," Vladislav said loudly as he pulled over a chair for N.

Mary was American. She worse a sleeveless black cotton dress and white tennis shoes.

"I saw her reading, that's how we met," said Vladislav cryptically. He picked up the menu. "Do they have anything with potatoes?"

"No," said N. as he sat down. "Still no potatoes."

"Doesn't it ever change?"

"No, never changes. Don't have, won't have. Get the prawns."

"How silly," said Mary, laughing for a moment.

Mary didn't drink the table water, pushed the vegetables to one side, and ate only her steak. During dinner Vladislav entertained them with wild stories from some trip to Senegal. A stream of jokes and anecdotes, his loud laughter, and, behind their table, the strange play of blinking lights at the bar.

N. flinched when fingertips touched his arm. He was tired, and two beers with dinner had made him retreat into his own world. Vladislav was leaning back in his chair, talking to someone at a nearby table. The fingers were Mary's. She touched one of the long scars, where you could still see the stitches.

"I'm sorry," she said when N. winced, though without embarrassment. She kept her hand on his forearm. "How's it healing?"

34

"Fine, I guess," he said, pulling his arm away and rubbing back and forth over the scar.

"Isn't it time to get those stitches taken out?"

"Maybe. I haven't really thought about it."

"It's not good to let them go too long."

"Irish," said Vladislav, leaning forward over the table. "Shall we end with one?" He'd gotten a taste of Weejay's Irish coffee a few nights back.

"It's too hot out," said Mary.

N. looked at the clock. "Just whisky for me."

"They can throw in a few ice cubes, if you'd like," Vladislav said to Mary.

"Right—ice, Nescafé, and condensed milk!" She said it with genuine disgust. Vladislav dismissed her with a shrug.

She didn't talk much more that night. Given the odd atmosphere, N. didn't expect to see her at their table again, but she showed up the very next day. Same black dress, same white shoes, took her seat royally without even asking. Vladislav, needing his audience and already starting in with his stories, gave her a warm grin. And so it went: he wrestled with the menu, she left her vegetables untouched and ate only meat, and N. longed for the anesthesia of his last glass of whisky.

Three souls at the same table, night after night.

# CHAPTER 7

Government Jet N50711

Night of April 26, 2008

S OMETHING ABOUT SHAUNA FRIEDMAN'S NO-NONSENSE personality convinced Grip to go along with her. If she wanted to hand him the puzzle piece by piece, fine, he could live with that. Sooner or later he'd find out what she actually wanted him for.

In the Cadillac they drove out of New York to a little airport, where a Gulfstream waited with crew. VIP atmosphere, private hangar, people in nice suits. The cabin of the small jet had two sections, and Grip heard voices in the rear as he boarded. A man greeted Friedman on his way to the back; otherwise Grip saw no one else during the flight. Grip and Shauna Friedman sat down in the saggy leather club seats, the color of sand. Facing each other by the windows, they drank sodas they'd taken from a cooler before takeoff, made polite conversation, and looked out. The weather was clear, and even though they were flying west—chasing a perpetual sunset—eventually the lights of midwestern towns appeared below them. When the last red stripe of twilight melted away, they had been in the air for nearly three hours. Friedman declined the sandwich offered by a crew member, then moved to the next seat so she could stretch her legs and fell asleep.

Grip nibbled a tuna sandwich made with too much mayonnaise. The cabin lights were switched off. Below him he saw small towns, their scattered clusters of lights, and after a while he could even pick out individual cars as they headed here and there. Lazily, he tried to imagine what people down there were doing, where they were going—was it an early or late evening for them? He had lost track of time. The topography was impossible to read in the darkness; he could see the lights of a bridge but not the water below it.

Engines humming, air-conditioning cooling: with his mind on low, his gaze turned inward.

"All the pineapple you wanted," Friedman had said, "as much and any time." Since they couldn't talk shop during the flight, they had to talk about themselves. Pineapple—it was Friedman who brought up childhood memories. Summers she'd spent with her grandmother on Lanai, the small Hawaiian island that was mostly pineapple plantation. A fruit company owned the land and everyone working there, and it was strictly forbidden to take the fruit, but kids always knew where to steal them. "You get tired of the taste though, really fast." Grip saw the painting from her office before him, the village of faded wood. By the middle of summer she'd always had enough of the island, and longed to get away. "I guess I haven't eaten pineapple since."

On her hand was a single gold ring with colored stones. She mentioned having relatives in San Francisco. Grip tried to put it together, the double-sided identity. Jews were easy enough to recognize—Friedman—and so were the Japanese—the grandma on that pineapple island, her almond eyes. She liked to talk about her parents. Grip was certain that she was an only child and that her parents had waited years before having her. Certainly there was some family money, but not in excess. She had gone to Williams, a private college in western Massachusetts. Nothing came free—her own words—and her father had been there before her. She joked about the fact that she'd played lacrosse.

Grip looked at her sleeping face. She was careful, her makeup almost invisible. Just a line above each eye. Her eyebrows made two distinct arcs on her bare forehead. She'd put her half-long hair in a clip behind her neck, but a few strands had come loose and fallen across her cheek. For a man who shared her bed, it would have been an irresistible sight.

Grip had noticed that her eyes never wavered. A self-assured look oblivious to whatever else was going on around her. This fit a pattern; she'd used her chopsticks the same way, with a kind of total self-confidence. She was the type who received help as soon as she walked into a store. The type who corrected others, and who never needed anyone to repeat what had just been said. The type who made men feel more insecure the more they fell for her.

That was not, however, Grip's predicament. While she slept, his gaze did not travel to her breasts or her lips. The beast in him did not stir. Instead, he thought about the puzzle: Newark, Topeka, a flight to California. What bothered him was that Shauna Friedman had told him too much about herself. A bit too much detail. Those descriptions of her grandmother's kitchen or of some rabbi in Los Angeles were not just friendly—they created a bond between them. It was nicely done. Her chattiness forced him to talk. The FBI had a folder on him, but she wanted more. That was it, right? The question she would eventually ask, she wouldn't address to a stranger. Yet that folder he had seen, it bothered him. On the flight, he had spoken about trivialities that could not possibly be in there. What had she gained from that?

Grip didn't mind offering her crumbs about his own past. Unlike Friedman, who'd grown up traveling the entire continent, he hadn't left the low buildings of his small town until adolescence. No damn pineapples, maybe a few kronor a row from weeding carrots one summer for a stingy farmer. She had seen volcanic lava run into the sea; he had sat in the summer cottage, gazing at the warm glow of the cast-iron stove. When she talked about swimming in the sea, he told her about swimming alone in a pond one August night. Her lacrosse, his soccer. Two seasons in Division I. A knee injury, no big deal, but so ended his dreams.

Then Friedman asked about his family. He had two older sisters, and Friedman amused herself trying to pronounce their names. Both sisters were married, unlike him.

By the time they landed, Grip had barely managed to doze off a few times, and it was only as they were taxiing that he actually fell asleep.

He woke to Friedman commanding: "Come on!" She was already standing, her hair brushed and collected behind her neck again. Three-piece suits from the rear cabin passed behind her.

"Where are we?" asked Grip. The cabin light stung his eyes.

"California."

Lacking the energy to ask for details, he leaned over to tie his shoes.

Outside the plane, a car was waiting. A thin young man in a US Navy uniform drove them through a deserted area of an airport. The buildings were tall boxes painted white. There were few doors, and even fewer windows. The brightly lit buildings stood out in sharp contrast to the black night around them, like a labyrinth in a computer game. Above an open hangar, where lights washed over some planes, were tall black letters: WELCOME TO NAS NORTH ISLAND.

"North Island?" said Grip.

"Yes," said Friedman. "North Island, Coronado, California— we're in San Diego."

Grip humphed in response.

They were driven to a hotel complex, dark and unmarked. In the parking lot, where there were a few cars, a man came out and gave them each a set of keys. Their young driver insisted on dragging their bags up the stairs. He refused to accept a tip when Grip stood like a fool with a few dollar bills fanned in his hand. Friedman hadn't even tried.

"See you tomorrow," she said simply and disappeared to her room.

Grip nodded, looked at his watch. He'd set it to New York time, but now he wasn't sure of the time difference or of how long they'd been in the air. He couldn't work it out—he'd spent too many hours in the plane's timelessness. He remained in limbo.

As he entered the room, he was hit by the cold of the air-conditioning. The TV was turned to CNN with no sound: a shouting mob, a news anchor, American soldiers. A corner of the screen showed a clock at half past ten, but nothing to identify the part of the world where that applied. Grip turned off the television, stripped naked, and pulled out the too-tight sheets. He fell asleep immediately.

Although his body didn't know it, outside the window it was morning. He saw some joggers; the few cars that went by seemed to drive slowly. From brochures in the hotel room's leather folder, Grip concluded he was inside the gates of a naval base. Was that important? He wasn't sure.

"Do you scuba dive?" Friedman had asked during the flight. "What do you like to do in New York? Where in New York do you usually stay?" There was a folder on him that the FBI didn't want him to see. What the hell was he doing in California?

There had to be an Internet computer down in the lobby. For a moment, he thought about sending an e-mail to the Boss, a sign of life, at least a line saying he'd left New York. But that was not what the Boss wanted. No official e-mail from a naval base in California—at most, a few pencil notes.

After breakfast, which he ate with Friedman under an umbrella at the base's golf club, she said, "We leave in an hour."

"Into town, or . . ."

"Make sure you bring your bags."

"Should I wear a blindfold?"

"Just allow yourself to be patient." Friedman smiled.

It was the reverse car ride, back to the base airport. Small military jets flew in wide circles, practicing takeoffs and landings; he heard helicopters but didn't see them. Their car had stopped on the tarmac where a large plane was being loaded. It had military markings.

"Another flight," said Friedman while Grip watched his bag being carried away.

The sound of her heels echoed on the concrete. A fresh breeze blew in from the sea. Grip was left standing there. An endless trip, just because of some note scribbled on a piece of paper. So far not a single word about Topeka, instead all those little questions about New York. He'd entered the States as a tourist, anonymous because others wanted it that way. Friedman said that she'd taken care of the hotel bill when he asked, and it was her card that had paid for breakfast. Just like at the Korean restaurant the day before. Nowhere had his presence been noted, not since his passport was stamped in at Newark.

Now a new flight raised the stakes—this time without so much as a destination. Who was busy deceiving whom?

It made him hesitate, at least for a second. But then he thought, the Boss had asked him to do this, after all.

"Just a stone in my shoe," he said when he caught up with her on the tarmac.

This plane also carried other passengers. When Grip entered the cabin, he noticed that he and Friedman were the only civilians on board. Most wore flight suits with their sleeves rolled up, squadron patches with wings, skulls, and gunslingers on them. They sat together in groups of eight or ten. Loud talk, forced laughter. On the seats behind Grip and Friedman sat a group of military police, all of them armed, but quieter than the aviators.

The engines were started, and the cool air poured in. Among the islands of men with crew cuts, the conversations intensified.

"Did you go home with her?"

"Hell yes."

Someone applauded.

"And we went out yesterday."

"Lucky bastard. The whole night?"

A whistle. Someone was being hassled.

"The wife and kids . . ."

" . . . I didn't call."

"You never learn, do you?"

Like a ship casting off, in tension and relief, leaving kisses and rubble behind. Warriors on their way.

The plane rose, and a sandy beach appeared for a second out the window, then only water. They headed straight out without changing course. San Diego, Coronado, due west, nothing but ocean.

The nose was lowered, the engines slowed.

"Garcia," said Friedman. "Diego Garcia, that is our final destination."

On the map in Grip's pocket almanac, it was just a dot with a name. They were headed for an atoll in the Indian Ocean.

# CHAPTER 8

*Weejay's, Thailand*

*Second week of January 2005*

T WAS INEVITABLE, THE ADDITION of Reza Khan. The first time they saw him, he was standing by the bar, shouting. Carrying a large backpack and various bulging bags, he had walked all the way from the village. The free glass of juice did not calm him down. He swore that he would walk all the way back just to repaint the sign with the true distance.

He threw all his bags in a pile and then, like everyone else, he stayed.

In the evenings he was the one who spoke to everybody under the palm-leaf roof. Mornings he slept away in his bungalow, called it meditation. He was generous and bought people drinks but himself never drank anything other than Coca-Cola. If someone offered something stronger, Reza raised his hand and said, "Sorry— Muslim."

"Is he gay?" whispered Vladislav to N. after a few days. Reza's bleached blond hair stood straight as a brush. He looked like a mad samurai and wore tight shirts. Yet no one doubted him when

45

he said he was Pakistani, with his dark skin and coal-black eyes. He said he couldn't remember when he had last been at home in Peshawar.

"So," asked Vladislav straight out, "the bleached hair, what's it good for?"

Reza's laugh was short as a cough. "I was tired of all the attention at airports."

Vladislav looked puzzled.

"What my kind suffers at border crossings."

"Your kind?"

"My type, yes," replied Reza, tapping his finger on the glass. "We Muslims." He nodded slowly a few times, as if he were speaking to a child.

"Did it work?" asked Vladislav, pointing to his hair.

Reza gazed at him. "Not so far."

"I'd say it looks fucking awful."

Just as Reza was about to hit back, a man at the bar muttered, "Idiot," behind Vladislav's back.

Reza rose up and half screamed, "Say that again!"

Everyone at Weejay's froze. The man, who was more than a head taller than Reza, recoiled slightly when the Pakistani jumped up and stood right in front of him. When his smiling lips began to apologize, Reza snapped, "Shut up! This is a matter between me and the Czech there."

He turned back, took his Coke from the counter, drank, and shook the glass so that the ice sounded like a rattlesnake before saying to Vladislav, "*You* are the idiot, but at least you do not think I will cut your throat. Not like that Yank there, who looks like he watched too much Al-Jazeera." He pointed at the man at the bar, who carelessly poked in the sand with his cane.

One morning Vladislav walked up with an old shotgun over his shoulder.

"Finish up those eggs," he said to N., who had just been served breakfast. "I have organized everything. We're going to have some fun." N. had no idea what he was talking about. "In the meantime, I'll get Mary."

N. ate quickly, and was just swallowing the last of his coffee when Vladislav returned with Mary in tow. She carried a folding deck chair in one hand and a paperback in the other. They brought along Reza as well—Vladislav had pounded on his door until he gave in and got up.

Besides the gun, Vladislav had brought a few boxes of cartridges, a carton of clay pigeons, and an improvised device for throwing them. They divided the things among themselves and set off down the beach. It took them half an hour to get beyond the headland Vladislav had indicated.

As soon as he said, "This is good," Mary dropped her chair and opened her book. The strip of sand was narrow, and she sat in the shadows of the palms so that they would fan her in the breeze.

Vladislav gave quick instructions to the other two and then loaded the double-barreled gun and fired the first shots. N., taking charge of the thrower, hurled the clay pigeons over the water. It took him a couple of tries to master the technique. Vladislav reloaded, and when N. managed to get the pigeons to make a wide arc through the air, they all came down in a shower of black chips. Four hits in a row, and then Vladislav handed over his gun to Reza. A throw, a shot, a single splash in the water—it went like that a few times before Reza began taking Vladislav's advice seriously. At the first hit, he raised his arms and cheered. Mary looked up from her book. A couple of hits, and then it was N.'s turn. The hits came fast; he had listened to the advice.

Reza wasn't interested in throwing pigeons, but instead stood and fiddled impatiently with a few cartridges while he waited. Vladislav did the throwing and gave commentary.

N. felt satisfied, hitting at least every other, and he let Reza and Vladislav take turns with the rest of the ammunition.

Reza couldn't get enough. He crouched with his gun as if wanting to pounce with every shot.

"Did you ever get more than two in a row?" He grinned at N. when he did it. Vladislav was silent when he shot, just nodding sometimes when he got a hit. Reza imitated his way of reloading the gun with a violent jerk, so that the empty cases flew. N. hurled clay pigeons until his arm hurt—throw, shot, throw, shot.

A flock of pelicans came flying along the beach. Reza and N. watched them, while Vladislav reloaded. They glided over the beach at the edge of the palm forest. Mary put the book in her lap and stretched her back.

"Coming right at you," she said unexpectedly.

Reza looked at her, puzzled.

"Well, why not?" she continued. The pelicans glided, without moving their wings at all.

Vladislav caught on immediately and fired two shots. He dropped the first two birds, then reloaded quickly. He passed his gun over to Reza. "Here!"

Reza licked his lips hesitantly. The birds flapped but stayed in a line, and then he fired. His first shot hit nothing, and the pelicans veered off in different directions. After the second shot was fired, a bird in the middle of the line winced and tumbled down in a spiral through the air. It landed in the sand a few meters behind Mary. She watched as it awkwardly flapped one wing, making it turn in a circle. Its large beak looked for something to peck.

"You must finish it off," said Vladislav. He took the gun back from Reza, who stood frozen, and reloaded it.

"Here!"

Reza took the gun again, walked a few steps toward the bird, hesitated. The pelican gave a hoarse cry. Mary remained sitting in her lounge chair, stroking her knee.

Reza's shot landed short, throwing a cloud of sand over the bird. Without the slightest flinch, Vladislav grabbed the gun by the barrel and walked straight up to the pelican. He stood and watched it for a while as it turned in circles at his feet. He crouched down, looked at the bird, stood up, took a step back—shot.

It was Saturday night. Everybody was treating everybody else to beers and oversize cocktails under the palm-leaf roof. People talked back and forth among the tables, laughing loudly, and some couldn't resist going out in the darkness for a swim in the sea. Pranks lasted as long into the night as anyone could keep a bar tab. N. made sure he was drunk into oblivion by the time people started talking about the Wave. It was always that way; something would start at one of the tables and spread like a disease. Half-truths and myths took hold. It was unstoppable. N. responded to direct questions with lies: he was traveling alone, had seen nothing. That way, nobody asked about his scars or bandages.

But then the conversation turned to the religious sect and their leaflets. The rejoicing over all the deaths, how the victims had only themselves to blame. Many under the palm-leaf roof had heard talk on the beaches about fights and demonstrations in nearby cities. Just as on evenings before, the mood turned ugly when the subject came up. Voices were raised. Someone spat in anger and threw his glass, which smashed against the side of the bar.

The man who'd called Reza an idiot the other night stood nearby, tossing out comments about Baptist mobs and evangelical wackos, which further fueled the debate. N. hated being reminded but listened to every word. He watched the tall man with the cane and wondered who he was. A young woman said she'd seen on television a group of people chanting, holding signs about sinners and God's punishment. They were Americans, she said, a Christian sect. This had happened in the States, and apparently was still going on. The news had spread from television to the Internet, and out into the world. And it was here in Thailand that the response had been the most intense. Angry crowds had tried to attack a couple of consulates and the office of some airline, but riot police had protected them.

"Americans," said a local bartender, collecting bottles, "the authorities here . . . they don't dare do anything else."

"I saw police beating people up," said the woman, her voice cracking, "just to protect America's interests, even for a bunch of sick religious fanatics."

The bartender made a gesture that suggested he was ashamed.

A few hours and several glasses later, when spirits were running high again and Vladislav was just about to tell the next table how he escaped from the bus, Mary leaned close to N. and said, "Come."

"What . . ." He looked around, confused.

"Come on." She stood up, and he followed her out into the sand.

They headed for Mary's bungalow, her skirt fluttering around her bare legs. His mouth felt dry, and when they stopped outside her door, he thought she was the more sober one. She held his wrist, and he tried to put his other arm around her shoulder.

"No," she said firmly. He stopped, some kind of misunderstanding. She lifted his arm again, turning it with interest under the light from a lantern on the path.

"We're going inside." She opened the door.

N. stood awkwardly in the middle of the small room while Mary lit a candle and looked around for something. As she bent over in front of him, her skirt slipped down and her tank top rose up her back. In the gap appeared a tattooed cat—a black cat arching its back, its tail straight up. N. hadn't seen it before; his first impulse was to touch it. Its eyes stared straight at him.

"Sit down," said Mary, standing up with a small bag in her hand. "On the chair there." She pulled up a stool and sat down beside it. The candle burned on the table beside them.

"Let's see now." She had unwrapped the bandages on one arm and felt with her fingertips over the stitches. N. closed his eyes, feeling only her hands and his own breath. His sleeve was in the way, and she made him take off his shirt. She felt him, up and over the shoulder. Again on the other arm.

When N. looked up, she had taken a scalpel from the bag.

"They've got to come out now."

N. didn't answer. She held the knife in her hand in a way that suggested habit, heating the blade by the candle flame without getting it sooty. He let her. It didn't hurt, only pinched a bit, as the stitches were eased out of the skin around the scars.

N. stretched out his arms and looked at them: irregular stripes that looked like something sewn by Dr. Frankenstein.

"Lift it up," said Mary, and clapped her hand once in her lap. N. raised one leg so that she could reach. He was wearing only a pair of thin shorts. With the bandages rolled off, once again she examined him with keen little movements. Felt around the edges of his kneecap, massaged a tendon in his knee, then touched a sore on the inside of his leg that extended down the calf.

Her fingertips subtle, he got an erection. His hips responded but, overcome by shame, he pulled back his leg and sat up. He avoided looking at her.

"Lift up your leg," she said, rolling the scalpel between her fingers. "Leg." When he didn't respond, she bent forward and lifted it into her lap again.

The small threads from the stitches looked like black pine needles when she laid them on the table.

One last tug as a thread was cut, and N. let the other foot slide down on the floor.

"Did I get them all?" she asked.

He looked down at his legs. They had been the worst. He looked at all the twisting scars that branched like white roots. He was about to say something when Mary leaned forward so that her lips just touched his shoulder. Felt her warmth, her hair falling over his arm. Her fingers found their way in between his fingers. A white stripe revealed where there had once been a ring. He didn't remember if he had lost it or taken it off.

"It doesn't matter," she said, "not anymore," and stood up. Once again, the tattooed cat's eyes in the gap on her back when she turned around.

"Not anymore," repeated N. He stood up too. Mary moved slowly in front of him, as if she were dancing. Slowly, lightly. She touched her own shoulder with her cheek and came closer. Like a wave.

"Did you have children?" she whispered.

N. floated inside, as if he had drunk a truth serum. She felt it.

He turned to her without looking. Her closeness there anyway, sensed as warmth, a scent. What he saw was his children's faces. As clearly as if they were standing right in front of him. Saw the color of their eyes. The blue.

He held up two fingers, but Mary had already put her index finger over her lips.

"Ssh . . ." Then she whispered, "No past . . . no future, just like me." She smiled.

He tried to smile as well.

"You can live that way," she said, with a slow shrug. "Can't you?" She stood with her back to him, hesitating. N.'s breath moved through her hair. He exhaled again, making the loose hairs tremble. Then he stretched out his hands, gently, as if reaching out in a completely dark room, felt the skin beneath his fingers. Brought them to her hips, saw her shoulder blades relax. Slowly, as when a tree starts to fall, she leaned back against his chest.

"No," she said quietly, but not wanting him to stop. Took hold of his hands and led them over her stomach, guiding his movements with intertwined fingers. The inviting indent of her navel. Then it was his power that carried them forward, still with her hands over his. The hip bones' relentless inward trail, fingertips balancing as if on a tightrope. Her gasp like that of a frightened audience. His own lustful sound when he brought his hands together over her mound. Thin fabric, a hint of hair. He pressed himself hard against her.

"Does it feel awful?" she asked and turned around, taking hold of his hand and gently licking the palm. "Is it terrible?" That same vigilant, fearless gaze as when the pelicans were shot.

She resisted when he forced her hand down and held it there so she could feel him.

"It is . . ." She squeezed so hard that he fell silent. Moaning, he heaved his hips. She braced herself and held her head so he could reach her neck. A slow bite, over skin and hair.

53

Swirling naked together on the floor. The tip of her tongue drew tracks, he bit where he could. The whole time she kept his sex in a firm grip, her hand at the root. He looked down, tried but did not want to pull free. There was nothing gentle in her movements—a thin silver bracelet and something blue twitched restlessly around her wrist. She shivered and swore quietly with her eyes closed when he took her breasts. The glaring cat showed his arched back when Mary stretched out in the dark. She said something loud and turned around, took him in, and he moaned. In lust, the teeth she bared were very white.

N. woke up during the night, a few moments of consciousness in the dark. When he moved, he felt the dirt on the wooden planks beneath him. He shivered, feeling sandy and naked. Behind his eyeballs, a headache from the whisky had taken hold, and his groin ached with exhaustion. Mary was no longer next to him, though he heard a sound from her bed.

He listened, sensed her there. Then he rolled over on his side, curled up, and fell asleep.

He saw a vast ballroom floor, light shining just above its surface. A man came walking, the sound of his heels against the wood. He was visible only up to the waist, his two legs and one hand on a cane. The tip of the cane was silent—nothing could be heard as it hit the floor, only the heels of his shoes. Its head was carved like the skull of a starving animal. The man paused, as if waiting, or seeing something. Then, from somewhere behind the man with the cane, came a gust of wind, a whispering wind. It was Mary's voice N. heard, saying, "Let's do it . . . Let's do it . . ."

# CHAPTER 9

IT TOOK A WHOLE DAY to reach their destination, with one stopover at a foreign military base somewhere in the Eastern Hemisphere. Nobody told them where they'd landed to refuel. Passengers stretched for a few minutes outside the airplane: heavy tropical air and fuel fumes, uniformed Asians dragging snaky black hoses over the tarmac in the heat.

Off again. Up at altitude, crossing over the next sea. The hours crawled by.

Landed.

Diego Garcia: a remote location in the Indian Ocean, where the land barely rises out of the sea.

"You know about the island?" asked Shauna Friedman when they got their bags.

"Not much," said Grip. Buses arrived for the other passengers; a car came for Grip and Friedman. In fact, he did know a few things about the atoll. Diego Garcia, a ribbon of sand and vegetation, made into an outpost for strangers. No one called it home. There were no permanent residents. A world of antennas, barracks, tanks, and depots—that was the picture. A deep harbor, that was important, and even more so, the two-mile-long runway. The biggest ship in the navy's arsenal could anchor there, and the heaviest plane in the air force could take off. All the eyes there were America's own. Surrounded by unbroken water, hundreds of miles in all directions.

A place out of reach, created mostly as a way to get to everybody else.

There were rumors about Garcia. Overheated websites suggested many things: blurry satellite images with arrows on buildings, lengthy records without references, testimony without names. People who tracked airplane routes saw flights that hopped all over the world and finally landed on Garcia. Excluding the supernatural nonsense, the UFOs and the superweapons, there were still a few items worth noting. Things that any security police analyst would mention in a follow-up meeting. True, it stank. There were those who said that Guantánamo was a place that did, after all, tolerate the world's attention. Not Diego Garcia.

But why bother to mention it? Here he was, Grip—a reluctant tourist.

They drove out of the airport and through buildings on the base. An entire community whose signs, flagpoles, and shops all showed unmistakable military style—soulless. Khaki, concrete, bare lawns.

"I'm a foreigner," said Grip after a moment of silence in the car. "Don't I have to get stamped?"

"That's not necessary," said Friedman.

"You're familiar with the rules here?"

"Unfortunately."

They were given separate rooms in a hotel reserved for officers. It looked like a cheap motel stuck in the 1970s. In Grip's room the walls, ceilings, and thick carpet were all beige, and the doors and dressers were paneled in fake dark-brown wood. As if someone had packed up a den in Alabama and moved it out to the Indian Ocean. The clattering air conditioner was wired right into the wall; the bed had only a thin cotton sheet.

A few hours later, a piece of grilled meat sat on a plate in front of him, bloody as an open cut. Friedman had been smart enough to get a salad. He took a few bites before his travel-battered stomach said enough. Not many had shown up at the officers' club.

"Still too early," said Friedman, looking at the empty seats. "The heat."

The evening disappeared mostly in silence. Fatigue, travel, the unlikely place: all those were excuses enough. But things were so cool between them that talking didn't help, as if they were on a bad date. She drank a dry martini, saying she didn't like the water on the island. After a few thousand miles too many on an airplane, Grip had decided not to drink, contenting himself with the water, which stank of chlorine.

One night, then reveille from a scratchy speaker off in the distance. Toast and a couple of fried eggs, which they didn't eat together. Not breakfast. For a while, this would be their pattern.

Friedman had picked up a car earlier in the morning. Distances on the island were small, but still too far to walk. She came and got Grip, drove a few minutes, and stopped.

The building was low and windowless with a plain entrance. Past the door, they had to go through a barred metal gate. Grip saw a camera in the ceiling; the lock clicked open. Around the corner, Friedman showed her ID, signed something, and they went in. All doors they passed closed as soon as they went through. It was strangely quiet, just the sounds of their own footsteps. The floor sagged slightly under them, and Grip got the feeling that he was surrounded by something makeshift, a facade.

Friedman walked first into a sparsely furnished room where a man sat balancing on a chair with his back to them, watching a small TV. He turned and mumbled a greeting when they entered.

"Clay," said Friedman, with a gesture in the man's direction that was both introductory and dismissive. Then she said, "Well, here we are," and pointed to the TV screen.

In black and white, they saw a room about the same size as the one they were in. The grainy image from the surveillance camera showed what clearly was a cell: bare walls, an open toilet up close, and at the far end of the floor, a bunk right on the floor. Distorted by the wide-angle lens, the toilet's curves loomed huge, while the bunk looked distant and tiny. There was someone on it. Nothing moved in the picture; the figure lay still in a vaguely unnatural position. Maybe it was just the perspective, or maybe he was dead.

Grip had been in many jails before, but seldom had he been seized by the discomfort he felt now. He saw that the man on the bed—for it was a man—was barefoot and wearing overalls. Had a beard and unkempt hair, he thought. A speaker crackled. The man in the cell shifted on his plastic-wrapped mattress. The sound was so amplified that it sounded like an insect, as if a microphone stood right next to the bed.

"We need help determining his nationality. We have indications that he might be Swedish. Is he?" Friedman asked abruptly. She said it as if she was expecting an immediate and uncomplicated answer. As if the person inside was someone familiar, a person any Swede would instantly recognize as a compatriot. Grip neither replied nor looked at her. The man called Clay held up a couple of photos for Grip.

He took them, the black-and-white mug shots, front and profile. The man's gaze was apathetic, telling a tale of insomnia, defiance, and something else that had gone on far too long. There was no name, no number, nothing to identify him.

"Is he a Swedish citizen?" repeated Friedman.

Grip turned from her. "Clay, isn't it?" he said, with a questioning gaze toward the man on the chair.

"Clay Stackhouse," she filled in.

Grip nodded. "Must Mr. Stackhouse be involved here?"

"Go get a coffee, Clay."

He was already on his way.

They were alone.

Friedman threw up her hands when Grip said nothing for more than a minute. "Well?"

"What is it you want *me* to tell you?"

"Just say whether or not you think he is Swedish."

"No," said Grip. "Clay's gone. Now it's your turn to talk."

"About what?"

"About what— You're making yourself look silly. Okay." He waved once with the photographs and then said with deliberate slowness, "What the hell is this about?"

"Determining the man's identity." Friedman shrugged, searching for words. "The FBI would love to know who this man really is."

"And this is how you go about it?"

"We are not going about anything in any particular way. We are looking at a fait accompli."

"Fait accompli . . . a lone man in a cell at Diego Garcia?"

"Something like that."

"He just showed up out of nowhere, overnight?"

She didn't answer.

59

"What is he suspected of?"

"Can we take one thing at a time? He isn't suspected of selling cigarettes to minors, okay. Soon enough, all right?"

"One thing at a time. Why would he be Swedish?"

"Because someone said so."

"But you don't know for sure."

"No."

"A Swede," said Grip to himself. Then he held up one of the pictures, pointing at it. "How the hell do you think I could identify someone who has been beaten up like this? Who did this to him?" He turned to Friedman again. "Or for the sake of being completely obvious, maybe I should ask why you tortured him."

Friedman looked completely unmoved. She didn't answer.

"It isn't very nicely done," said Grip. "Maybe it wasn't meant to be." He nodded, for drama. "Nothing you feel responsible for?"

"Not the FBI. We just want to know who he is."

"And how many are working with you on this?"

"Right now—just me."

"Stackhouse—"

"Stackhouse isn't FBI," interrupted Friedman.

Grip suddenly felt an unseen audience in the room. "But Stackhouse doesn't belong to the military. He's wearing civilian clothes."

"No," said Friedman. "Stackhouse isn't military."

The repetition was a whispered insight. Shauna Friedman was conducting an investigation in enemy territory. Perhaps trusting reality in that room as little as Grip himself. The perspective shifted—he needed to buy time. Time to think.

"But the cell is here?" he asked, just to say something.

"In the same building, a short distance away."

Grip nodded. "I'm thirsty," he said. Then, "Maybe Stackhouse can bring us something?"

"When we pick up Clay, we can get ourselves a drink."

Clay Stackhouse was obviously CIA, or part of their loosely affiliated enterprises and covert agencies known by other letters. Grip could tell after only a few minutes. Stackhouse was the type who could have done a hundred push-ups in a row twenty years ago, when he was in the marines. A guy who thought of himself as still in good shape. But many belt holes later, after the years of barbecues in the Virginia suburbs and the heavy-bottomed glasses of Jack Daniel's, he'd be lucky to do five. The type who thought he knew the Middle East, who liked to drown out everyone else by saying what his Arab friends thought whenever he heard arguments he didn't like. Friends who in fact were mostly businessmen from Beirut and Riyadh, whose sons already went to private schools in the United States and who hoped their useful American contacts would help them get out when everything collapsed and the jihadists took over. These days, you bumped into Stackhouse types all over the world. A dime a dozen.

All three were back in the room. Stackhouse sat on the table next to the television screen, holding a cup of iced coffee. He called Grip by his first name and talked about the food that the man in the cell could soon look forward to. How the prisoner would be able to shower the next day. It gave Grip the feeling that someone had captured a rare animal and got stuck taking care of it.

"He answers when spoken to?" asked Grip.

"That was a long time ago, Ernst."

"When?"

"Several months ago." Stackhouse looked down at the TV picture whenever sounds of movement broke the silence through the speaker. Only when the picture was still and the sound had stopped did he look up again. "He spoke English, in case you're wondering."

"With an accent, any accent?"

"No one who attended the sessions was trained to determine that."

"Trained to determine . . ." Grip let it go. "Is he a Muslim?" he asked instead.

"We haven't noticed anything that would suggest that."

"So what *have* you noticed?"

Stackhouse looked at him blankly.

"What do you know about him?" Grip repeated.

"He has dark hair."

"Colombian, perhaps," suggested Grip. He gestured toward the photographs on the table. "No one can tell anything about him, not from these." Neither Stackhouse nor Friedman looked at the images. "Half his face is bruised. He was still bloody when those pictures were taken. He could be Portuguese or he could damn well be Japanese. Christ!"

Stackhouse spun his cup so that the ice cubes rattled around in the coffee. "We have very reliable intelligence, Ernst—"

"That may be true," interrupted Grip. "And I look forward to receiving it."

Stackhouse continued to spin his cup. The man on the bunk lay motionless with his back to the camera. A cautious silence filled the room.

"You want me to interrogate him?" said Grip eventually.

Shauna responded first. "We are offering you the chance to find out if he is one of yours."

"Mine?"

"If he is Swedish."

Grip humphed.

"Shouldn't you take the opportunity to go in to him?" asked Stackhouse, chewing on a piece of ice.

"Not today."

Stackhouse shrugged.

A moaning sigh could be heard through the speaker. As Friedman signaled that they were leaving, Grip noticed cool air blowing in through a vent behind him. That and the prisoner's moan made him ask, "How hot is it in there?"

"Hot enough," said Stackhouse.

Friedman turned, her hand on the door handle, and Grip felt her gaze from the side.

"Is the air-conditioning even on?" he asked.

"He refuses to talk." Stackhouse looked at the last ice cube, which spun on the bottom of his cup. Then he glanced up again, satisfied at having given the perfect response.

"Brilliant," said Grip. "His mind is frying. It's unbearable in there."

"Not unbearable enough, apparently. All privileges are available to him, it's a simple question of cooperation." Stackhouse crumpled his paper cup and tossed it over the top of the desk. "There's water in there. He can drink as much as he wants."

Grip looked at him and then turned to Friedman. "If you want *me* to cooperate at all, turn on the air-conditioning." He opened the door and went out.

Friedman lingered in the doorway. The door swung closed again, but it was too thin to block out her short "Damn it!"


Afternoon. The sun had passed its zenith only an hour before, and the heat lay like a lid over the island. But he couldn't sit and stare at his hotel room. Grip decided to go out for a run.

Keeping his pace slow, he got to know the base through its streets and back roads. There was no risk getting lost: the main part of the island was barely more than half a mile wide. He ran past the harbor, located on the inner side of the atoll, saw a couple of ships docked there, a few gray-painted warships anchored farther out. Ten minutes to the south, he came to the airport. A path ran alongside it, a few hundred yards away. The air was filled with engine noise, but he saw no aircraft taking off or landing. Where the runway came to a stop, the road continued farther south. Here the vegetation was higher, but the trees still weren't tall enough to cool him with their shadows. Humidity rose up from the greenery, making the air hard to breathe. Beside the paved trail were white patches of coral sand, and between branches he caught glimpses of the sea. But he couldn't hear it, not with the airplane engines howling somewhere behind him. Then a passing convoy of trucks drowned out his impressions.

Grip slowed down, walked for a minute. At the signs for ammunition stockpiles, he turned and started running again.

New lines of trucks came from behind, belching out black diesel smoke. He glanced up at their flatbeds. They were loaded with bombs. Hundreds of them.

What were they doing, the Americans? Were they planning to start a new war, or had they not yet ended the last one? What the hell were they doing, and what the hell was he getting himself into?

# CHAPTER 10

"RIP IS FICKLE, AND GRIP likes art." Little more was ever said when someone at work sized him up. Then they turned to the usual: punctual, loyal, and well dressed. Everything that said nothing. (If you wanted a security police assignment as bodyguard for the royal family or a government official, you had to look sharp.)

The art, that was the easiest to handle. Asked during a coffee break what he'd done over the weekend, he could honestly answer that he'd been to a gallery. No one was really interested in that, not there. Occasionally a young lawyer in the hallway would ask who his favorite painter was, hoping he'd say Dalí or Matisse. These types loved to have their good taste confirmed. Grip always replied "Lucien Freud," which drew a blank look—and then they changed the subject, which was the goal. Moreover, it wasn't true. Freud was good, but his naked yellow-gray bodies made Grip think too often of Auschwitz.

Not that he was ashamed of his taste, but it was simpler. Or rather, it was predictable: exactly what a policeman who suddenly takes an interest in art would fall for. Mainstream. Reproduced on posters you could buy at Åhléns department store and slap up over the couch. But Grip had liked Edward Hopper's paintings as long as he could remember. Their names alone: *Cape Cod Evening, Nighthawks, Early Sunday Morning*—this was art for lonely people.

The fickle part was harder. Some saw him as a hero. Grip and the women, world champion of one-week relationships and one-night stands. Two in a single night, a colleague's estranged wife, many more. There were stories about him, one more outrageous than the next. The attic apartment he'd inherited on Norrmälarstrand, overlooking the Stockholm waterfront, didn't hurt. At least, that was what he said when drinking a few beers with colleagues in the sauna.

Grip had been hungry ever since the first youthful spots on his sheets. Wanting to try what others only fantasized about, finding his way to the fearless ones who laughed back, the ones who also wanted it. Games with new positions had started before the end of adolescence. Later: bruises, leather straps, and candles—anything that excited—on airplanes, in hotel elevators with the emergency stop button pushed. A grunting nocturnal animal, a machine of flesh and blood who wasn't ashamed of himself.

But he never found redemption. He came and came, without any sense of peace. The game went on for far too many years. The cursed hunger devoured him, demanded the next level or simply something different. A demon to be exorcised every time. In the end, he could only make love—or as he put it, *knock off, clear himself*—in complete darkness. He couldn't bear to look at faces.

Waking up together, that he could sometimes do. Sometimes. Sometimes even a relationship. But he could never stand the ones who wanted to share closeness in the morning light. He was like a vampire. The dark was made for that—after the final trembling, it was every man for himself. Some shared that need, could live like that for a while. But then he always hit the point where some triviality would start to irritate him beyond reason. They ate from the refrigerator without asking, or dug around too much in his cupboards and closets.

For a while he dated a morning-TV host with big hair. She was young, had her own apartment, and never said a word about wanting it any other way. She liked the darkness and was as restless as he was; it worked. They showed up together in the tabloids—in the captions, he was "the policeman." Her breath smelled like a warm orchard breeze, she hated wearing skirts, and she screamed into the phone whenever he made excuses for sometimes wanting to spend a week alone. On the way to bed, she would braid her hair in a split second. And at a couple of ambitious restaurants in upscale Kungsholmen, her drinks were always on the house. Then came the rumors about her and some theater actor with sleepy eyes. Grip was surprised that he didn't care—he still thought he was getting what he needed. But when he saw all the empty white-wine bottles in her nightstand, and realized what the mints and apple scent were hiding, he'd had enough. Couldn't tolerate that kind of weakness.

That was a few years ago. Since then, most of his women had closed the door on him. Among his colleagues, a few stories hung around. Immortal feats, the prey in mink coats, the untamed Amazons, those far too young and far too old: "What about the one that . . ." A question to kill the boredom during a three a.m. stakeout. A colleague hoping for entertainment. Grip shrugged. None of them saw that the temple had collapsed, the tide had reversed.

The change was spelled New York.

It happened in the fall, but really it began in early August of the same year. A Belorussian lost his shit while being arrested in Stockholm and pushed a bookcase over onto Grip. It landed on him full force, dislocating his shoulder. The Belorussian was deported, shouting of excessive police violence, with two broken ribs and a black eye—but even though Grip had paid back, he was the one who needed surgery. A few titanium screws in his shoulder, and for that, he was out for ten weeks.

When he came back, the security police's own doctor—a moody type who ruled over his own arbitrary little kingdom of sickness and health—wasn't happy with the number of hours Grip had put in on physical therapy and barbells. Without even asking him to take off his shirt, he took Grip out of action for another two months. There was no point arguing. Causing trouble could trigger the sudden mention of a heart murmur in your record, leading to years of examinations. Such was the power of the white coat.

Another two months. Grip could stand it for about three days. He'd already been stuck at home for ten weeks, hardly getting out except to the weight room at the gym. His shoulders and biceps grew while everything else in life stood still. The dead time burned in his head as soon as he woke up in the morning. He had to make a break, get away.

One night he thumbed through his address book, made a call, and reminded someone of an old promise. She lived in Stockholm but also had an apartment in Brooklyn, on the outskirts of Williamsburg. No elevator, but brick walls and hardwood floors. Views over the balconies of Orthodox Jews, and to the west you could supposedly see part of Manhattan. "Feel free to borrow the place—any time." Said on a whim once (they'd spent a handful of nights together; she also loved predictable art, Jirlow and Grünewald, and was married)—but still, on the phone she seemed to remember her promise better than she remembered Grip. At any rate, it was enough; she stood by her word. She still needed someone to let in the workmen—a renovation that had dragged on too long, she herself never had time to be there. There was a doorman to give him the keys. "Stay as long as you want."

Everything was ready with a phone call. Grip threw out his few potted plants, put a plastic basket under his mail slot in the door, bought a ticket via London, went underground.

Williamsburg, New York. It started out predictably enough. Galleries and museums, and in between Grip searching for shops that sold the food he missed. Keeping up with his weights in a gym that overlooked barges on the East River. Letting in the workmen, who spent a few days replacing the old tiles in the bathroom with travertine and then disappeared again. He made a few attempts at the local bars. Halfhearted attempts, paying for drinks. No luck.

How many personality tests had he taken for the security police over the years? A dozen, twenty, something like that. Pages filled with tricky timed questions, hypothetical moral dilemmas, boxes to tick, yes/no. *We want to identify trends among our staff members.* After a week of interviews, hired psychologists would summarize you in a ten-minute briefing. "I see that loneliness does not scare you. You seem to enjoy danger." Yet never more than tiptoeing around the edges of who you really were. Had anyone been able to predict what would happen, who he'd become after his houseplants were thrown out? A security police officer on sick leave, between borrowed sheets in New York.

Instead of all checkmarks and contrived statements, he should have shown them a picture. "There, that's me," he could have said, pointing to the smuggler at the back of the boat in Hopper's *The Bootleggers*. Calm, blue-gray water in the foreground, a crude little wooden boat making its way along the coast. In the background, a character on shore watches the boat and the two men in it. "There I am." The figure in the stern, with his back to the viewer. He's right where he wants to be, but he doesn't belong anywhere.

What nobody could have predicted had occurred by chance. Or at least afterward, that's the way it seemed. One coffee too many, perhaps, he was out on some errand one afternoon and needed to find a bathroom. The door was black with a pane of glass at eye level—a bar, just what he was looking for. He opened it, walked in. There were only a few customers. Nodded at the bartender when he passed the counter to avoid issues and looked for the bathroom, among unmarked doors in the gloom at the back. Did his thing, went out again. Then continued as before, back up the street.

But that was when something caught up with him from the bar, an overwhelming feeling. His steps slowed. For a moment, for a few seconds, he felt like a child coming home to his bedroom after a trip. A sense of loss and familiarity at the same time. But he hadn't seen anyone he recognized inside the bar. He'd simply noticed a hand patting someone else's shoulder, and from a table at the side heard a low, sincere laugh. Grip passed a street sign, memorized the address. He returned a few days later after getting up the courage. A Friday night.

There were a lot more people now, crowded, a haze of faces. The familiar tingle more intense in his body. "*It's the dark night of my soul . . .*" Tracks of Depeche Mode lay like a carpet over the din. Suggestive guitars, French 1980s pop, "*avec son sabre, attaque les cavaliers . . .*" The air was sweet, the interior black. There was a suppressed restlessness. Everything floating. A state of preparation: short conversations, smiles, ice spun in half-full glasses. The bartender nodded, recognizing Grip. Two mouthfuls of whisky at a time; the skin on his back felt the slightest touch. There were glances he let slide, and others he eagerly devoured. All that remained of his other life was the name Grip, and hardly that. His entire life was on idle on the other side of the Atlantic. Two months that didn't exist. Another *I* began to form: caterpillar, chrysalis, empty shell, butterfly. Ernst Grip saw only men around him. A hand groped next to him. He took it in his and led it inexorably up between his legs.

The first time he came, man to man, there were no names, just lips, thighs, and greedy nakedness. Not the second or third time either. For more than two weeks, he gave in to it—he counted sixteen days, or more precisely, sixteen nights. It was as if he had been lame and suddenly learned to walk, never wanting to stop. To express himself in a way that did not require darkness, only the anonymity of bars. Tips on where he should go next whispered as golden chain letters between blow jobs and caresses. A nocturnal pilgrimage between beds and bars. First mostly around Williamsburg, but soon enough also to Manhattan and Chelsea. He woke up sore and empty, always naked, always as himself.

B enjamin Hayden was the first Grip met in daylight. He was wiry, calm, and squinted whenever he poured something into a glass.

The first time they crossed paths was at a vernissage with good champagne but lousy art. Benjamin had a small entourage around him, his thin, tanned arm carrying a bottle of champagne he'd stolen from a waitress. He poured for himself and others, pointing casually with the bottleneck at the row of paintings, and said something about how here was yet another American who painted Tuscany as cheap orgasms in ocher. A woman laughed loudest; he filled her glass again, squinting. Then he came up to Grip, standing by himself a few steps away, looked at the canvas in front of him, and said, "Don't you think Italian customs should seize the paints and brushes from every American who lands at Florence airport?"

A pair of heels clicked sharply across the floor, a masculine woman in a suit. A pair of long earrings dangled, while in the doorway behind her the waitress stood pointing.

"Excuse me," said Benjamin to Grip. Apart from the sound of her heels, he couldn't have caught more than a movement in the corner of his eye, but he turned to her with warm and open arms.

A few nights later they passed each other at a bar. Benjamin stopped Grip with one hand over his chest and held out the other to shake.

"Ben," he said, presenting himself without the condescension of the vernissage, as if it were obvious that they should get to know each other. It was evening, night thirteen in Grip's new era.

There was an undercurrent in Ben that made Grip hold back a little. His first instinct was that Ben was married—a sensitivity he carried from his past. Later he would understand that it was Ben who saw more, who could see what glowed beneath the surface of Grip. He recognized the newcomer, one who had just taken the leap, insatiable, wanting only to devour. Ben was beyond playing at something he was not. Although there were suggestions, and they circled hungrily around each other, they never made contact beyond the first handshake. When decision hung in the air, and Grip pressed on again, Ben took a business card and tucked it in his breast pocket.

"Please, let me know when you're ready," he said. "We can . . ." He paused, struck his finger against the rim of his glass on the bar, looked up again. "Good luck."

Later that night and for the next three nights, Grip found other men to be devoured by. He needed to recuperate, didn't realize it then, didn't even think about it, but was surprised by his own relief when he called the number on the business card, and Ben suggested that they meet early afternoon at the Whitney Museum café. Just meet the way most people do.

They sat beside the huge plate-glass windows, just that, a couple of relaxed hours, parted, and from there everything swept forward. That week Grip's daily rhythm returned to something like normal—he even woke up alone and at home, and ate breakfast before the construction workers' jackhammers had stopped for lunch across the street. He ate dinner out with Ben every night, accompanied him to parties a few times. They hung out with Ben's circle. But no night together, not even close.

Finally one evening, Ben asked: "Are you ready?"

Grip understood perfectly. There had been no contract between them. Even after his daily rhythm had been restored, and Benjamin Hayden became Ben, Grip had still desired other men. Lust was lust. As Ben himself said of him, "With that accent and those bulging arms." It wasn't complicated, firefighting that had nothing to do with Ben.

Are you ready?

To swear an oath, even if the fine print hadn't yet dried. There and then, at the kind of crossroads in life where at most you get a second to think. Yet he lived for the spirit of that, for the few moments in life when everything hangs in the balance. Grip nodded.

"Say it," said Ben.

Perhaps the realization came just then. "Now I am," said Grip. It sounded defiant, even if he didn't mean it that way. Something trembled in Ben. It disappeared. He laughed briefly and said, "You think you are, but warn me beforehand. For God's sake, warn me."

But Grip would never have to do that. Because Ben wasn't the type to need constant reassurance—when Ben touched him, he did it in a most natural and obvious way. Grip had never experienced that before. Someone whose presence made him feel calm. Nothing more, just that. It changed everything, and a different kind of life began.

White shirts and a tan can hide a lot. Age was one thing— Ben turned out to be almost ten years older. The other was the virus. That Ben's fragility could be contagious, Grip wasn't at all

73

concerned about; instead Ben was the one careful about certain details. He was, after all, the person busy keeping death at bay. His bathroom cabinet was filled with pill bottles, and too often he clung to articles about new findings, and to rumors. There was a certain vanity in it, given that his prognosis was hopeless. Being forced to use condoms, and not kissing, those were trivial, under the circumstances.

For several years Ben had been the manager of a gallery on the outskirts of the Flatiron District. The owner had made a fortune in industrial properties in Jersey, and his third wife convinced him to open their own gallery. But his wife soon lost interest, and the owner wasn't around, so it was Ben who ran the place. He had pretty much lost interest too, but it kept him afloat. The gallery survived mostly on its annual show by a Jewish artist from Massachusetts. He was best known for his unsavory insects made from parts of real bugs, for his huge ball made from thousands of pieces of chewed gum, and for once having carved a bust of himself in an aspirin tablet. Some noted collectors had invested, and then David Bowie bought a piece; after that prices had only gone up. The artist himself was said to spend his money on high-stakes poker; for the gallery and Ben, it meant they kept going, no better.

"Security police," said Ben, thoughtfully rubbing his beard-stubble when Grip told him about himself. By then, Grip had moved in with him in Chelsea, and there were only two weeks left before he had to leave New York.

"Security police—I thought only Bulgaria and banana republics had them. Security police, that's what they say on the news when some human rights activist has been beaten or people have disappeared, that the security police have been on the move." He gazed at Grip and crossed his thin arms. "In the real world, they're

always three letters: GRU, CIA, MI5. Am I right?" Ben was originally from Houston and could never shake the fact that he was a
devout Republican.

"You a good shot?" he wondered. "Two bullets from thirty
yards, and both within an inch of each other, in the chest?"

Grip shrugged.

Ben liked it. Also Miles Davis, of course, though he never admitted it, and an occasional Hopper painting would be all right too.


G rip went back to Stockholm. Farewell was no farewell; between
their two cups of coffee that morning, they both knew that something had just begun. After breakfast Ben picked up clean shirts
from the Chinese laundry on his way to the gallery, while Grip
took a taxi to JFK.

In Stockholm, Grip went to see the doctor again, this time at
least getting to take off his shirt. And with that, he was back for
real. The first thing he did on the job was submit an application for
transfer. He wanted to join the bodyguard detachment, not least for
the overtime. When they worked, they worked round the clock,
and afterward were off accordingly. His old boss was furious, called
it a hell of a waste. But Grip had performed enough unholy services
under his direction. "I'll still need you sometimes." Grip nodded,
and with that, the man who would always be the Boss had signed
his consent. Then Human Resources did their usual thing: checked
his loans and bank accounts, asked him to fill out some routine papers about his family. Dad was dead and Mom senile, no problem.
And really, what would they ever find out by asking people to tick
boxes? If something happened, a real scandal, a juicy revelation,
at least they could pick up their sheet and say, We did our best to

screen out people with black marks in their past. Ticks in the box. Everybody happy.

Grip got his royal family assignment and bought two new suits with room for a bulletproof vest underneath. Then it was business as usual: some official state visits, strolling down the cobblestone streets of a market town, subduing drunks, Solliden Palace in summertime, then a trip to the Riviera. He trained in rapid firing on the shooting range and listened to the latest concoctions from the threat analysts. Like everything else, these went in cycles, sometimes fixated on the stone-throwing Left, sometimes just blurry pictures of bearded Palestinians. They never talked about the lone crazies, the outliers, the ones they never could get to anyway. And so Grip gazed out over the public gatherings, over the people with their outstretched hands, looking for the ones in the background who just stood quietly, staring, preparing to leap.

He got to knee two German paparazzi, that was all. Autumn came.

The bodyguard detachment was the security police's refuge for the divorced, newly divorced, and never married. Their stories were mostly of compassionate lies and failures. Life without the earphone was life on a different planet; for many, their civilian time was a wasteland. In any event, everyone minded their own business. Their mountain of overtime compensation was the captain's biggest problem, and what his staff did when he could find gaps to send them away, nobody cared about. "Lundgren, von Hoffsten, Grip, take ten days—now!" Lockers were slammed, cell phones turned off. Maybe they took the time to have a beer, usually not. A few brief nods. And so each headed out on his own.

Grip didn't even pack—he already had what he needed in New York. He usually landed sometime after lunch and then headed to the gallery. It took no more than a glance and a smile over Ben's shoulder as he stood talking with a customer. Certainly they missed each other, but there was no jealousy or worry. The state of affairs was completely clear. Till death do us part. In the fall they went up to Cape Cod for a long weekend. Stayed at a small hotel with a yellow facade that Hopper had once painted, walked between the lighthouses under the clouds.

One night they sat in one of the few restaurants that hadn't yet closed for the season. Ben had downed a couple of martinis before dinner, and they were on their second bottle of red. Ben squinted so it stretched even the corner of his mouth when he poured the last in Grip's glass.

"You're security police," he said, waving the bottle to the girl at the bar. "Most art is just stuff. Dead things." He took a big gulp from his glass and cleared his throat. "I appraise art, you know. All kinds of fools want to hear what a man like me thinks." He rubbed his mouth drunkenly. "Their eyes shine when they find out what it's worth. Then if you can find some new thing for their walls or their pedestals, they'll pay anything. It has to cost them, that's the thing." He let the knife spin on the tablecloth.

"Jean Arp," he said then, "what do you know about Arp?"

Grip was only half listening to what Ben was saying. "Nothing," he replied.

"Sculptures," said Ben, and raised his hand dismissively. "There are people who"—he paused, drank of the wine—"people who need help."

Now Grip knew it would be about money. That was the dark side, the eclipse—until death do us part. They needed money, lots of money, to postpone the prophecies that faced them. Sums that caused them to sit up at night staring at each other. Until the moment nearly twenty years ago when the nurse handed him a slip that said "positive," Ben had been living like an immortal. He couldn't afford anything else anyhow: as a freelance art writer, at best money meant paying the rent on time. He knew better, knew damn well he needed to do better, but health insurance, he'd get to that later. Later, later, later, until he sat with that slip in his hand. He tried to fix it, but it turned into a gauntlet of pitying glances. Sooner or later a remark about the disease always came up, and the insurance agent would shoot the application forms a little too far to the side. He had to take out a loan, he had to have care. In those days, the doctors in their white coats offered a lot, but nothing that would help. He arranged creditors, endorsements by others wandering in the same desert. They signed for each other. Almost every one of them was dead now. And then the probates ended the pyramid game against the banks. Ben came to dread phone calls from lawyers more than the notes saying that another emaciated friend had given up the ghost, among addicts and homeless people in some county hospital. While the insurance agents had at least been sympathetic, the faces of the bankers and the lawyers they hired were cold.

To save himself, falsity became second nature: to throw out mail, to lie under oath, to question the authenticity of his own old signatures. To hunt for medical certificates that said he was dying and therefore not available. Everything was about procrastination. It was a decades-long war of broken promises and betrayed confidences. Everyone and no one was the enemy. Or—the banks and lawyers were the enemy. Always.

And it had worked, it had just barely worked. These days Grip took care of the most pressing bills, the overdue fees that keep Ben from being sued by his own lawyers. But more than that he could not manage, and Ben needed doctors more than ever. His lungs rattled, and now and then the shortness of breath forced him down on his knees with blue lips. But the doctors who could treat him only took cold cash.

" . . . people that need a bit of help," said Ben. "They pay well." Drinking deep drafts of the wine again, Grip lowered his eyes from the deserted street outside the restaurant.

"Help?" he said. They had both agreed that Grip would never get mixed up in the paper war over money, that his name or signature would never show up in those battles. There were many reasons for that.

"Help, with Jean Arp," said Ben, putting the glass down. "I will certify its authenticity."

"The sculptures are fake?"

"No, everything indicates that they are genuine."

"Wait—to certify the authenticity of something authentic, does that pay much?"

"It depends on the context." Ben's eyes grew clearer.

This was about more than money and perjury. Out of habit, Grip looked over his shoulder. No one was near them.

"First, they must get their hands on them, the Arp sculptures," said Ben.

"Theft," said Grip, giving it its proper name. He weighed the word like a tool in his hand.

"A person with a lot of money pays so that someone else, just as wealthy as he, will in turn lose them. In the process, I examine the sculptures and say that they are what they are."

"Should make a couple of thousand," murmured Grip.

"Usually something like that," replied Ben with a shrug.

That's how it was; Ben earned extra money by appraising stolen goods. And of course it was something Ben never talked about.

But now he wanted more. A few thousand dollars at a time, under the circumstances, was like collecting bottle deposits to pay for a space flight. Grip shifted in his chair, uncertain about where they were going. At the same time, he knew that Ben was so drunk he'd drowned any reluctance to say what was on his mind.

"Now they need help, planning a few details for the next bust." Ben's hand seemed to lie on the table, but in fact it hovered a few millimeters above. Apologies already prepared, and a thousand phrases that said "Forget it" as soon as he'd laid out what he needed to. But Grip was sitting perfectly still. He understood. Understood perfectly. The idea was to bring him in next time. With him being part of the planning, they could pay off a lot more bills.

"A robbery," Grip said then. Not even a question. Not even a flinch.

Ben wasn't sure. "Of the wealthy, they have—"

Grip struck his palm on the table: "Don't ask!" The girl behind the bar looked up, but couldn't hear the rest. Grip stopped a second and then said in a low voice: "I'm not a child and I'm not a toy. If we are something, you and I, then we don't pretend. We talk about how it is. I know what a robbery is, and I know exactly what's at stake."

Ben's hand kept hovering. His splayed fingers trembled. Not even three martinis and two bottles of wine could keep away his fear of death.

They went back to the hotel that Edward Hopper painted. Complete silence between them. Not war, just silence. It was the third and final night in the same room, and what over a weekend had become familiar now seemed completely foreign. Decorations, light, furniture.

It was five o'clock in the morning when Grip woke Ben up, a hand shaking his shoulder.

"What have you told them?"

"Nothing," replied Ben after a few seconds, coming back to the surface, "only that I know someone."

"Security police?"

"No." Ben slowly turned around. "I met them, understood that they need people, I said I knew someone."

"Is that all?"

"A Swede, I said. You know, Europeans always arouse interest in those types."

"And the connection between us?"

"They have no idea. I said you could be reached through an intermediary."

"But Swedish, you said?"

"Your accent, you would meet . . . It was hardly a revelation."

A car's headlights shone through the gaps of the blinds. Nothing more was said.


Back in New York, three days later. Ben stood bony and curved like a bird carcass, coughing his lungs out over the sink. When he sank deeper in exhausted recovery, Grip walked in behind him in the bathroom. Their eyes met briefly in the mirror.

"How much do they pay?" said Grip.

Ben turned his eyes away, panting.

Grip slowly stretched his back against the doorpost. "Be sure to talk with them," he said, and went out again.

# CHAPTER 11

I T WAS DURING A STATE visit with the royal couple in Hungary
that Grip got an e-mail from Ben, saying a "sponsor" wanted to
meet him in New York ASAP. A second e-mail contained a link
for works by French sculptors. Scrolled past the Rodin bronzes,
found the Jean Arps. Rounded, sensual shapes in granite, made by
someone who must have liked touching women.

Grip opened his datebook as his earphone roared: "The queen
wants to leave early." It was dinner with the president, already past
midnight. Grip sat at a computer in a single room that he'd found
away from the dinner buzz. No response, on the radio. Grip glanced
at some possible dates, marked one with a pencil, shut the calendar.

"I'll take her," he replied, getting up.

L ess than a week later. Back from Hungary. Off duty. Another
flight, then New York again.

The meeting was in a brick no-man's-land near the Brooklyn
Navy Yard. Grip had an address, took a taxi. The place turned out
to be a workshop for theater scenery and large department-store
displays. Seven men were waiting inside, but two did most of the
talking. It was obvious who they were, definitely pros—a group of
cash-in-transit robbers with a few add-ons: extra muscle, capable
drivers, that type. They used only first names, and the two talkers

had no visible tattoos. So far, so good. Eventually they unfolded a worn-out tourist map of New York, and the two walked through their plan. A truck was supposed to leave a freight forwarder's storage facility at a specified time. That was all there was to it. No escort, no armored cars, no coded lock. Just a truck carrying a lot of stuff and two sculptures by Arp. Piece of cake.

But the men in the Brooklyn workshop were used to hitting armored cars, and they had a certain way of doing things. Guns, handcuffs, getaway cars, tire spikes. All undeniably well-thought-out, a surprise raid, complete with escape routes and torching of gasoline-soaked cars to destroy the evidence and fry the DNA. The sticking point was the loading—the Arps did, after all, weigh several hundred pounds. And that was the reason they'd brought in Grip.

Grip sensed that they already looked up to him. Without him saying a word, they seemed to treat him with respect. Ben had made up extravagant lies about his background. Although he hadn't told Grip much, Ben confessed he'd told his contacts that the Swede was an experienced art thief. "You damn fool," Grip had sworn when he heard about it the first time. "Art thief!" He had no idea what that meant anyway. What could he say? He wanted to call it off, had come close to postponing the meeting when Ben's cough made him shut up. After the taxi let him off outside the workshop and he saw the lights and the men in the windows, he did a lap around the block—he was *that* close to getting the hell out of there. But really, what were the options? " . . . good money . . . you'll be rewarded for your services . . ."

A first time for everything. He'd spent years among scum, but had never been one of them. That's why his heart was hammering when he walked into the workshop, the pounding heart and sweaty hands of a goddamn amateur. They shook hands and looked him over. Any second, he'd be thrown out. He was convinced of it. Beaten up and thrown out—at best. But nothing happened. Someone kept talking, mentioned names he'd never remember. His mouth was dry, he felt transparent, his back tensed whenever someone moved behind him. But then he saw the torn map and heard their plan. And at that moment, he got his nerve back. Not thinking about Ben, just about how easy this was. How easy it would be to pick up something that wasn't his. It was the first time.

The men in the workshop weren't idiots, but their plan was over the top, almost cartoonish.

"What about loading?" they asked.

Grip crossed his arms over his chest, said, "Just a sec," and went back to the beginning, when fingers had started tapping the map. He scrapped the whole plan. Told them to forget about the weapons, the gasoline, the tire spikes. "Give the police a day off," he said. And with little nods to places on the map, he rewrote it. The two who'd laid out the original plan stood there, the others sat. Grip explained the critical parts—how they could take the truck before it even arrived at the warehouse, just by switching drivers. No car chases, no flaming fireballs, no bloodthirsty guys shouting with stolen automatic weapons in their hands. It wouldn't be a hit to brag about in the clink. But one peaceful afternoon in September, the Brooklyn police would keep driving right down Ocean Avenue, while not far away, someone with too much money was stripped of his two Arp sculptures. That was a security policeman's perspective on things, if it had to be done.

Grip put the pen on the table and turned around with a look that said he was finished.

It took a second, then said one of the two leaders: "We'll see."

There was silence again.

From the start, instinctively, Grip disliked a man in the room named Romeo. One of the hired guys, an overweight jerk with a cap who jiggled his legs up and down like a cocky teenager. Now he snorted, but when everyone turned around, he said nothing, just smiled with contempt at Grip and shrugged.

"Shut up," said one of the leaders.

Romeo pulled down his cap and shrugged again.

"So where do you come into this?" asked Grip, with a nod toward the leg jiggler.

"Who's asking?" Romeo, older than Grip, rocked backward on his chair.

"He drives," replied the one who'd told him to shut up.

Grip stared at Romeo. "People can't drive with their head up their ass. Try to remember that."

The chair's front legs hung in midair. Romeo lifted his hand, urging Grip to come closer. He was just about to say something when the other man hissed: "He drives!" Cutting it off. Grip shrugged again.

Then the two leaders threw him a few what-if questions. It was mostly for show; there were no holes in Grip's plan.

"We'll be in touch," they said then.

Grip stood for a moment, legs apart, and looked at them, memorizing their faces. Ben had assured him he'd only have to listen, give advice, not participate, not get caught. That was for laborers. A paid job that brought people together, with someone invisible pulling the strings. The men in the workshop didn't know anything about an art expert—how Ben's eyes and hands would eventually confirm that the pieces of granite were indeed authentic sculptures by Arp, protruding from the Styrofoam in broken crates. And Ben was never one to mention names. So far, everything seemed fine. So far.

"You do whatever," he told them. Heart not racing, palms dry. "If you use my plan, you pay."

He left. Walked all the way over the Brooklyn Bridge and back to Ben's apartment in Chelsea.

When he woke up the next night, it all seemed like a costume party. A kind of game. Like when drunk cops sat at home together and, instead of playing cards, slurred over the heists they'd dreamed up—how easy it'd be to pull them off. This time was hardly worse: a workshop, some first names, a torn map, and some good advice.

Nothing really, just a little talk. Right?


Back in Sweden again, Grip bought the *New York Times* every evening from the Pressbyrån newsstand at Central Station. Twenty-six days in a row, twenty-six front pages about Bush and Iraq, before the article finally appeared. Not large, but not small either. Two stolen sculptures by Arp, a fuzzy picture. A truck that disappeared, no violence—a footnote.

Ben phoned later that evening. Began by saying that he loved Grip, talked nonstop, maybe had been drinking, and ended by saying that *they* had paid. There was no shame in the silence between them. It was done. They said good-bye and hung up.

Autumn rolled along, a doctor treated Ben, and his cough went away. It could have been fine that way. It could have been enough, right there.

# CHAPTER 12

W HAT IF YOU ACTUALLY DECIDE to take action?" It was Bill
who said it, Bill Adderloy. Bill had slowly slipped into their
circle. After calling Reza an idiot, he'd repeatedly turned up
at their table with his cane, which was, it turned out, mostly for
show. Slightly older than the others, Bill Adderloy had a grizzled
beard that rose when he spoke. He smoked, wore long sleeves, and
had a large ring on one hand. Like other Americans, he jingled
coins in his pockets and constantly asked for more ice in his drinks.

"I mean—actually decide."

He didn't take the sting out of what he'd said with a laugh—the
usual way out when someone touched on something serious under the palm-leaf roof. Instead he waited them out: Vladislav, N.,
Mary, and Reza. Bill Adderloy was serious.

By the time Bill joined them, circumstances had already
changed. N. suffered from severe restlessness. The night with Mary
had left him with an inexplicable anxiety, as if at the beginning of
a good-bye. He was forced to drink more and more to fall asleep
at night, and the fat bundles of banknotes in his bag now fit too
easily in one envelope. The others were also down to eating fruit

for lunch, and even the generous Reza often paid for only his own Coke at the bar. Mary showed up later and later every morning and had started sleepwalking. Or at least, so N. thought. He woke up in his bungalow one night to find her standing next to his bed in just a white T-shirt, nothing else, looking at him. His first instinct was to lift the sheet for her, but then he hesitated.

"What is it?" he asked, seeing the whites of her dark eyes, not much more. She stood like that for an eternity, motionless as if he were a stranger, before she turned around and walked out. N. hadn't been able to go back to sleep, not until he got up and locked the door from inside.

Everyone felt it, the undercurrent of untamed energy. Vladislav ran longer in the mornings, and on his swims his little dot of a head disappeared at the horizon.

"Fuck you," he spat out between waves to the boat someone sent out after him one day.

Then Reza knocked out an Australian with a single punch at the bar. When the man's two friends pounced on him, he shouted "Come on!" with such a vicious look that they all backed off. Afterward he wept, and said something about being immortal.

It was at such times that Bill would show up at their table.

"Impressive," he told Reza that time, and sat down. He didn't give a damn about the commotion right behind his chair, but raised a couple of fingers and a waiter came over immediately. The staff at Weejay's were like flies on a sugar cube, or rather, like hyenas—hyenas around a lion that had just taken down its prey. He left good tips, never just coins. One served while two others calmed the screaming Australians. No one dared to say a word against the American.

With Bill Adderloy's cigarettes came discussions. He rarely

puffed on them; his cigarettes burned down like incense between his motionless fingers as he laid out his ideology. He didn't think much of his own country. Reza nodded in agreement without saying anything. N., unimpressed, stayed to get a couple of whiskies at the speaker's expense. Mary was more engaged, argued on Adderloy's side, while smiling Vladislav amused himself by provoking people for the sake of it. Their evenings turned predictable.

N. drank and tried to suppress his yawns.

One day Adderloy said, "No, you deserve it," when they found out that he'd paid the Weejay's bills for all four bungalows and their food. No one argued.

Another time, Adderloy seemed to know that Mary was from somewhere in Kansas. N. couldn't remember ever hearing her say anything about it. Vladislav looked at Adderloy suspiciously.

"But what if you actually decide?" That was the instant their discussions took a different turn.

"Decide what?" Vladislav sat, his jaws tight. Mary listened intently.

It had started the night before, when Adderloy snorted at Reza: "Immortality—what's your secret?"

Reza had responded with a malevolent gaze. He hadn't forgotten that Adderloy had called him an idiot.

"That's what you feel like," said Vladislav, conciliatory, "when you've survived."

"You feel immortal too?"

"Not immortal," said Vladislav, and smiled his broadest white grin. "But strong."

"I am truly immortal," said Reza then, and leaned forward. "Right now, I mean—you do not understand. That day, the wave." He ran both hands through his hair. His lips were moist, his mind tuned to its inner images. "I went to bed late the night before. I fell asleep surrounded by relatives, thought I was sleeping in a city. It really was a city. There was a whole city around me when I fell asleep, but then when I woke up . . . My bed was in a room on the second floor, and I went to the window as I usually do." He made a motion with his hand, as if he were in a vast, open field. He swallowed. "Everything was gone," he whispered, "everything. Just me and the house left—nothing else, no one else. God forgot to count me in, I was overlooked." He leaned back. "You understand?"

"God?" said Mary. "You think it was God. That's . . ." She went silent.

"Immortal," said Reza grimly.

"How can you believe . . . God, so silly," Mary went on.

"Those hit by the tsunami, they died for our sins," said Adderloy. "There are people who believe it."

Vladislav shook his head. He looked at Reza.

"You've heard about them too," continued Adderloy, raising his chin. "About the American church that celebrates what happened as God's punishment. About their minister, Charles-Ray Turnbull."

He looked at N., recalling the night they'd talked about the minister and his followers. N. wasn't drunk enough yet. The anger took his breath away. His hands trembled. He remembered the pictures: the bloated bodies, the smiling minister called "Beloved Father." *Thank God.*

Adderloy fiddled with his ring, shrugged. "Those struck down were sinners, as simple as that." He tapped his cigarette, and the ashes fell in the sand. "That's the price, some say, the price of freedom in a country"—he kept looking down at the sand—"where anyone can say anything."

"Is it really a church?" Vladislav wondered.

Adderloy paid no attention. "You know they celebrated, right? They were especially happy about the children. They think that—"

"Bastards, they deserve to die," interrupted N.

Reza hit his palm on the table. "An American church." He spat something in his own language and continued: "No American church can come here and talk about my sins."

"Where's that church?" It was N. who asked.

"In Topeka," replied Adderloy. "Topeka, Kansas."

"But aren't you . . ." Vladislav looked puzzled.

"Yeah, I'm from Topeka," Mary said.

Adderloy waited as glances went around the table, watching the glow of his cigarette.

"Mary and I happened to be sitting at the same table one evening when people got started on the fanatics and the demonstrations. That's when we made the connection." Then he said to Mary: "Go on, tell them about Charles-Ray."

She said, her voice low, "Charles-Ray Turnbull is a hideous man. He often came to the hospital where I work, or worked." She paused a moment. "He used to donate blood. I'm sure he still does. He needs the money."

"They deserve—" continued N., angry again.

Adderloy looked up quickly at him. "Deserve what—deserve to be talked about?"

N. shifted uneasily in his chair, as if he had hit on something.

"And what if you actually decide to act?" continued Adderloy.

Reza replied with a snort.

"Decide what?" said Vladislav slowly.

Mary listened with narrowed eyes.

"They deserve to die," repeated N.

"To give them payback," replied Adderloy. Vladislav measured him with his eyes.

"Look at yourself, look at us," said Adderloy. "We don't exist. Beyond this stretch of sand . . ." He hesitated for a moment. "We're all lost. From now on, we make our own choices. We have to seize this opportunity, the time is now. Convergences like these come only once in a lifetime."

"For the chance to get revenge on the fanatics, sure. But you can do better," said Vladislav. "Why us?"

"We all need money. How long can you keep up this life? A couple of months, and then what? Rent out lounge chairs, or buy a gas stove and a wok to cook for tourists when they eventually return to the beaches? Or become hippies like the other westerners who never made it out of here? You've seen them, toothless fucking hobos with their fifteen-year-old girlfriend on the back of their moped. No, we're going to rob a bank and get a hell of a lot of money, and then lay the blame on someone more deserving. With a bang that gets the whole country's attention. We frame the minister— and we kill two birds with one stone. We give Charles-Ray what he deserves, at the same time as we get a shitload of money."

Vladislav gave a short laugh. "To give the loudmouth fuckers a taste of their own medicine." He looked at Reza. "I like that."

Reza jiggled both legs in his chair. "But he's a blood donor— what does that have to do with it? How—"

"No one gets it," said Vladislav. "Mr. Adderloy has worked it out, but he's not going to tell us everything yet."

Adderloy acknowledged him with a gesture.

"But to help him, he needs a few people who are invisible. And immortal," Vladislav added, taking a fresh look at Reza.

"We don't exist," said Mary.

"Whether we do or don't," said Vladislav with a toss of the head, "we need money, obviously, for the life we want to keep living."

"I have enough to start us off," replied Adderloy.

"Once we get to Topeka, we can stay at my place," said Mary. "It's secluded, and big enough for all of us."

N. hesitated. What was it they were about to do? He broke in: "What are we talking about here? Are we going to America to rob a bank?"

No one spoke.

"Well," said Vladislav finally in a loud voice, "crusading has never been my cup of tea. But I have to do something. I need the money, and you, Bill, need me. I'm in."

Adderloy's eyes narrowed to slits as he took a drag on his cigarette.

"See you," said Vladislav and got up from the table. When he left, it was with the same implacable calm as when he took his gun out of Reza's hand and walked up to the wounded pelican.

"Not a big talker, but he makes his point," said Adderloy when Vladislav disappeared. The only reply was the rush of the sea in the night.

"I think most everything has been said," he added, dropping his cigarette into the sand. "Sleep on it. I can hardly be the only one tired of paradise."

# CHAPTER 13

**Transcript of Hearing. Tape: 2 (3), N1315263**

**Date:**       April 12, 2008
**Location:**   El Dorado Correctional Facility, El Dorado,
                Kansas

Appearing:

Examining Officer Gordon Zachy (GZ), FBI
Assistant Shauna Friedman (SF), FBI

Defendant Reza Khan (RK), sentenced to death for five counts
of complicity in murder; bank robbery; seditious conspiracy;
terrorism; obstruction of justice; kidnapping; and aggravated
assault

**GZ:** But Reza, you were born in Peshawar, isn't that correct, in
Pakistan?
**RK:** Must we go over that again?
**GZ:** Yes.
**RK:** [*Says something unintelligible.*]
**GZ:** Reza, you're slurring. I know it's hard, but try.

**RK:** I said, I have already answered that question, on at least twenty different occasions. And I am suffering from a headache again.

**GZ:** You always have a headache, Reza. Were you born in Peshawar?

**RK:** So it states in my passport.

**GZ:** I'd like your answer.

**RK:** Is it a matter of consequence?

**GZ:** Yes, some of our investigations are ongoing.

**RK:** And do you genuinely believe I will be affected by that?

**GZ:** Very much so.

**RK:** [*Laughs.*]

**GZ:** There's nothing funny about this.

**RK:** No. [*Clears throat.*] Judgment has been made, I am going to die. For five murders, quite impressive.

**GZ:** Accessory to five murders, and a bank robbery.

**RK:** Right, accessory, absolutely right. My lawyer tries to keep my spirits up, sweating over endless contingencies. Contingencies! A judge has already sentenced me to death.

**GZ:** The conviction could be appealed.

**RK:** Not in Kansas. Not given what happened. Someone's blood must be sacrificed. And look, they even got ahold of a Pakistani. America cares about its Muslims, when they are dressed in orange jumpsuits.

**GZ:** There are extenuating circumstances. You know that.

**RZ:** You mean this here.

**GZ:** Mr. Khan was shot in the head in connection with the arrest, it—

**SF:** I know the facts.

**RK:** Suddenly *she* opens her mouth. [*Silence.*] Gordon and I are already well acquainted, but you . . . you are new—correct?

**SF:** Yes.

**RK:** And we have not met before?

**SF:** Never.

**GZ:** Mr. Khan's memory . . .

**RK:** She knows, she sees the damage to my head. Everyone does. You, Gordon, I have not seen in several months, and now you appear with a new woman by your side. Ongoing investigations, you say—how many additional life sentences do you hope to pile on me? Surely you can only kill me once.

**GZ:** It's not that.

**RK:** Do you hear how Gordon here is always trying to keep me calm? He knows that I sometimes start a fight. That is what he fears. Where did you say you were from?

**SF:** FBI.

**RK:** Kansas State Police, US Marshals, FBI. Is there no end to how many police you have—DEA, ATF, Secret Service—

**GZ:** Reza, stop with the tirades.

**RK:** Shauna, Shauna was it?

**SF:** Yes.

**RK:** [*Inaudible reply.*]

**GZ:** Reza, we cannot hear you.

**RK:** My apologies, Shauna. It was the shot, you know. My psychology, there are many explanations for it now. For how I function. Memory loss in connection with murder—so timely, no? But even the doctors concede that the damage is there. My skull is sunken, look for yourself.

**SF:** Thank you, that's enough.

**RK:** But that's just it, a shot to the head was not enough. I will be strapped down, given the injection, and only then will you be satisfied. And it all takes so much time.

**SF:** Do you still claim that you were not involved?

**RK:** Are you sure that we have never met before?

**SF:** Quite sure.

**RK:** Did you have long hair?

**SF:** That was a long time ago.

**GZ:** You missed her question, Reza.

**RK:** Yes, I miss questions, and I slur a little. What was it, right, whether I was involved. I never said that I was not involved. It is very likely that I was there, but I do not remember. They say we robbed a bank.

**SF:** What about the others, the ones who were with you, do you remember them?

**RK:** Gordon, weren't you asking just now if I was born in Peshawar?

**GZ:** We can come back to that later.

**RK:** No, no, the doctors have specifically pointed out my need for structure. The brain damage, the slurring, the memory—after so many operations, structure is the sole path to rehabilitation. Before I am strapped down for the final injection, that is. Given this, we must finish what we started. I believe I was born in Peshawar, because that is what is written in my passport. Can anyone have a reason to question that? And my answer should be consistent with all my other answers to this question. I thought you had given up long ago, Gordon?

**SF:** It was I who asked Gordon to ask you again.

**RK:** He could have given you the answer.

**SF:** We have not been able to trace any members of your family.

**RK:** No, you say that, and I do not remember them. Now what was your second question, Shauna?

**GZ:** Ms. Friedman is the proper form of address, Reza.

**RK:** [*An angry scream.*] Half my brain is gone, and you give me this shit!

**GZ:** Sit down, Reza.

**RK:** You heard the doctors, we have gotten sidetracked. Focus! I need to focus.

**SF:** I'm wondering about the others you were with, do you remember them?

**RK:** [*Breathless.*] Right, the others. You have not worked very much with those who have investigated this, right, Shauna? With Gordon here and all the others. [*Silence.*] My memories of the past few years are like scattered pieces of a puzzle—I cannot tell them apart and many are missing. I can speak perfectly well, except for the slur, but I hardly know who I am. Certainly, I remember many different people, and Gordon and others from the FBI have patiently tried to sort out those that are of particular interest. They are certainly noted in the reports.

**SF:** I've read some of them.

**RK:** I think they are interested in a tall man with large glasses, and also someone with an animal tattoo. Perhaps a monkey, perhaps a dog, perhaps the tattoo is located on the back. Then there is Adderloy, the only name I remember, Bill Adderloy. He is an older man with a beard, a very unpleasant man with a beard. He sometimes carries a cane. It has a handle carved like an animal skull. You would only need to hear his voice, the kind of voice that persuades people to do almost anything. Adderloy is as dangerous as the devil himself. [*Silence.*] Certainly there are one or two other people, but we have not had much luck with them, right? Also, two or three in the group spoke English with an accent. That should make four including me, perhaps.

**SF:** Is that all?

**RK:** There were also two brothers dressed in white. But they turned out to be the owners of the restaurant across from the house where I was arrested. I cannot help it, my mind. Blame it on the damn police officer, he said he was aiming at the legs but shot me in the head.

*[Silence.]*

**RK:** Does it surprise you that I am cooperating? I feel no guilt for the crimes I am convicted of, I do not remember them. I am just convinced that a few of these people are very dangerous, certainly Adderloy. That is the only feeling I carry with me from what happened, that they would be capable of killing any number of people.

**SF:** What about pictures?

**RK:** You mean of people. Are there any?

**SF:** What do you think about this one?

**RK:** Oh, I recognize him.

**SF:** Is he one of them?

**RK:** He might well be. He might also be a taxi driver I encountered at some point, or a movie star, or a former neighbor.

**SF:** It's not a movie star. We think he was with you. Do you know his name?

**RK:** No idea.

**SF:** Do you remember where you met him?

**RK:** No idea.

*[Silence.]*

**RK:** However, I think that he is Swedish.

# CHAPTER 14

URING THE POLICE INVESTIGATION THAT followed, it became clear that the Weejay group did not meet up again until they'd reached Toronto. An itemized credit card receipt from a hotel bar showed: Scotch, mojito, Bloody Mary, and a Coca-Cola.

Vladislav had, as usual, turned the drink menu inside out, and then asked the waitress, "What's in style?"

"Now?" It was morning. "A Bloody Mary, I guess."

"Is it colored?"

She didn't know what to say. "It has tomato in it."

"As in, food?"

N. sighed and raised his hand as a stop sign. "It'll be fine, he'll have one." He waved off the waitress. N. had left last and traveled farthest, via Tokyo and Vancouver, and he was wrestling with his jet lag.

When the drinks arrived, Vladislav took out the celery stalk, which baffled him, and emptied half his glass. Mary wanted only water. N. sipped his Scotch and then sat motionless, leaning his head against the corner. He opened his eyes when someone spoke, sucking on an ice cube.

Adderloy had picked the route each would take to Toronto. Since it was his money, no one had questioned him. "Getting to Canada, that's the way into America" was all he said. They'd been separated, fanned out, each with a stack of tickets, reunited a little more than a week later.

Adderloy got to the bar first, was already on his second drink. He smiled and told little stories about his trip. But every time he drank from the tall glass, he looked around nervously. Reza was still missing.

Vladislav was busy again with the waitress, trying to order a meal. Said he wanted something with fruit or fries. He'd made it to Toronto via a longer stop in South Africa. His stubble was several days old—he seemed to be growing a beard.

Another of Adderloy's instructions had been to buy new clothes. "Get whatever you need," he'd said before they left, handing them enough dollars to cover it. By then, Vladislav was down to ragged shorts and an undershirt. Now he sat in a shiny brown leather jacket so new that it squeaked. Paisley shirt, black pants. No trace of the tourist, bohemian, or whatever he'd been at Weejay's. Mary was more familiar, even if her smoky eye shadow was neater. A new black dress, thin sandals with straps up the calves. Didn't fit the season, but it suited Mary.

Every time N. opened his eyes, he looked at her. They'd nearly tripped over each other an hour before in a hotel hallway. For a moment, they stood like strangers. He wasn't expecting to see her, and she looked at him as if he were dead. As if she wasn't expecting to see him again—ever. But then, he'd been the one who'd hesitated the most over Adderloy's scheme. The awkwardness had lasted only a second, then they made polite conversation. She'd asked to see his arms, how the scars had healed.

Now she slowly rocked the glass of water between her fingers, with her usual nonchalance. She smiled at him, but only with her mouth.

Vladislav was served one plate with a sliced orange, another with what appeared to be hunks of fried fish.

Reza appeared. Looked around disoriented, as if the fact that everyone in the bar immediately noticed him had made him incapable of recognizing people. Blood-red Converses, white jeans. A black jacket with thin white stripes and oversize lapels. Inspired by the centerfold of some fashion magazine no one was supposed to take seriously. The jacket obviously expensive, the sunglasses too.

Vladislav laughed—that was how Reza found them. N. waited for Adderloy's reaction, surprised that all he said was "Welcome!" His expression made N. realize Reza was the one Adderloy most wanted to see again.

Reza sat down, looked around the room. Vladislav reached out to feel his short, newly bleached hair. Reza gave him an annoyed look, looked at the others around the table, and took off his sunglasses.

"What?" he said. No one answered. "Airport security fucked with me as usual, otherwise it was no problem. None."

"A Coke," he told the waitress, who was heading over. She turned around. "I've been here three days," he added, taking a fried piece from Vladislav's plate. "Toronto makes me nervous, it is too perfect." He took a bite. "When do we leave?"

"Soon enough," replied Adderloy, "maybe in a few days."

"Soon enough," repeated Reza low, as if he had already forgotten his own question.

N. saw that his eyes were bloodshot.

There was silence for a moment. Reza's Coke arrived.

"Look," said Adderloy, taking out newspapers from a briefcase that he'd left on the floor. There were papers from Kansas City, Wichita, and other cities in the Midwest, one from Dallas, and also the *New York Times*. Adderloy flipped through the pages and showed them articles from the past weeks. Photos from where the tsunami had hit, but also images from inside a church, where the minister who made N. flinch stood smiling among the pews. He beamed with self-satisfaction. "We have saved Sodom and Gomorrah, driven out Satan's demons." It was unclear whether the newspapers took a stand for or against. The only critical voice was an opinion piece clipped from the *New York Times*. There was also a picture of a desperate Asian woman—reportedly, she had lost all her children. "Another two million dollars," said the newspapers that interviewed the minister at his church, "that's all it takes to find final salvation."

"Turnbull's minions collect the money," explained Adderloy, "and organize demonstrations, make flyers, and take care of everything else that's going on right now."

"Those bastards will stop at nothing," said N.

"Why would they?" replied Adderloy. "It's not in their nature."

"Then we will behave the same," said Reza.

Adderloy started picking up the newspapers. "But let's not talk about that now. It's time to start making plans."

He pointed to a real estate ad in one of the newspapers: "It looks like Charles-Ray hasn't been doing so hot—forced to sell off all the land he owned outside of Topeka. The pockets of the crazy minister and his Westhill Baptist Church will soon be empty. But we—we are going to rob a bank for them."

There was silence around the table. The words, now that they were out, seemed to echo. Vladislav was the first to regain speech.

"What about weapons?" he said, without looking up from the orange slice he'd just bitten off.

Mary looked around, but no one else seemed to have heard him. N. felt hot, uneasy.

"We're all here now, that's the important thing," said Adderloy.

N. sucked up another piece of ice. The whisky had made him nauseous.

"Ideally MP5s," said Vladislav, picking a seed from his mouth.

N. sat, closed his eyes again, and winced when Vladislav nudged him, pointing to the bowl of sugar packets.

"MP5s?" asked Reza.

"Submachine guns," replied Adderloy, eyeing someone who walked past their table. Vladislav tore the corner off a bag and sprinkled an untouched slice of orange.

Another four days in Toronto. They ate well, but always separately. Didn't socialize, stayed at different hotels, while Adderloy prepared something. N. rarely left his room, surfed cable channels, ordered room service for breakfast and lunch, and forced himself to get dinner at some tavern he'd found in the yellow pages. Left most of it on the plate, before he took a taxi back through the night. He was surprised by his emptiness; it was only when he flipped past a TV evangelist that he felt something, a moment of confused rage.

He would get revenge for his girls, under Adderloy's scheme. After that, whatever miserable scrap remained of his life wouldn't matter.

On television, the same news over and over: shattered cars, bodies, women screaming. Iraq, Palestine, Afghanistan. The weather never seemed to change: cloudy in Singapore, a hundred and four degrees in Cairo, risk of thunderstorms in Topeka. N. went to sleep, woke up, noticed the time passing only from the television's red digital numbers.

They met in the garage of Adderloy's hotel. Three cars, still wet from the rental agency. Adderloy handed out keys, maps, new cell phones. They piled in and headed out into the daylight. Mary had to travel alone—three adults in a car might look unusual, demand an explanation.

Border crossing, half an hour between each car. They decided to blend in with the stream of tourists and commuters crossing the Rainbow Bridge at Niagara Falls. At border control, traffic was bumper-to-bumper, but they kept slowly advancing, like cars on an assembly line. Beyond the concrete and guardrails, mist rose up from the cauldron of the falls. Sign after sign listed the border control rules. Vladislav sat and smoked beside N. in the car. Uniformed people everywhere: creased shirts over body armor, sunglasses, weapons—a short greeting, a few questions. Then a row of poles with the star-spangled banner, and the cars in front of them took off and disappeared one by one. Nothing more, it was that quick. They'd made it. Then back on the highway, south again toward Buffalo. Vladislav both drove and handled the cell, sending text messages, receiving answers. "Even Reza is through," he said, snapping a new butt out the side window. Half an hour later they'd reached the ring road around the city and made it to the airport. A pimply Mexican complained about the smell of smoke when they returned the rental car. Vladislav pushed him a few smooth notes.

Check-in, boarding passes, a quick coffee on the go, coins in the plastic bowl, belts off before the X-rays and metal detectors.

They still traveled two and two, with Mary ahead and by herself. Buffalo—Chicago—Kansas City. The last flight was delayed, and Vladislav and N. landed at dusk. They got another rental for the last stretch to Topeka. It started pouring rain as soon as they got out of the parking lot, and for sixty miles on the Kansas Turnpike, the wipers barely kept up. Evening lights shone around them in the watery darkness.

The cell phone rang. Vladislav answered and said they were on their way. At an Exxon gas station the rain stopped suddenly, leaving a silence that was almost uncomfortable. Plains extending either side. The total emptiness between Kansas City and Topeka.

To find the address in Topeka, they'd been given a hand-drawn map. It wasn't hard to follow; Mary had written down all the details. The street they were on was the right one, but it didn't feel like a place where anyone would live. Old brick buildings stood tall and black in the dark, along a street of uneven cobblestones with patches of asphalt. They passed facades with rows of windows, but without seeing a light in any of them. Low steel doors with thick layers of paint, sometimes a shiny new padlock. It was hard to tell where one building ended and another began; everywhere there were alleys, courtyards, exterior staircases, overhanging structures. High above, steel beams jutted out like cranes; silhouettes suggested outmoded machinery in a courtyard. Not many lights, only random ones above facades and in elevated windows. Still, there were a few parked cars, and on a side street a beer sign shone outside a small pizzeria or maybe a store.

"Number forty-four," said N., and pointed.

The entire first floor was glass, hundreds of windows divided into small panes—unmistakably an old factory. None of the panes were broken, and somewhere inside they could see diffuse light.

Vladislav and N., carrying their bags, looked for the entrance and found the door that would be open, among a long row of doors.

Inside, the building had a pleasant echo. Factory halls led off in both directions, with badly worn wood floors. Red-painted steel beams formed regular columns between floor and ceiling. A few lights shone like beacons from thick wire cages. The halls were clean, and the place was completely empty.

Vladislav and N. found the staircase noted in their directions and groped along the walls for a button. Fluorescent tubes flickered on, and, squinting in the harsh light, they started climbing. Three floors up, through a heavy metal door, then down a stalesmelling hallway with a curling, threadbare carpet. The hallway ended at a gray door with a small tempered-glass window at eye level. Where the mail slot would normally be was a piece of paper that read "Mary."

"Welcome." It was Mary herself who opened. "You turned off the light in the staircase?"

N. nodded.

They stood in a large open space, everything around them suggesting an old factory of some kind. It smelled strange.

"There was a soap factory here once," said Mary. "The stuff seeped into the floors."

The floorboards were dark, with an oily shine. At the bottom of a short stairway stood Adderloy, leafing through a magazine. Around him was furniture, scattered along the walls. It looked like a stage set, with wide gaps between the pieces. A single gas stove without a counter beside it, a blue couch that broke up the monotony of the worn brown brick walls, a few odd bookshelves, some equally odd chairs around a table. There, where Vladislav and N. had entered, the ceiling was low, while above Adderloy it rose as high as in a church. In the other direction from the door stretched a long, wide corridor. There the light was dimmer, and one could see no end to the row of plain doors.

Mary made a gesture with her hand. "Your bedrooms are down that way, as many as you want." She moved hesitantly, as if she herself did not quite feel at home yet.

"Is this your house?" asked Vladislav, looking quizzically at the ceiling, which was a jumble of dusty pipes.

"No," she replied. "The guy who owns it just wants someone in the building. It costs me nothing."

"Nothing?"

"No, as long as I keep out of sight when the authorities come here to inspect."

"They can't find their way up here, can they?" said N.

They went down the little stairway. At the bottom Reza got up from a chair they hadn't been able to see from above.

"What happened—why did they keep you?" he asked.

"Nobody kept anybody," said Vladislav. "The flight was just delayed."

Reza sat down again. He looked tired, and seemed to be annoyed by something. "You are also foreigners," he said.

"Did they mess with you?"

"It is only in New York that nobody stares."

"I'm Czech, you're Pakistani," said Vladislav. "What the hell do you expect?"

"I mean"—Reza pulled at his shirt as if he was too hot—"it is the only place in the world where no one stares at anyone."

"Is that supposed to be a good thing?"

Adderloy was still reading his newspaper. N. sat down on the couch and looked absentmindedly at a mounted fish head, placed on the table for decoration. Hundreds of tiny barbed hooks spilling out of its mouth.

Mary turned the stove's gas burners on and off, as if to see if they still worked. She cast a brief glance at N. Then she said quietly, "I always fast after I've traveled. If you want something, there's canned soup—tomato or cheese." She pulled out a drawer in an old file cabinet that served as a pantry.

# CHAPTER 15

*Diego Garcia, 2008*

ERNST GRIP WAS STUCK. REGARDLESS of the half-truths they poured over him, he had to find out whether that broken heap in the cell on Garcia was a Swedish citizen. No way around it. At dinner that evening, Grip said he realized he'd be there longer than he'd originally thought. Friedman said the formalities with Washington were no problem, and she'd make sure that someone informed Stockholm.

"Skip Stockholm," he said, then: "Can you get me newspapers?"

The answer took a few seconds. "The largest US dailies get sent regularly to Garcia."

"I mean foreign newspapers."

"You need newspapers for your job?" asked Friedman.

"You could say that. For the man in the bunk." Grip handed a list of foreign newspapers to Friedman.

"We should be able to round up some of these by tomorrow," she said, reading over the list.

"No rush. First, by tomorrow I want somebody to bring him a table and a chair."

"Shouldn't be a problem," said Friedman with a shrug.

Grip had expected more of a fight. "You give Stackhouse orders, despite the fact that he doesn't belong to you?"

"In this case."

"Did you know that the air-conditioning in the cell was turned off?"

"I'm not here to crusade against my own side."

"But you accept what they're doing."

"My privileges are limited."

"The torture—who was responsible?"

She removed a strand of hair from her shorts. "You know the talk and walk here as well as I do. Who acknowledges what and who doesn't. The man in the cell has been in a third country. He arrived here only recently."

"Which country?"

Friedman hesitated.

"Do you know what country it was?" Grip went on.

"Oman, Bulgaria, Saudi Arabia, Malaysia—you choose. I don't know."

"But that's where they did it?"

"Yes."

"And you sent him there."

"Not the FBI."

"The United States sent him there."

"Give up," said Friedman, setting down her glass.

"And now you have a goddamn mess to sort out."

"We . . . we have a goddamn mess."

They were both silent for a while, condensation dripping down their glasses.

"And you need my help," continued Grip. "So let's stop pretending that I'm here out of charity. What do I get in return?"

"Maybe a sunburn," Friedman shot back. "The real prize could be saving a Swede's skin."

The first newspapers arrived two days later. Grip sorted them into stacks. One stack for each day. Then he took the first and headed with Shauna to the building with sagging floors where the prisoners were held. Stackhouse, sitting in the monitoring room, said he'd bring in the papers after lunch. Apparently Friedman had already given him instructions. On the TV screen, Grip saw a small table and a chair. The man, the prisoner, whatever he was, half-sat in the corner at the head of his bunk.

"Air-conditioning?" said Grip.

Stackhouse finished drawing a meaningless figure on his paper before he replied. "It's on."

"That must have hurt," Grip said, and left the room.

Shauna Friedman had accompanied him only on the first few days. After that Grip was trusted. She never asked him what he was doing—the daily stack of newspapers, but no attempt at questioning inside the cell. Grip figured the explanation was simple: he would get the job done. She had all the time in the world.

Diego Garcia: eternal sunshine, cottony clouds over the atoll, sometimes a late-afternoon storm. Each day the same, unchanging. Every day Grip left the newspapers and then watched the previous day's surveillance tapes. He fast-forwarded through them. At first the days were pretty much always the same. Apart from eating some of the food he was brought and using the toilet a couple times, the man in the cell stayed on his bunk. It was like watching an animal in hibernation—asleep, or half asleep. His movements were slow and ineffective when he had to get up, as if gravity itself tormented him. As he lay, he sighed and scratched himself often. The newspapers remained untouched in their stack on the table, every day new ones. When he ate, he didn't leave his bunk, wedging his back against the wall. The table and chair were simply obstacles on his way to the toilet.

"I'll leave the old ones there," said Stackhouse on the third day, about the newspapers.

"No, replace them," replied Grip, tapping the fresh stack.

"Should I put out warm croissants too?"

"If you want, absolutely."

On the fifth day, the man took his plate to the table and sat there and ate. The next day, he gently pushed apart the papers with the end of his plastic spoon. As if to see what they were, without seeming too interested.

Grip played through the sequence on the tape a couple of times when he found it. Watched how he moved his hand, looked at his eyes.

"And he doesn't say a word?" he asked Stackhouse, who was leafing through a glossy boating magazine behind him.

"Not to us," Stackhouse muttered.

"And his hair?"

"It was already long when he came here."

"Came from where?" Grip tried, halfheartedly.

Stackhouse didn't even bother to reply.

The swelling in the man's face had gone down, but Grip couldn't yet analyze his facial features, only imagine. His movements were still fumbling. Grip thought he'd like to see him naked, to see how bad it was. If he'd only been roughed up, or if they'd been more sophisticated. The loose overalls hid most of it. With only a TV image, Grip couldn't see if he still had nails.

The days went by. The man, the prisoner, ate at the table and spread the newspapers apart with his spoon. Friedman didn't ask Grip what he was doing. Nor how long it would take. He still hadn't been in touch with Stockholm.


Grip met Shauna Friedman at the officers' club every night at seven. It was their baseline, their checkpoint at the end of the day. They started with a drink and usually sat at the same table, a little apart from the flight suits and the other uniforms, who sat closer to the bar.

"No, they don't," Shauna had said on the second night, stopping Grip when he tried to order a mojito. "A place like this serves three or four kinds of drinks, period. Look around"—she nodded toward a group of airmen—"beer and whisky." The waitress who'd stood waiting for his order wore the blank look of someone who'd been waiting too long for a bus. She appeared to be Filipina.

"He'll also have a dry martini," Shauna said.

That was then. Now it had been a week, exactly. The same waitress had just placed a dark rum on the rocks in front of him.

"I told you," said Shauna, "the ice is disgusting."

"I know, chlorine," said Grip and drank.

They'd talked about New York. What seemed to be small talk. A little competition over showing you knew your way around. From the huge stone lions in front of the Public Library to the gallery at the corner of this street and that avenue, the sandwiches at the Polish deli, the clock tower in Brooklyn. Grip held back, let himself sound initiated but basically still a tourist.

"Other places then. Where do you like to spend time?" Shauna glanced toward the bar and away again. "Someone like you?"

"Someone like me . . ." He drank again, tasting the chlorine. "Where I like to go?"

"Yes."

"The well-known places are just clichés."

"What does that mean?"

"I like Cape Cod."

"*That* is a cliché." Shauna laughed.

"Exactly." Grip nodded.

"Sand and sea and outrageously priced ice cream in August."

"Have you been there in April?" he asked.

"The thought never crossed my mind."

"The light . . ."

"Hopper," she interrupted, lifting her glass.

Grip flinched. "Hopper, yes . . . Edward Hopper."

"Paintings of a different kind of sand, a different kind of light."

"Don't you agree?"

"Maybe."

Grip pondered for a moment. Thought it wouldn't cost him anything. To make his case.

"In one of Hopper's paintings, there's a small hotel. It's in Provincetown, and it looks the same now as when he painted it in 1945. Whitewashed wood, two stories. If you walk past, you hardly notice it—but if you look at the painting, you long to spend the night there. Two ways of seeing one place. "

"Mm."

"Two realities."

"There's a lot of Hopper to see in New York," she said. "Have you—"

"I think I've seen everything."

Shauna nodded slowly. "That hotel," she continued, "you've obviously stayed there. If the painting was so irresistible, I mean?"

"It is."

"Hopper's subject being loneliness?"

"I wasn't there alone."

"At Hopper's hotel?"

"The painting is called *Rooms for Tourists.*"

Shauna smiled, sat with her glass in her hand. "You made love?"

The empty glass from her first martini was still on the table, next to the drink she was now working on. Grip held the silence for a moment.

Then he said: "We did, all night in fact. Until it hurt."

"Hopper," she said, unfazed, and smiled again.

Then she raised her napkin and dropped it like a parachute over her empty glass.

"Have you ever heard of Chung Ling Soo?" she asked. "Speaking of things you care about."

"Chinese?"

"Yes, a magician. Around the turn of the last century, Chung Ling Soo was the biggest thing in London, legendary performances, everyone wanted to see him." She took a sip of her second martini and put the glass down again, half full.

"You and Soo . . . ," said Grip, not entirely following.

"Not me, Dad. My dad needed an expensive hobby, so he started collecting posters from Soo's performances. Originals—the most sought-after can go for a few hundred thousand. May I?" Shauna reached for Grip's napkin, lying beside his glass. She unfolded it, continued: "Dad bought posters, and when he told me about his tricks, I got interested in magic."

His napkin fell through the air and landed on her half-full glass.

"The thing was, the posters weren't enough. I wanted to do it myself."

She took hold of the second napkin, pulling it off the glass with a quick gesture.

Not only the martini but even the olive had disappeared. A lift of the other napkin was simply confirmation. What had been in one was now in the other.

"You . . ." Grip was speechless. He glanced under the table. "Impressive."

She took her once-empty glass and drank again. "Nothing to it, really," she said. "Like this . . ." She slid off her ring, and for several seconds made it appear and disappear everywhere in her hand. "It's just dexterity, something to do when you're bored."

A group of officers started yelling down by the bar. Shauna looked at them and then at the clock. "Shouldn't we order? It'll take forever to get our food if we let the flyboys get there first."

She called to the waitress.

They were in the middle of their meal when she came back to the subject. "Art," she said, "that's what we were talking about when I interrupted you with those martini glasses."

"Not interrupted," said Grip, with a dismissive wave.

"In any case. You like Hopper, and for me, the Soo posters weren't enough, I had to get to the magic itself. For me, art needs to be more tangible. Have you seen the sculptures of Jean Arp?"

Grip chewed. Nodded once.

"Their shapes, almost human, but not quite. You can't resist wanting to touch them. Even own them. That's what explains the prices, you know."

"They're beautiful," Grip got out.

"Man and woman, in the same form."

Grip sat in his underwear and a T-shirt at the desk in his room. He'd stacked up the next day's batch of newspapers. Most printed in languages he didn't understand, foreign alphabets and characters. Next to them lay the copy of *Expressen* he'd saved from his flight to New York, wavy from being stuffed into seat pockets and bags. The tabloid reminded him of Sweden, made him think of Stockholm. He hadn't made himself known yet, hadn't even sent an e-mail. Something made him resist—Shauna Friedman. She ordered newspapers for him but asked no questions. And Stackhouse, who rocked in his chair and had something on the tip of his tongue, something he so wanted to spit out, that look in his eye—I know something you don't know.

And then. Suddenly Shauna Friedman started talking about art. Hopper, even though he'd been the one going on about his paintings, but then—Jean Arp. Women always liked Jean Arp, but within the space of ten minutes, first the magic, switching stuff around, and then she started talking about Arp. Why the hell had she done it? Jean Arp, of all bastards.

# CHAPTER 16

New York, autumn 2004

THIS TIME, BEN DIDN'T NEED to get drunk before telling Grip. His cough was only the tip of the iceberg. The problem wasn't his health, now in a fragile equilibrium, but the havoc the virus left behind. It was the money—the old debts threatening to sink them. The total amounted to many times more than what it had cost to end Ben's hacking over the sink at night. As with icebergs—one to ten—people get blinded by the part above the surface, and can only imagine the immensity below. But the law offices' stream of white envelopes could no longer be pushed down among the takeout cartons and eggshells. Dates were now written in stone, orders sent without any deadline for appeal, all exemptions expired. No longer was anyone willing to sign anything new, no pen was raised to an appeal. Cash only. Pay!

But the town was full of money. New York rolled along with its usual extravagance—supply and demand. And now Christo, the monumental artist who had wrapped bridges and tropical islands in cloth, would transform all of Central Park into a billowing orange temple with his draped gates. The newspapers wrote that he'd worked on the concept for nearly thirty years, and now it would happen. *The Gates* would show up one morning, gates by the thousands, on walkways, paths, and roads, stand for a few weeks, and then disappear in a flash—every single gate. According to the concept and agreement with New York City, nothing in the park would be permanently impacted, and every component of the gates would be recycled: ground up, melted, incinerated. Only the memory would remain. It became an unbeatable slogan, a sort of impossible dream.

Seven thousand gates that New Yorkers and visitors from around the world would feel compelled to wander through during the month of February, while Central Park was leafless and gray. This was art. A Braque oil of a village, or one of Giacometti's figures in bronze—wait long enough, and they'd eventually come up for auction. All art has its collectors. But Christo's *The Gates* could never be bought like a Giacometti or a Braque. This aspect appealed to the rich who had everything. Surely, the fingers of one of those fuckers would start to itch.

"They don't need me, but they want you," said Ben. They both knew, though at first Grip pretended otherwise. Ben stood in the door of his small office at the gallery and fixed his sober, anxious gaze on a lone visitor.

"So now they want *The Gates*," Grip said at last. He sat in Ben's desk chair, flipping through one of the books that had already been published on Christo's project. It was still a few months away.

"Not all the gates," said Ben. "A couple, maybe one. I don't know."

"I could do ten jobs like that, and it still wouldn't be enough." Grip turned several pages at a time as he went through the illustrations, all of them billowing with orange.

"It's not your opinions they want, they want you to plan the entire job." Ben gazed out at his gallery with fragile pride.

Grip opened the book to yet another spread before he said anything. "Are you the one who convinced them?"

"It's only art. People don't need to get hurt."

"Not art, just plastic and cast iron, so it says here."

"Picasso's bull was nothing more than a handlebar on a saddle."

"So you figured that if it's called art, there would be money involved, and then there are always collectors—and you told them I should be their man."

That made Ben turn around to look Grip in the eye, and Grip saw less hope there than fear. Ben turned away again. "Yes, I offered them the Swede, the Swede who's becoming quite valuable around here."

"They pay well?"

Ben mentioned the sum. Grip flipped another page. Ben continued: "They want it to be you and one of the others who did the Arp job."

Grip was surprised that Ben suffered more than he did. This was obviously their unholy opportunity. It was a fact that as Grip crossed the Atlantic Ocean, somewhere in the middle he became a different man. But even if he gave in to attractions and cravings here that were impossible for him to play out on the other side of the ocean, still there was always something of the security police left in him. Certain guiding instincts. Such as, he didn't want to deal with cash-in-transit robbers. Better to keep those types at arm's length. But then there were all the other parts of the equation too. Such as, life as he and Ben knew it would be over on the last of February—that was the date carved in stone. Then the bankers and the bean counters would come break down their door. The sum Ben had mentioned would go a long way toward covering the debt, but not all the way. So why not shoot down the foreclosure and overdue notices for good, and make the insomnia go away with one stroke?

"Tell them to double it, and I'll do the whole plan myself."


It took two days. *They*, whoever they were, went for it. And it was a gate they wanted, at pretty much any price.

This was November, and New York would wake up to *The Gates* at dawn on February 12. The artwork would remain in Central Park until the twenty-seventh. Then there were just a few days left before Ben's loan inexorably came due on March 1. The time frame was crystal clear. Grip began to read up, received packages of things Ben sent him in Stockholm. Sat during the day in his bulletproof vest in the car between Drottningholm Palace and wherever the king or crown princess were going, then sat in his own kitchen late into the night, browsing and sketching in catalogs, books, and maps. The late-autumn darkness arrived, with all the rains. Then came the clear frosty mornings, and his captain called him up for extra weekends. He drove the royal BMW to inaugurations, sat next to the king when he wanted to drive himself, went to Brussels a few times with the princess.

*Grip likes art.* A plan for a New York theft took shape. It wasn't hard to get hold of the sketches he needed. Several books on *The Gates* had a map you could unfold to show all of Central Park, with the location of each gate neatly plotted. Same with everything else. As if no detail was too small to be mentioned: the gates were 4.87 meters high, the fabric that would hang from them had been woven from nylon at a factory in New Haven, one of the seamstresses was named Sandy, the cast-iron pieces that would keep the gates in place weighed 275 kilograms each. The park map showed 7,503 lines, exactly where there would be gates. The whole setup fell right into Grip's lap, ready for him.

Overall, it was obvious. Where Ninety-Sixth Street entered the park on the Upper West Side, at the Gate of All Saints, leading to a tunnel with a sidewalk. A string of Christo's gates would follow the road's curve down toward the tunnel. They would take the last gate. To do it fast, they'd need to set up a truck right beside it, so it could be done on the spot. Besides, there wouldn't be many people around at that hour. Didn't everyone know to stay off Central Park sidewalks late at night? The gates were designed to be quickly set up, so they ought to disassemble just as quickly. A truck with a crane, a few simple tools, Grip figured it would take no more than two or three minutes. Put some little plastic cones on the street, blinking lights, men in yellow vests, reflectors—it would all look completely legitimate. And then doing it on the last night, when everyone expected *The Gates* to disappear. Was it even stealing, when the gates were going to be removed anyway? No weapons—Grip underlined the words. *The Gates* would be cut into pieces, ground up, melted down. It was a prank to sneak off with one. They didn't need to arm themselves for such a thing. Despite all that money.

Three minutes. Something so simple—what could go wrong?

December. Christmas was the time of year when Ben lived with lies. He went home to Texas, even brought along some of the ties his mother had sent him. During these days, Ernst Grip and the rest of Ben's real life didn't exist, not even the virus. Ben would eat breakfast on Christmas morning with the Baptists, share a brandy with his father the night before, and hide all the medications he still needed in the lining of his suitcase, because his mother shamelessly went through everything.

"I guess you'll meet them at my funeral," Ben would say in the apartment, when some old family photo appeared or his father's drawl played on the answering machine.

Ben's white lies around Christmas didn't bother Grip; on the contrary, they gave him some maneuvering room. While Ben loved a fit man's body, he'd given up on his own. He exercised only perfunctorily, under doctors' orders and at the gym. For him, the sea was something nice to observe, not go on or in. The closest he got to waves was the beach terraces of art patrons in the Hamptons. Since Ben had made it clear that he'd go to Texas alone, Grip could revert to his old habit of going away over Christmas for windsurfing and diving. He'd always chosen the sun over elves and fir trees.

So it was only for New Year's that Grip got back to New York, and then with a temporary passport arranged by the Swedish Embassy in Bangkok after the tsunami's terrible devastation. He had come away unscathed, actually hadn't even noticed when the wave came in, but his luggage got lost in the chaos that followed. Things being what they were, during those days in Southeast Asia—confused—he'd still been able to get to New York.

Now he would celebrate with Ben and some friends, and also arrange the handover of a few detailed maps of Central Park and a memory stick with the files describing his plan. A few days into the new year, he put everything in a cheap briefcase and left it in the cloakroom at the Whitney Museum, hid his number tag in one of the bathrooms, as agreed, and then took a lap among the familiar paintings.

When he came back, the briefcase was gone.

"Your wife was here," said the woman behind the counter, uncertain.

"Exactly," replied Grip, and left the museum.

Just a prank, he told himself as he stood on the street outside. Just a collection of hypothetical plans. No harm done. He kept it at arm's length, met none of them in person, nothing could go wrong. As long as they didn't bring guns. Just wait. The money would be deposited two days before the loans came due.

On Saturday, February 12, the morning news was orange. Christo and his wife strolled satisfied through *The Gates*, and already by lunchtime it seemed the rest of New York City realized they needed to get there too. Grip watched the story on Swedish TV's *Rapport* that evening, and the images made him feel restless. Beside him stood the king. He'd been receiving new ambassadors at the palace, and then watched the news, along with bodyguards and an adjutant, before Grip drove him back to Drottningholm Palace. The king said something about his youngest daughter wanting to go to New York to see it. Grip nodded without listening. When the news switched to what had become the usual fare—the wave that had washed away half the Indian Ocean beaches, all the Swedes who were still missing—someone turned off the TV with the remote.

"Shall we go?" said the king.

It took a second before Grip responded. "Sure," he said, "of course," and started walking.


Days became weeks. Grip kept himself busy, but even if he tried to think of other things, he was constantly reminded of *The Gates*. It was like trying not to scratch a mosquito bite: a TV commentary, pictures in the paper, an orange plastic bag that blew past. Buddhists may have believed that the color brought peace, but Grip felt only unease when reminded of it.

He was practicing two-shot series at the shooting range in the police station basement when Ben called. Three days left in Central Park, and a few more before the loans came due and the predators came. The kind of inner state in which he just wanted the time to pass, and was sensitive to phones. Despite the ear protectors, he'd heard the cell phone ring. Grip pulled the ear protectors down around his neck.

"They refuse to take it!" was the first thing Ben said when he answered.

"Wait," said Grip. His heart tumbled as he walked away to be undisturbed.

"Who, Ben—and what?" he said when he lifted the cell phone again.

"They refuse to take it unless you go with them."

"Who refuses?" repeated Grip.

"The ones who will actually steal it, who else? That gang, the crew, whatever you call them."

Grip hadn't met them, but he imagined their faces. Some would probably be familiar. "What did they say?"

" 'Honor among thieves,' they said."

"What fucking honor?" Grip spat out. In truth, he understood exactly.

Ben's voice sounded unsteady. "Drawing up the whole plan means you're in," he said, as if it were something he'd just learned by heart. "Someone talked to someone who talked to me. Yes, I don't know . . . but they won't do it."

There was silence. Maybe it lasted half a minute.

"Say nothing," Grip began. He was interrupted by a few bangs from the shooting range, then continued: "I know. The calendar's turning, the days running out. I'm on my way."

"Tummy bug," Grip said, calling in later.

"Fish, you know," said von Hoffsten, with whom Grip was supposed to share a shift for several days. "Never eat sushi on a Monday. I'll see to it. Later."

There was a flight from London that evening. Ben was white as

130

a sheet when Grip opened the door to the apartment. Guilt and fear, from floor to ceiling.

"It's all right," said Grip, with a smile that wouldn't attach to anything.

Still, when he saw Ben, it was settled. In the dark as they went to bed, with the lights swarming anxiously outside the blinds, the coward within Grip hissed in his lair. The one that wanted to pull out. The one that had always wanted to pull out. The deliberation, the two sides to everything, how plus often turns into minus. The dark truths emerging from the disgusting little creature of selfishness. "Go on, pack up and leave, just choose, will it be one or both of you pulled into the abyss?" It was a slap in the face when he heard Ben's breathing. That he slept. People like von Hoffsten could always find someone to cover for them, but not Ben. Ben believed in him, even now, with only a few days remaining of what seemed to be life itself. He trusted him, and he slept. Grip could just barely make out his silhouette. The silhouette that was his home, and finally, when he had to choose, his everything. It was then that the coward died, forever. Something collapsed, and all the room's impressions forced themselves upon him. Not that they were unpleasant, but clear: the smells, the lights from the street outside. As was the pure, hot fear that washed over him when all his escape routes were closed. What remained then, when he finally fell asleep that night and woke up at dawn, was a sense of almost biblical determination that would follow him for many years.

He went to a meeting like the one where he'd explained his plan for taking the Arp sculptures. A new address in a bad neighborhood. This time, the difference was that Grip would be physically present, albeit in the background. That he was in, that was the important thing. Briefly, they singled him out as "the Swede." Someone else, a new face, went over who should do what. The man stuck meticulously to the plan Grip had laid out in the briefcase left at the Whitney Museum. Among those gathered, some looked familiar from that night in the Brooklyn workshop, others new. Someone saw him and nodded. It felt like being on the wrong side of a witness confrontation. The edgy driver, wearing the same mottled sweater and hat as last time, tried to pretend he didn't recognize him.

Grip had been taken hostage by his own plan. They already had enough men as it was for the hit itself—they'd put him in a place that made no sense, at the last minute. It was obvious. He would stand and "keep track" with a cell phone in his hand, standing on a sidewalk two hundred yards from where the truck would stop. Stand there and watch—to make sure he really had thought of everything, and that he couldn't sell them out. If it all went to hell, Grip would be along for the ride. The Swede would burn with them.

They'd gathered in a closed-up pizzeria. The men pulled chairs off the tables to sit with the people they knew. It exposed a division: one side of the room asking questions, while the other already seemed to have it down. Two gangs brought together for a bigger job.

"No guns," said the one who led it all. Mutters in reply.

"But Central Park is full of muggers," someone said, getting a few laughs.

"Exactly," said the man who stood in the middle, and no one laughed. When he wasn't speaking, his jaw muscles twitched as if he longed to bite into something.

"It's a lot of money," said someone from the side that asked questions.

"I cannot fucking afford to lose this," someone beside him added.

"You, motherfucker, cannot afford to do time either." It fell like a whip, because it came from the other side of the room. Grip sat on that side, and the man who stood in the middle never even bothered to glance at that side. The support was obvious.

The driver (Grip remembered that his name was Romeo) took off his cap and threw up his hands. "Should we crack some skulls instead?"

"This is no bank robbery. Just do the job. No guns." The man spoke calmly and forcefully, as if dealing with a child. A child he wouldn't hesitate to thrash. Grip liked what he saw—at the time, he did.

The murmur of distrust continued.

"You heard me." The man's jaw tightened again. "Are you in or out?" Sirens passed outside. "Well?"

It was Romeo who eventually stretched, slowly, as if about to yawn. "Obviously, we're in," he said, and turned to Grip with a smile. "Now we're talking."

Grip stood completely still in his new short leather jacket and jeans. He would throw them away later that same evening. It was almost two in the morning, and there were more people in Central Park than he'd expected. They were about to dismantle *The Gates*, but the sounds and voices seemed far away. Sometimes they disappeared altogether. Grip had the lights of Central Park West on one side and the park on the other. A few pathways of *The Gates* came together on the sidewalks leading away from the park, behind him. A single row continued down in an arc toward the tunnel. In the distance he saw it, the last gate. It was cold. A frosty mist was in the air; ice crystals circled the lights with shimmering halos.

He'd wanted to get a coffee first, had looked for an all-night spot—but no luck. It gave him an odd feeling of desolation, being in the middle of the city, finding nothing open. He was barehanded, and the thin pockets of his leather jacket gave no warmth. He looked like a pimp shivering on his dimly lit street corner. Another figure stood a hundred yards away. The same silhouette as his own: hands in pockets and elbows straight out at the sides. Stamping now and again in the cold. Eyes checking to see that Grip was in place.

When some of the men had gathered a few hours before, to take a head count and distribute cell phones, Grip smelled Jack Daniel's on several and noticed that some had oversize pupils. Romeo had also been there. The mood was anxious. Grip had just picked up his phone and walked out.

Ten minutes to go . . .

Five . . .

Grip blew a little warmth into his hands. A truck came and went. Ten past two, then quarter past. Now they were five minutes late.

The truck came from the north, not the south as planned, but then turned where it was supposed to. Grip didn't care about the rest of the surroundings anymore, just followed the truck with a wary gaze.

A pause, some running around, and then the traffic cones were put in place and the warning lights started flashing, making the reflectors on their jackets shine. Clatter, whiz of pneumatic tools, the crane's arm stretched out.

The cold made Grip stamp the asphalt again. The gate's crossbar was lifted up onto the truck bed, then the two vertical supports. He heard the scrape of metal on the pavement before the first cast-iron foot was lifted clear by the crane. As Grip slowly clenched his hands in his pockets, killing the pain from the cold, the missing coffee crossed his mind. He glanced at his watch without pulling his hand from his pocket. Half past two. Then it came to him, a place that stayed open all night, off in the other direction. He knew it for sure.

A shiver made him pay attention. A voice, a bit far away, but still too close. Wrong tone, too many fast words. It echoed, at first he didn't know where it came from.

It was down by the truck. There was movement around the truck, and the voice was a woman's. He couldn't make out the words, but she was protesting—loud accusations.

Where had she come from? Grip hadn't seen anyone. The second figure with hands in his pockets stood as still as he.

What did she want? Why didn't the truck clear out? Grip saw only reflections and moving feet. No confrontation, but something going on. He couldn't see her, only heard her voice. Had they gotten caught?

Then he heard more clearly, a man: "Fuck you, fuck you!"

And then a shot.

Grip flinched from the muzzle flash before the sound even reached him. And so the little world of footpaths and trees, not far from the intersection of Central Park West and Ninety-Sixth Street, went still. Calm and quiet, a hole in time. Grip didn't move from his spot. But soon the truck started to move, on its way. Then it was gone, the gate was gone, leaving behind a heap.

A small movement—it puffed fast, exhaling mist a few times. Just a shapeless figure at a hundred and fifty yards. Grip turned away and started walking. The second watchful figure did too. Away, along different paths. Grip had houses on one side, the park on the other. He sensed vague sounds and voices, but all infinitely far away. Shifted to another world. His feet got faster. A taxi slowed down and took off again when he didn't look up.

"How'd it go?" asked Ben, in a pretended half-asleep voice

from the dark bed, when Grip tried to quietly shut the front door behind him.

"Completely . . ."

He'd thrown his clothes and the mobile phone into a Dumpster. The clothes he was now wearing had been lying in a box beside it, waiting.

" . . . no problem. Let's get some sleep. I want to sleep now."

The following day, when they were together just before Grip left for the airport, Ben told him that a woman had been shot at night in Central Park. "You . . ."

"Nothing like that, no. No one there. No one." Grip shrugged. "The flight," he said then, pointing at the clock. "Can't have food poisoning forever." He smiled.

Accomplice to murder.

Nowhere was it said or reported that a gate had been stolen. Nobody was heard from, not about anything. But the money came in, and the lawyers were never heard from again.

That night in the park, the last white breaths out of the heap on the ground. Others had made the mistake; the burden had shifted. There was never anything to remind him. Not until three years later, when Shauna Friedman couldn't seem to get enough of talking about art.

# CHAPTER 17

*Topeka, Kansas, February 2005*

A COUPLE TIMES A DAY, HUGE diesel generators went on inside the factory building. Automatically, without warning. The floor shook. It was hard to make yourself heard even at close range.

The first tremors traveled across the floor just as Adderloy was about to say something. Then came the noise. He paused and sat down, knowing the routine. They waited it out.

They were in their third day. Some kind of plan had taken shape, and they lived on pizza and Thai food. They went out, sometimes one at a time, more often two and two, learning the roads into town and the escape routes. They sketched maps, bought stuff. Adderloy had gotten rid of the rentals and bought three used cars in town. The papers were in the glove compartment. (To be on the safe side, he'd gone over what they should do if stopped by traffic police. All the registration and insurance documents were legit. No sense doing anything rash.) But Vladislav nixed the first batch of guns that Adderloy brought, saying the weapons should be the same caliber—9mm—as the submachine guns he'd been promised. Adderloy never questioned Vladislav's opinions on guns, though in pretty much everything else he was used to getting the final say. He'd claimed one of Mary's armchairs, where he usually sat and handed out directives, cigarette smoke coiling above his head. He didn't seem bothered by the fusty air of the factory, always wore a jacket and tie. N. never saw him head up to any of the rooms off the hallway to sleep. If N. got up in the middle of the night, Adderloy was always sitting in his armchair, reading under a single bulb.

When the generators went off, the stillness startled them, as if a film had snapped. They fumbled a moment.

Adderloy shifted in his chair. "Yes . . . ," he began. Before the interruption, they'd been ticking off items in the master plan. "Suits?"

"We got everyone's size," said Reza sleepily. "Mary and I will buy them tomorrow."

"Cooler and toolbox?"

"Making a run to Walmart tonight," said N. "I'll get the dry ice tomorrow."

There were lists.

"City maps?"

Vladislav gave a thumbs-up.

Everything was broken down into detail, in matériel, in sequence. One at a time, in cardboard boxes and plastic bags, the critical events took physical form.

Everything else disappeared. Reza could tell you about a fight he'd seen in Toronto, and Vladislav joked about the newlyweds getting tangled in the wedding-dress train, posing for a photographer at Niagara Falls. But no one talked about anything farther back. Even Weejay's seemed to be forgotten. All memories had begun to fade. Certain things would be bought today, others things get done tomorrow. Looking ahead, never mentioning a date. Time was becoming blurry and soon would stop altogether.

When Adderloy brought in bags with the right guns, Reza began to act nervous. After the submachine guns arrived, he stood by a window and aimed out over the city roofs in the night.

"We are not going to kill anyone?" he asked.

"We're going to rob a bank."

Time and again, it had been said. But what remained unspoken was that their plan would require someone to face the death sentence. That's what it would really take, to give the minister payback.

"Cartridges?"

"A thousand," said Vladislav, pointing to bright orange boxes on the shelf.

'll just be a minute," said Mary, picking up her shoulder bag and disappearing into a bathroom.

N. was with Mary, back at her former workplace: the hospital. It was two o'clock in the morning. The idea was that no one on the night shift would recognize her. "Crabby night nurses—they won't remember me," she explained. She'd come to the hospital dressed in her usual black, but without any makeup. To N., it was a different face. Her eyes looked small, and she looked older.

N. sat in the empty waiting room. He looked around, took a magazine off the table. Celebrities smiled vacantly at him from the worn cover. He leafed absentmindedly, stopped at blurry paparazzi pictures of suntanned bodies on a sandy beach, then flipped through more pages of smiles and dresses hanging on scrawny bodies.

The bathroom door opened, and Mary came out again.

Although N. was expecting her, he looked surprised. "All white!" he couldn't help saying. Not just dressed like a nurse, but transformed.

"Around here, you don't exactly have a choice," she said. She had sharp creases on her short-sleeved blouse, a name tag, pens. It was Mary, but then again it wasn't. She dropped her bag on the floor in front of him and slipped a bill into the soda machine in the corner. Down fell a Dr Pepper—she took a few quick gulps, and the cold took her breath away. She looked at her watch. "We're going this way."

Without the slightest hesitation, she stepped into the small office. "It's pretty urgent, will you excuse us?" The nurse at the computer muttered and walked out without looking at them. The minute the woman disappeared, Mary sat down at the terminal. N. stood in the doorway so he could check the hallway. He'd come to the hospital dressed as a janitor, or maybe an electrician, the kind of workman who always shows up unannounced in stained clothes. Behind him, he heard the clicks of Mary's keyboard. A doctor, busy tagging a small bottle of medicine, passed by.

"Now the sun goes down, Charles-Ray," said Mary, and stood up. She drummed her fingers impatiently on the printer that just started up. "He still gives blood," she said to N.'s back. "Type AB, Rh negative." The paper came out. "What's yours?"

"What?" said N.

"Blood type?"

"No idea."

"Something you should keep track of."

They set off farther into the hospital. Mary went first, looking both homely and anxious. N. read the signs as they passed by: UROLOGY, ELECTRICAL ROOM, SURGERY . . . A big toolbox rattled against his legs with every step. Mary pushed the elevator button, and they went down a few floors.

N. knew from the silence that they were underground. Dull green hallways with fluorescent lights, a vague chemical scent. A sign said BLOOD CENTER. They could see a figure moving behind the frosted glass.

Mary drew N. aside. "Right now they're trying to save an old woman up in surgery," she said, taking a sip from the soda bottle she still carried. "There's a man in there too, quite young. Traffic accident. Soon he'll be brain-dead. With bodies leaking like sieves, there's an exhausted team with each, pumping in the blood and sewing them up. According to the computer, the young guy has already received ten pints, the old lady six, and now I've placed another order. It's urgent, and almost three in the morning. She's here in the Blood Center alone. Surely there are rules, saying this and that about how it should be done, all very carefully. But not at three in the morning, when up in surgery they're letting the stuff flow all over the floor anyway. So I'll go in and won't even say hello. Just tell her that I'll get the bags myself. The papers are already in order—she'll be happy not to have to take out bags again, after all the running around."

Mary dropped her half-full soda in the trash. "You can wait here," she said, pointing to yet another empty waiting room.

Even Mary's sneakers were white. When she disappeared, N. looked down at his own, which had left black lines on the polished floor. He sat down on a chrome bench and leaned his head against the wall. Felt the night burning behind his eyelids, and the ventilation fan's humming. The hospital's smell pressed into him, its sweetish chemical. Something unhealthy, the odor of bodies. He remembered a hospital far away: the heat, the shapeless, swollen sores, backs covered with marbled bruises. He rubbed his hands over his arms, felt a chill up his legs as if someone had sliced them with a razor. Shivered.

He'd started to search for something to drink when Mary came back.

"Here!"

There were two bags of frozen blood, in separate sleeves of protective foam. N. took them and opened his toolbox.

Mary looked out into the corridor, turned again. "The freshest you can get out of Charles-Ray Turnbull."

The toolbox was big enough for N. to store a small cold bag in the bottom compartment. Soft, filled with blocks of dry ice. When he opened the zipper, white mist slowly poured onto the floor.

"So simple," said Mary. Her look was triumphant. "Just like that."

She slammed shut the toolbox, and N. started walking. As it banged against his leg, he read the signs: MRI, TRASH, MORGUE . . .

Mary's industrial loft didn't have a freezer, but the twenty-four-hour pizzeria on the corner did. So after a few kind words to the Lebanese guys who ran the place, they squeezed the cooler into the back of a big icy freezer, which otherwise held nothing but ground beef.

# CHAPTER 18

To look their victim in the eye, to meet Charles-Ray Turnbull once before they struck. The idea had been floated before, but in the end it was N. who convinced Adderloy to let him be the one. To watch Charles-Ray in action—a cat toying with a mouse, nothing more. A certain malicious satisfaction. To lay eyes on the man who had celebrated his losses, his suffering. Under Adderloy's ingenious plan, the minister was going down.

"The two of you go, as a couple," said Adderloy, and Mary raised her beer bottle in a toast.

The groundwork had already been laid, mapping Charles-Ray's habits. A simple thing, completed in a matter of days. Not much of a challenge in Topeka, not with someone whose life was as straightforward as Charles-Ray's. Besides, for their plan, they only cared about his mornings. There were few landmarks, really only two. His house—large, wooden, two-story—in a run-down area, where every little bush looked like a Christmas tree adorned with trash; and the sign-painting company he ran across town: TURNBULL—SIGNS OF THE TIMES. The company sign was peeling, just like the paint on his house. Between the two sites, he drove twenty minutes every morning in his red Lincoln. Reza and Vladislav had followed him a couple of times. When he got to a strip of car dealers, motels, and fast-food joints, he'd stop at a random drive-through for coffee. He didn't always buy coffee at the same place—that was as unpredictable as he got. A couple of times he'd gone by his church on some errand, but that was just a stop on the way.

Not much more to it. The final act would be getting a look at him, but at the right distance, among people. At church.

In the half-full parking lot, N. and Mary saw his Lincoln parked near the entrance. The low building had no steeple, no cross, nothing but a sign with red plastic letters. Dusk had already fallen, half the sign disappeared in the twilight from the burned-out bulb inside the glass. When N. walked past, he saw that the plastic characters for church-service times and a Bible quote had fallen out of their grooves. They lay like dead flies at the bottom.

Mary looked, as usual, as if she were dressed for a funeral. Perhaps this was what caught people's attention, drawing belated smiles when the two of them passed through the church doors. Soon an elderly man came up and introduced himself. He greeted Mary closely, squeezed her paternally on her arm as if testing her strength. Launched into a tirade about premonitions for the future, then asked if they were from the city.

"No," said N.

"Not so, not so," the man said, without taking his eyes off Mary. He stood a little too close. "Welcome, you are always welcome."

Soon after, as if someone had whispered a message, the people around them started moving. Quickly people hung up their coats, ceased their chatting, and made their way toward the sanctuary.

The church hall was white, with high ceilings, but obviously the place hadn't been built for masses or preaching. Maybe it was an old warehouse. Transformed, it looked like a huge lamp shop, lights suspended everywhere. As if to banish the shadows: lamps at the end of each pew, sconces on the walls, and three brass-and-crystal crowns hanging from the ceiling. The too-bright lighting made a newcomer feel not so much hot as anxious, although soon people's foreheads began to shine. Everything sparkled, glittered, and shone. On one of the all-white walls, tall gold letters shimmered: JESUS—SAVE US ALL.

While people took their seats in the pews, a man paced back and forth on a platform that resembled a school stage without the curtain. His lips moved, mumbling, as the hall murmured.

Mary pulled N. to her and whispered, "That's Charles-Ray," with a nod toward the stage.

"Mm," said N., continuing to stare straight ahead.

"Sit," said the minister, in a low hiss from the dais.

Some of the buzz ceased. Turnbull, legs spread wide, looked at someone on one side, and then fixed his gaze along the aisle.

"Sit!" He swayed. His deep sigh expressed not annoyance but deep satisfaction. A black leather-bound Bible hung low in his hand.

It was quiet. He looked over the crowd, watching. Nodded.

"Thanks for this, what a night." A breath in between, then almost shouted: "Thanks for this!" And stretching his free hand straight up, he grinned.

It was that face—it was true. N. remembered the sidewalk by the park: the evening after a rain, it was that face. From the flyer that he picked up, the image of a minister. *Beloved Father.*

"Sinners," shouted the man from the dais, now with clenched fists. Someone clapped excitedly. "We are surrounded by the riffraff, we are led by them. Homofascists, lesbians, surrounded by creeping decay." He sighed loudly. "The Muslims came flying over to obliterate the Sodomites in New York. And still, and still, no one understands." He shook with the Bible at the ceiling, as if hordes of flying devils were about to descend on him.

"The Lord's wave, the Lord's wave left the pedophiles, rapists,

and self-abusers to rot in unmarked graves. And yet. And yet"—
the words tore from his throat—"no one understands!" His lips
were already wet from saliva, his nails struck loudly against the
Bible's leather. " 'They sow the wind, and reap the whirlwind.' "

"Amens" sounded here and there. Beloved Father Charles-Ray
Turnbull pulled on his lapels and shook his head, as if his mouth
had filled with something nasty.

Mary leaned next to N. "It's brilliant," she said. He looked at
her, uncomprehending. She closed her eyes. "So completely . . .
such reckless hatred."

"Every day," said the minister, pointing out over the congregation and then to himself, "we are forced to witness homosexu-
als who marry. Pictures of smiling dykes and sweaty queers who
can barely contain themselves. That even marry in the good Lord's
name. We ask for retribution." He lowered his head, stretched
his hand in front of him. "We ask for retribution, Lord, Lord . . .
Amen."

After a few seconds of silence, just as the most zealous started
swaying in the pews, he drew in a fresh breath of air like a drowning
man. "And they multiply"—he beat his fists against his chest—"a
crawling avalanche aided by science. Artificial inseminations, eggs
and sperm from who knows where. Children born already degenerate, bred from paired male and female slime and scum. Have you
ever seen such children, have you? I can tell you that a light shines
from them. But it is not a Lordly light. Instead they desire their own
death, these pitiful mutations of human flesh."

N. looked at the people around him, their hands trembling, their
eyes moist, while others panted, "Yes, yes . . . ," in an incessant
murmur.

Charles-Ray bent his torso into an arc as he read: " 'Shall I not punish them for these things?' says the Lord. 'And shall I not avenge myself on a nation such as this?' "

"Jeremiah," someone shouted.

Seeing Turnbull, his blustering style, his wrinkled jacket, his flabby neck, and the sweating assembly, nodding and swaying—it filled N. with rage. He wanted to cut the man's throat. Never in his life had he been so overpowered by such a desire to kill someone. It was a strange feeling, sweet and driven. In one leap he could be on him. His legs wanted to do it; they trembled with anticipation.

A single leap.

"Just look for now," said Mary, so close that he felt her breath on his cheek. She took his arm with both hands, pulled it next to her. "I know," she whispered, "but just look for now. Soon . . . soon you will get to act."

N. felt a cold, dead streak in his chest, and his hands started to sweat. He lowered his head and closed his eyes. One might have thought him sunk in prayer.

From the stage, the fire-and-brimstone extravaganza circled round and round: whores, homofascists, sodomites, sinners. The minister kept rising to his toes.

"Exterminate them," he moaned. After a few screams and amens from the congregation, he stood perfectly still, closed his eyes, and in a monotone between breaths urged them to rally: "Our defiant army . . . constantly we shine the light . . . on nests of sin." He ranted about foreign countries and places, to an increasing murmur of "Yes . . . Yes" and "Hallelujah!" Others in the room had feverish faces. They held hands over their foreheads and chests, someone spoke softly and incomprehensibly to himself, a person in the back was weeping uncontrollably. The minister was soon up and running again on the syphilitic and self-abusers.

The veins on his forehead and neck swelled when he shouted: "Our prayers have deprived the godforsaken of their children."

N. struck his fist on the counter and shouted: "You bastard!" But amid all the fervent responses, his didn't even make worshippers in the next pew turn around. Mary forced her hand into his and intertwined their fingers.

Charles-Ray Turnbull dropped his voice as low as he could: "Sacrifices . . . sacrifices against the devil's legions." The hall resounded with sacrifice. In a final eruption, he screamed about how the world's gluttons and pedophiles rotted from the inside, and how the horsemen of the apocalypse now stormed, while voices called out "A hundred" and "A thousand," as if all the world's sins were being auctioned. The checks were passed from hand to hand toward the stage.

When Turnbull fell silent, an electric organ began playing, its looping hymn and the assembly's urgent shouts feeding the flow. A hat was filled, and a last few crumpled bills passed forward. A couple of young men with a fumbling sense of rhythm began playing electric bass and drums. An elderly woman sang into a microphone. She drowned out the murmur of the hall as she gazed somewhere high up, singing to the ceiling and the sky outside.

Charles-Ray Turnbull nodded, smiling, and wiped the sweat from his temples.

# CHAPTER 19

N. LAY AWAKE A LONG time in his room. Had lain there, listening to the others through the walls of the factory, and hearing them fall silent for the night in their hall of old offices, with no windows and only a single toilet. That was the last sound he'd heard, the toilet flushing, probably several hours ago now. He was lying on a mattress on the floor, lying on his back shirtless, sweating. The air felt thick and motionless, the old soap factory smells inescapable.

Five rooms in a row, a room for each of them—and there were more farther down in the darkness, he had no idea how many. Beyond his own room, the map was blank. Mary lived at the other end, closest to the factory hall.

Now all was silent through the walls, sunk deep into the night. N. rose slowly.

Out in the hallway, the only light came from somewhere below the stairs leading to the factory hall. It was Adderloy. Couldn't see him, only the light from the lamp where he sat. He too was silent. N. stood at Mary's door, hesitant and warm. He held his breath, looked toward the yellow-green light, then pressed down on the door handle again.

He opened the door and went inside.

Gently, Mary pushed the door shut behind him. She took a step back and looked him up and down.

She wore a paint-spotted smock as a nightgown, the kind you'd otherwise think of an artist wearing. It hung unbuttoned and left most of her revealed. Then she came close, but only so that they barely touched. N. inhaled the air around her head, but in the factory she was scentless. He smelled only the old soap from the floor and walls, not her. That strange thing with Mary—dimensions where she did not exist.

He made an attempt against her neck, but she slipped away like a cat—an impossible evasion to one side, so that he brushed past her skin with his lips. Her eyes shone with delight.

She crouched down by a bag, picked up something. Whispered: "Keta . . . Keta . . . Ketalar."

It was a vial, held so that it spun between her fingers. "Do you know what this is?" She gazed at the liquid in the glass container. "Good and evil, mingled together. It numbs without affecting breathing." Her lips formed a ring, almost like a kiss, and she inhaled, whistling in the air. "But then there's the downside." The vial spun. "You experience what others only see in horror movies—unspeakable nightmares. You can't begin to imagine, the anxiety. All of Turnbull's demons gathered in a bottle. With just a pinprick."

"Is that what he'll get?"

"A pinprick, then he's at the mercy of his own demons."

The whole house shook when the generators turned on. Mary said something more, but it was drowned out by the roar that descended upon them. N. already had his hands on her hips. It was as if freight trains rolled past on every side of them. Her hand pinched his chest. First, just in a playful way, but then she dug her fingers into him. The nails made brands. His mouth felt dry from the pain, and when the blood finally surfaced he jerked involuntarily—but she pulled back and held him tightly to her. He felt the sensual pleasure of her weight against him and let himself be pushed back against the wall.

Her hand moved from his chest and lay like a mask over his face. They both breathed violently. She circled one finger in his mouth. Noise, waves of excitement, a furious erection. He tasted her thin finger and found the saltiness of his own blood.


Hard on his back. Sunburn in a remote place had turned his arms dark. Only the scars were winding white, untouched by sunlight, under her clutching fingers. She kept him inside her, braced, the floor shook, her legs clenched his hips in an iron ring.

His body was studded with small darkening fingerprints of his own blood.

# CHAPTER 20

### Diego Garcia, three years later

THE PRISONER HIDDEN AWAY BY the Americans poked at the newspapers brought to his cell. The days passed by. Grip spent them fast-forwarding through the surveillance tapes, running in the afternoon heat, or lifting weights at the gym.

His hotel room looked lived-in: spread-out running clothes that never dried in the humid air, shirts under plastic on wire hangers from the base's dry cleaner, a half-eaten bunch of grapes on a plate, corn chips and a package of cookies on top of the humming refrigerator.

On day eight, Grip found the man sitting and reading a newspaper. Grip played it back and forth, studying the bent figure, verifying the times—he read the paper for almost two hours.

Grip interrupted the playback. Thought for a moment, glanced at Stackhouse, who sat engrossed in some papers.

"I'm going in to him," he said.

"Huh?" said Stackhouse, who'd understood perfectly well. "Now?"

"Yes. I want to go in to him now."

"Okay," said Stackhouse, "but keep him guessing, and no names."

"I've questioned people before." Grip stood up. "Can I go now?"

"No names," insisted Stackhouse.

"I promise."


The heavy door closed behind Grip. The air was surprisingly cool; somewhere, a ventilation fan buzzed. The cell seemed smaller than it had looked through the surveillance camera. The man lay on the bunk. He didn't move. Grip couldn't see his eyes through the long hair, but felt that he was awake and very wary.

"Hello," said Grip in Swedish and nodded. He took two steps forward, pulled out the chair, and sat down with his back to the cell door. The man on the bunk held his fists clenched. Grip looked around with slow and slightly exaggerated head movements, as if becoming acquainted with a newly discovered room.

Clenched fists, and now the man's chest started to rise and fall in forced gasps. He struggled in vain to hide it.

Grip placed an elbow on the table. "I'm representing the Ministry of Foreign Affairs, but actually I belong to the security police." He paused. No reaction. Continued. "I've been called in because they're wondering who you are. The Americans are wondering. Myself, I know precisely nothing."

He squinted up at the fluorescent lamps hanging below the ceiling grates. "I was the one who got the air-conditioning turned on, got you the table—and the newspapers, of course." Grip looked down again, spinning the top paper in the stack his way. A Polish daily. He straightened his back a little. "I suspect that you've been sent to many places, and have been through all kinds of questioning. Lots of tricks. To suddenly be showering, have

air-conditioning, newspapers—is this yet another one, you wonder? A man who seems friendly, that's the oldest trick in the book."
Grip exhaled loudly. "I'm Swedish. I will not lie to you, and I will
not make you any false promises. That's what you must consider."

The man was breathing as violently as before, but now he no
longer tried to hide it.

"The date here is a little misleading," said Grip, tapping the paper with his fingertip. "This was printed a week ago, and today is
the sixth, the sixth of May."

The man moved his head, a short flick. His hair swept across his
cheek, but Grip couldn't see more of his face. His hair was dark, as
dark as Grip's own.

"Admittedly, the newspapers were a trick," he continued. "But
I had to try something." He tapped his finger on the pile again.
"You've poked at them, glanced at a page here and there. And like
me, with most languages, you have no idea. But this . . ." Grip took
a corner and pulled it out from the other papers. "Of course, you're
Swedish." It was his own well-thumbed *Expressen* he held. "You sat
and read it for two hours. Even the TV listings."

The man opened the fingers of one hand and clenched his fist
again.

"Yeah, I didn't do it to get some sort of advantage. I might as
well have asked, but they said you don't answer when spoken to. So
I thought this might save us some time. You're Swedish, and now
we both know it." Grip followed the man's breathing, kept his eyes
on his chest. "If I stand up and kick you a few times, hard, then
you'll be on familiar ground, right? Then you'll know my type,
what to expect. If instead I place something to eat on your table,
and leave, then you'll simply think it's another trick. That's a problem. Mostly for me, but probably for both of us. I am neither good

155

nor evil, I'm just from home, and here to find out if you are Swedish. Now I know you understand Swedish, but I'd also like to find out who you are. One more thing. I don't know how much time I get with you, that's something the Americans out here determine. It's not good, but that's the deal. And it makes us equal—maybe I eat a little better, but right now we're both their pawns."

Grip got up, made a gesture in front of the camera's Plexiglas, and then turned back. He stuffed his hands in his pockets, looking at the man and his whitened knuckles until the door lock rattled.

"Is he Swedish?" said Stackhouse, once Grip was back in the monitoring room.

Grip replied: "How much have you thrashed him? He curls up in a ball and starts to hyperventilate whenever a human comes near him. "

"Is he Swedish?"

"How much? Every other day for a year—more? A guess: first electric shocks and waterboarding, then just kicks and punches when people got tired." Stackhouse didn't respond. Grip tucked his shirt into his waistband. "The nails are growing in again, but they look lumpy. Usually takes six months to get them back."

"It hasn't been handled professionally," said Stackhouse effortlessly, but without looking at Grip.

"Thank you. And during all that, no one can be completely silent. How many identities has he claimed?"

"Many. A mess. I've said before, nothing we've been able to document." Stackhouse raised his voice. "And regardless of where he was before, he's here now. That's enough. A straight question—is he Swedish?"

"I don't know," lied Grip. "He said nothing. He only hyperventilated."

156

# CHAPTER 21


Topeka, 2005

WATER RAN OVER REZA'S HEAD. The metal bowl between his feet echoed with the rivulets. He was about to shave his head.

It was the night before.

Adderloy stood by the row of windows at the factory hall, looking out over the evening lights. A folded newspaper hanging in one hand. He hummed something, its tune unrecognizable. N. sat on the couch and picked among the handwritten notes and maps on the table. On top lay a couple of sheets taped together, Vladislav's sketch from memory of the bank—First Federal United. By the door on the drawing, he'd scrawled "2:30." That was all the time they'd have. An absolute, at three minutes they'd have to be back outside and on their way. Vladislav could prove it, had worked out all the details—distances to police stations, alarm times, police responses during armed robberies. There was a city map on the table where he'd drawn lines and written down something like formulas.

"Actually, two thirty-*two*," he'd said, "but let's say thirty. That's something you can remember." This was one of the few things the tall Czech took seriously. "When those doors open and you enter the bank, your memory goes blank."

That was then, a little while ago. Now Vladislav stood by the bookshelf, flipping absentmindedly through some volumes. A few seconds per book, though longer if there were pictures. He wasn't the type who sat down to read; always some other impulse took over. N. looked at him and remembered the story of the bus. How Vladislav had sat perfectly still as the water rose, how all the others around him drowned in panic. Two and a half minutes. It wasn't much. Certainly, there were people who could hold their breath that long.

Reza poured another bucket of water over his head, dragging the razor across.

"I told you to burn them," Adderloy said, with an irritated glance at N.

N. let go of the bank sketch, shoved it into the pile with all the other stuff in the middle of the table. In it were all their notes, checklists, and maps. Adderloy started humming again, watching some distant movement in the night.

"Are there smoke detectors?" said N.

Mary was sitting and flipping through a fashion magazine, eating bacon chips out of a bag. "Some . . . maybe . . . I've seen a few." She turned the pages in the pauses between words, smiled slightly absently down at her magazine. She was swinging one leg impatiently over the other, looking as if she sat in a waiting room. She was the only one who seemed to enjoy the idea that there were only hours left.

"Hey Mary, smoke alarms—if I start a fire then it could—"

"Just burn it," repeated Adderloy without turning around.

N. filled a pan from the stove with his stack of papers. He

splashed some nail polish remover from a can he found in a cupboard, and set it on fire. The flames burned a fierce blue, big flakes of ash rising straight up as the smoke disappeared in the dark. He didn't have to poke around for it to be completely incinerated. The flames died down, and soon there were only embers eating their way, like thin glowworms among black leaves.

"Anyone still not have it down?" said Adderloy loudly. All that remained of their lists and plans were specks of soot that slowly floated into the room. Adderloy had been taciturn and short-tempered all night. N. saw behind his gray eyes something like the vigilance of a predator. Capable of anything—flight or furious confrontation.

A few blocks beyond the old mill stood two newly stolen cars: a black Impala for size, and a Nissan with scraped-up rims for invisibility. On a banister inside the factory, four new suits hung in a row, still in their plastic, with matching pairs of athletic shoes and robber hoods in a neat pile on the floor below. The weapons were packed in their trunk, magazines loaded. The medical bag with all the vials was ready. The next morning, they would pick up the blood from the freezer of the Lebanese.

"Are you ready now, you freakin' suicide bomber?"

If Mary's smile was inscrutable, Vladislav's was the opposite. An outright sneer.

"Huh?" Reza turned toward the bookshelf, as if sleepwalking. He was still holding the razor in his hand.

"That's what you look like. Is this some kind of ceremony, first you cut off that blond shit and then jihad?" Vladislav shoved things around for no reason on the bookshelf, a few inches here and there. "Is this what you have to do to get those waiting virgins—those heavenly fucks?"

Two days before, Reza would have thrown himself at him in blind rage. Now he just looked at Vladislav. Maybe his nerves were already on overload. As of a few days back, he'd stopped asking his contentious questions about everything, and his jerky way of moving, his wandering gaze—those too were gone. As if everything he did was a little too slow, as if he could only do things he'd decided on far in advance. And now the attack was too quick for him to follow. Maybe this saved Vladislav, or whichever of them was being saved.

Vladislav wasn't satisfied. "You need some kind of fucking ceremony. Don't they always have shaved heads, your brethren, on the pictures you see afterward, after they've killed a bunch of people? Virgin horny fucking martyrs."

Reza groped for a moment. He pulled his hand through the hairy water, his lips hesitating at first, but then he said, "But we won't kill anyone."

"No, that's right," said Vladislav, pushing a bookend into a few paperbacks. "Everyone will live happily ever after."

Only Mary's turning of the magazine pages broke the silence.

Vladislav waited. No one said anything.

"Poker, anyone?" he said then, suddenly, and kicked the base of the bookshelf. "Where's the deck?" He started to look around.

"And what would the stakes be?" said Adderloy. His voice was low and self-assured. He straightened his ring and looked sternly at Vladislav.

Vladislav had started a poker game once before. After absurdly cautious bidding, the game had run out of steam. No one wanted to admit it, but who had the nerve to bet, when all that sat in their pockets was Adderloy's money?

"Oh, all right," said Vladislav, throwing himself into an armchair. His legs stuck straight out across the floor. "Who knows," he said, slapping his hands on the armrests. "Maybe things will be better tomorrow?"

A few hours earlier, when the generators went on and the building was drowned in shaking and noise, Adderloy had pulled Vladislav aside. Earlier, he'd said he wanted to practice shooting, claiming it had been a long time since he'd held an automatic weapon. Best to fire a few rounds when the generators were on—no one would hear. And he wanted Vladislav to instruct him. So with the first tremors, they each took a submachine gun and vanished. Toward the vast halls downstairs, N. supposed.

Soon after the generators died, they returned.

But there was something about their behavior that made N. send himself off on an errand, to the weapons trunk. They kept glancing around too much. While he was checking on a pistol, N. swiped his finger around the muzzles of the submachine guns, just replaced at the top of the bag. On his finger, he found only a hint of shiny weapon grease, but no trace of burned powder. Not a single shot had been fired.

Adderloy and Vladislav had been alone for a while—the generator had hidden not bangs from automatic fire but rather the lack of them. It was then that N. had looked into Adderloy's gaze, to where the unsafe predator stalked, although Adderloy himself stood still. By now it was clear to him that Adderloy's intentions didn't include any of them. An obscure agenda that only he knew. And Vladislav, sneering in mock offense at Reza, had possibly sensed what was going on.

Suicide martyrs, Charles-Ray Turnbull, and First Federal United.

The new world N. had almost unconsciously become part of was a minefield of unspoken threats and creeping conspiracies. He felt the currents around him, they would all converge eventually, but the only thing that mattered to him now was his goal: to get revenge for his girls. As long as that happened, the rest didn't matter.

He looked at Reza. The water poured over the top of his head again, he ran his hand over the skin, shaving where the stubble was still rough.

# CHAPTER 22

*A Friday morning in February 2005*

C HARLES-RAY TURNBULL, BORN IN OKLAHOMA, was as irascible as his father. Afterward, some would recall his bad mood that morning. The church was paying a visit to the state prison, and during the morning parishioners stopped by with homemade pastries. Charles-Ray arrived a quarter-hour late, already a bad start, and when someone thoughtlessly asked how on earth Bethany found time to bake all those cranberry muffins, he snapped something inaudible in reply.

The reason was that Bethany, Charles-Ray's wife, didn't bake. Didn't even try. She was upset by the world's decay, or at least that was the explanation Turnbull gave for her absence on Sundays. A degenerate humanity was to blame for her red-eyed gaze and hands that never quieted. She spent long stretches in the closed wards at St. Francis Health Center, a convalescence that often began with a high-speed ambulance ride. After treatments, she'd sit in her pew for a few weeks with a smile that made young children curl up in their parents' lap. And most—not all—knew that when you asked for help with homemade baked goods, then Charles-Ray drove to the Dimple Donuts across town and put his purchases into plain brown bags.

Charles-Ray Turnbull and Bethany had a childless union. It was Turnbull Sr., Charles-Ray's father and the church's founder, who had married them himself. For many years Charles-Ray had made his living providing Shawnee County with road signs. A job that, while not very demanding, he had severely neglected in recent years. Charles-Ray devoted his time to the church, to his mission. Delivering signs on time for Topeka's new school crosswalks, or keeping accurate accounting records—those were not Charles-Ray Turnbull's strengths. His talent lay in getting people to pay attention to Jesus Christ, when they were at their most receptive. That he could do.

But the more time he devoted to one, the less Charles-Ray had left for the other—and a few months later, the state's attorney would repeatedly point to the shaky finances of Charles-Ray and the church as aggravating circumstances.

As usual, the young people in charge of the pastry tables felt insecure in Charles-Ray's presence. He made a parting comment about how they should devote themselves with whole hearts to the prisoners, unembarrassedly tucked his shirttail into his pants, and then, to everyone's relief, left. In general, he liked prison visits and invariably reeled in a fish. But today he had yet another pointless meeting with the bank.

He pulled out of the church parking lot in his '91 Lincoln Town Car. A car that, at least at the time Charles-Ray bought it, carried some prestige. It was red with a black top. Back then, when he and Bethany had their good times, he called it the Demon—a preacher's joke. Now it was nameless. Its varnish had turned white, and the back fenders were streaked with rust.

It was not quite nine a.m. when his Town Car bumped out onto the street outside the church. That they could all agree on, but then the stories diverged. Police and prosecutors would claim one thing, defense lawyers another. What actually took place was that four traffic lights past the church, the fat doomsday minister's car stopped at an intersection. Of the few people around, no one noticed enough to be called later as a witness.

H e's still in there buying muffins, and he's late." Mary sat alone in a parked car outside a bakery, just past Charles-Ray Turnbull.

Eventually, he came out from Dimple Donuts carrying four grease-stained bags.

"That's a hell of a lot of muffins." Mary was talking on a cell phone with a two-way radio function.

"Plenty of time." Adderloy sat at the fourth-floor window of a hotel room in the center of town. N., alone in a car, could see both Mary and Turnbull in the distance. Reza and Vladislav, each with an earphone, sat on a bench in a dirty city park with brown grass and overgrown bushes.

"He's back in the car now."

"Switching around the muffins." It was N.'s voice.

"It looks like he's putting them in plain paper bags," said Mary. "Can you believe . . ." She let go and pressed the talk button again. "He'll probably stop by the church."

"Plenty of time," Adderloy reassured.

Reza sat in the park with a Coke, while Vladislav blew on a huge cup of American coffee, which he'd strengthened with packets of Nescafé from his pocket.

"Now he's rolling again."

Adderloy had pulled back the curtains from the hotel window. The air-conditioning was broken, and soon the morning sun would make the room too hot. He grinned at the light coming in through the window, lifted the phone from the desk beside him, and pushed to get an outside line. Coolly, he calculated that the call would eventually be traced.

The phone rang a few times, before a woman replied: "*Topeka Capital-Journal.*"

Adderloy was quiet at first, then exhaled with foreboding. "God no longer tolerates your impurities. The fallen will die and their corpses pile up. Punishment is imminent."

"Who are you?" The voice sounded surprised. "Is this a threat?"

He didn't answer.

"Hello?" The woman sounded fearful, her voice cracking.

Adderloy gave a forced cough and then hung up.

The police station was only a few blocks away, and a pair of blue lights sped by the Hotel Century.

"He has arrived at the church," roared the radio. Mary remained closest to Charles-Ray, watching him from across the church parking lot.

"Did he bring the muffins?" That was N. He couldn't see him, but had stopped at an intersection where he could safely watch Turnbull's Lincoln pull out.

"The bags, yes."


It took Charles-Ray Turnbull ten minutes to deliver the pastries. When he came out, he walked across the asphalt with quick steps. He seemed annoyed, slamming the car door twice before he turned the key.

N., waiting, saw the dirty vinyl top roll past. "I got him."

"We're off," Vladislav said over the phone. Reza was already up. He forced his empty soda can into an overflowing trash basket.

They'd left the park when Mary began to read aloud into her cell phone, as she crossed the streets: "Baseline . . . Indian Hill . . . red light . . . now he's moving again."

Reza wiped his forehead with the back of his hand, Vladislav slowly stroked his beard. They stood and waited on the sidewalk at the designated intersection. Next door was a parking lot, where the attendant scratched lottery tickets in his little wooden shed, with his back to the street. Painters ripped posters off a facade.

"Montclair Street."

That was N.'s signal. He drove past Mary and caught up with Turnbull, pulling into the outside lane, just behind him.

"Abbott Place."

Vladislav stretched, trying to see the incoming traffic.

"Miller."

N. passed him and turned so he was in front.

Vladislav first caught sight of N.'s stolen black Impala. Although the wide hood obscured his view, he glimpsed the dull red Lincoln behind.

N. began to brake. They needed Turnbull to slow down to walking speed. Mary eased up alongside and boxed him in—in case Turnbull decided to swing out and speed up from there.

Turnbull drummed hard with his fingers on the steering wheel, still looking annoyed. The eyes that followed him from three directions couldn't read what he said, but he shook one hand in front of him, and his cheeks quivered.

Vladislav timed his move carefully, stepping out into the street when Charles-Ray Turnbull's speed was low enough but still far too high. Turnbull slammed on the brakes, his seat belt throwing him back. Vladislav swiveled so he stood with legs apart in front of the bumper, then put both hands on the hood and leaned forward. Vladislav's huge and sincere smile looked scarily hypnotic. The minister's gaze was fixed, the way a hunted animal stands frozen in the eyes of a predator. Still alive, but already defeated.

Quickly, Reza climbed into the backseat, the gun up and leading the way.

When Turnbull got into the car, the countdown had begun—everything coordinated so that the right clues would be left behind, deliberately confusing.

Adderloy left his hotel room and took the elevator down to the lobby. On the way to the front desk, he removed the gloves he'd worn all morning.

"Checking out, please!"

The only thing the receptionist could tell the police later was that the man had had no luggage.

"Anything from the minibar?"

"Absolutely not."

Adderloy held out his card. The same card that would later be shown to have paid for a round of drinks at a hotel bar in Toronto.

Mary was already waiting in the car when Adderloy came out onto the street.

"We're moving," she said over the radio as soon as he got in, and they headed out toward the outskirts of town.

N. had parked the Impala at the factory and walked eight blocks. He opened the heavy padlock on an old door, painted black. The warehouse, with its row of metal gates, reminded him of engine sheds in a rail yard. It was quiet within the thick walls, like being inside a ruin in the middle of the forest. The light fell in oblique bands through the skylights, catching the floating specks of dust. He scraped his shoe on the gravelly floor to hear the echo. Emptiness around him, high ceilings. He waited. The gun holstered inside his jacket.

Vladislav and Reza circled around the neighborhoods with Turnbull at the wheel. It was Mary and Adderloy who raced against the clock, just outside of town. Twenty minutes to go.

Mary pulled into an open space in the middle of the parking lot at Waterstone High School. The lawns were brown with patches of dirt, the bushes overgrown. A group of Latino kids gathered around the hood of a car at one end of the parking lot, while a dozen cheerleaders walked lazily down the slope to the sports fields carrying black and yellow pom-poms, whitewashed wooden rifles, and stiff nylon flags. A whistle blew, someone laughed. Adderloy snorted and got out of the car, carrying a gym bag.

Not even ten a.m.; the school cafeteria was open but hardly anyone sat inside. Adderloy left the bag in the empty foyer and walked back to the parking lot.

Two pounds of saltpeter from a hardware store, an equal amount of confectioners' sugar from the Cake and Candy Supply at Fairlawn Plaza, a digital kitchen timer from Walmart, along with a few cables, batteries, and a lightbulb with its glass removed to spark it all. "Nothing lethal, just a real good scare," Vladislav had said when he'd finished wiring the thing in the factory.

Timer set for two minutes. Addeloy checked his watch in the car. Then, not even a bang, but somebody running out a side door yelling, and a second later a billowing cloud of black smoke pushing its way out the entrance.

Another thirty seconds, and Mary dialed 911.

"Help," she pleaded in a low voice, as soon the dispatcher answered, even closing her hand over the phone.

She played it well, the incoherence, the vagueness. The flat male voice on the other end wanted to clarify details, assured her that a patrol car was already on the way. Who was she, where was she, who had done what? In response, she whispered single words rather than sentences, stopped, changed direction. She seemed to be hiding, while observing something unmentionable. One person had been shot, maybe more, smoke, people screaming and begging for mercy. She saw one, had seen several figures running in black hoodies and boots, shell casings rolling away.

"Help, for God's sake!"

She hung up.

Twelve minutes left. Mary started the car and pulled out. They saw the first cars halfway to downtown, as three police cars shot past with blue lights and sirens. Soon after, a pair of black vans marked POLICE in small letters, no sirens but lights flashing. The stragglers that followed, just as loud as the first, swerved ominously through the traffic.

"Bloodthirsty," said Adderloy when they sped past, "like piranhas."

Downtown Topeka was about to be left without police officers. Soon they were on the scene, taking aim and screaming behind skidded cars, while lines of men with black gear poured in through the school's emergency exits. First, a threat called in to the local paper, then this. Wholesale panic. It would take more than an hour before they figured it out. Only then would the dark realization sink in, when the casings were swept up and the real corpses counted. At any rate, all the schoolchildren were fine.

Mary and Adderloy had parked next to the Impala and waited now with N. in the warehouse. Two minutes to go. They heard a car stop, and then steps.

"I have a family," came Charles-Ray's voice.

"We all do."

Vladislav led Charles-Ray Turnbull, with one hand on his shoulder. They'd put a hood over him, and with every panting breath his mouth drew the fabric into a taut little bowl. Fearful, as if anticipating the chair in front of him. The medical bag was open and ready on the floor beside it. Mary had drawn an entire vial into the syringe she held in her hand.

"Sit!"

Adderloy behind, N. and Mary on either side. Vladislav grabbed him with both hands. Mary held her syringe, N. his gun. Charles-Ray Turnbull sat down with his head lowered in resignation, as if awaiting a punch, or a shot to the back of the head.

Mary pushed the thick needle right through his jacket fabric and into his upper arm. It was the only time he fought, and for a few moments they all had to restrain him.

"There, there," said Vladislav with the voice of someone comforting a dying animal in the presence of a child. The fabric tightened when Turnbull turned his face up to the ceiling. Like the crude outline of an African mask. His movements were already confused.

Charles-Ray Turnbull thought they had bound him with restraining rope, but in fact the injection caused paralysis. After waiting ten seconds, Reza grabbed Turnbull's left foot, straightening the leg. He looked away when N. stepped forward, aimed for the underside of the thigh, and pulled the trigger. Turnbull twitched so violently that his chair fell over.

The bang rang out, and a thin streak of blood splashed out a few feet across the floor. Turnbull murmured low, and moved slowly, like a larva in the dirt. Mary sat with the medical bag beside him on the floor. She waited, poking around the entrance and exit holes in his pants. The thin fingers of her rubber gloves were shiny red. The wounds had slowly started bleeding, but didn't spurt. He let out a long-drawn cry while Mary quickly bandaged his thigh. That was it. He was gone, stunned. Now all that remained was to let the nightmares descend on him.

All five of them sat in the Impala, the men in suits and sneakers with the machine guns and some bags at their feet. Reza stroked his head, N. smelled powder from the gun inside his jacket. Mary, after turning off the car radio, drove upright and confident.

"Do you feel it?" said Vladislav, his eyes in the distance. "It's like it was then."

"What do you mean?" said Reza, who sat nervously, jiggling his legs.

"Exactly like after the wave. Don't you feel it . . . everything disappearing. The world disappearing." No one said anything. He added: "Now you can do anything."

First Federal United. In front of the bank, a no-parking zone, completely empty. The lone black Impala disappeared as soon as the men got out, Vladislav going first through the glass doors. White athletic shoes, black suit and hood, submachine guns like exclamation points as to why they were there. From a vast mosaic on the wall behind the tellers, Indians in garish robes stared down at the invaders. N. and Reza leaped and slid, half sitting, across the counters into the office landscape behind.

"The money—all of it!"

They tossed nylon bags to the tellers. A young man stood paralyzed, but the woman next to him picked up a bag from the floor and started throwing cash into it.

Adderloy stood, supervising, by the entrance to the vault with the safe-deposit boxes, while Vladislav went farther in to take care of the teller booths at the other end himself. As he turned the corner, he fired a few shots straight up. The echo was painful and paralyzing, off the black marble floors and mosaics on the walls. The ceiling was so high that it took a few seconds before the clouds of plaster debris rained down over the crouching customers.

"Hurry up!" roared Reza, behind the tills.

Adderloy had locked his focus on a single person. A man wearing a white shirt, blue pants with dark stripes. And a holster. Adderloy tried to keep his eyes on the bank guard's hands, but they were hidden by the elderly women customers who surrounded him. His face was visible: narrowed eyes, as if staring straight into the biting wind, and his chest was heaving. Something slid along the floor as a bag from Vladislav's side of the bank appeared from behind the corner. N. and Reza, hanging their bags over their shoulders, started moving.

In all their detailed planning, they'd never discussed the guard. It wasn't something they'd overlooked, it was something they'd avoided.

The guard's first shot tore a white streak through the brownish-red mosaic of a buffalo herd. The next hit the back of a woman standing near him. She fell headlong as the others threw themselves down around him. The guard, one Stan Moneyhan, retired vice squad, had never once during his career as a police officer drawn a weapon. This time it was different.

He had tripped over one of the elderly and fallen over. Now he lay on his back holding the gun in both hands between his knees. It looked odd, a low-profile shooting tower, using his heels to turn.

Maybe just doing his best after his fall. Getting some initiative back. Only he wasn't in control. He aimed at Adderloy but kept the gun too low and his head too high. His whole body seemed to shake. He was never even close to hitting him, not even when he aimed. If he saw anything at all. It was totally random—a senseless shooting.

Wood splinters flew through the air, seeming to fall from everywhere. N. and Reza threw themselves flat on the floor. Cashiers and clerks disappeared under their desks, someone shouted, the bullets ripped through the plywood of the furniture. N. saw a face falling forward near a table leg. Eyes closed, as if in sleep. A few muffled blasts, a pause between each. Adderloy returned the fire but never hit the guard. Instead, their view of the street and the town square disappeared, as the huge glass panes cracked all the way out to their frames, whitening like ice. As if Adderloy didn't want to hit the guard, but instead incite him even more.

It was into this situation that Vladislav came running, low and fast. Passed right next to Adderloy, who had fallen back against the wall from the recoil. A moment of consensus between the two men, amid the chaos. Adderloy's barrel moved aside, giving way to Vladislav. Stan Moneyhan lay on his back and twisted himself to reload. Legs floundering, he swayed as if he couldn't get up, when in fact he was trying to reach an extra clip somewhere at the back of his belt.

The silence was palpable as everything hung in the balance, Vladislav's blunt submachine gun resting against his hip. He kept a hand on it, cool, even taking the time to give Adderloy a long look. There was something flagrant in it. As if all his waiting was a provocation, just standing there, not even looking at the guard.

Moneyhan found the clip, fumbled, lay on his back again, got the gun ready.

Vladislav's movements were the same as on that beach once,

when Mary sat in her deck chair and Reza hesitated. They hadn't even gotten to know Adderloy yet. The same steps, the same smoothness. Something you barely had time to perceive before it was already done.

The guard took all three shots in the chest.

Until that moment, everything had had an explanation.

N. didn't know, had his face in the carpet behind the booths. Reza, however, who'd stood up immediately when the bullets stopped tearing around them, had seen it all.

Watching him from the floor, seeing how Reza winced but wasn't scared by the three shots, N. instinctively realized that something was over. In an instant, he got to his feet and moved forward. His breath snorting, his mouth dry, hurting from the unwieldy nylon bag hitting against his back. He saw people lying helter-skelter on the floor on the other side of the booths, but it was only an impression, no thought of who was dead or who only hunkered down.

Reza also ran. When he got to the counter, he shouted something in despair. A stream of foreign profanity.

Afterward, it was difficult to get consistent stories from witnesses, beyond that it was the man suddenly appearing from the back who put an end to Stan Moneyhan. The guard's death had seemed like an execution, so they said. The people in the bank had lain and waited, praying, while the men in black suits and hoods moved carelessly among them. In the hearings several witnesses believed there were at least six black-clad men. Someone considered particularly reliable claimed, under oath, that there were three. One had seen hand grenades. Another had heard the robbers speaking Spanish. A scrap dealer from Wisoma County rattled off all the types of weapons he'd seen during the robbery, as mechanically as an evening prayer.

The bank surveillance cameras proved inadequate. Two were completely out of focus. The little that could be determined from the tapes showed, however, that there were four people who robbed the bank—but in general the tapes were used to support a variety of groundless claims.

No one noticed how Reza stood and yelled, gesticulating at Vladislav. Or how Adderloy took out a pouch of blood from his bag. How he cut it up and let the contents flow out across the floor as he left the bank.


R eza was the first to take off his hood after the car picked them up. He threw it on the floor, didn't say anything, only let his eyes wander between Vladislav and Adderloy. Mary floored it for ten blocks, ignoring the traffic lights, then turned and began to zigzag.

When she slowed down, everything seemed to be normal around them: women with strollers, teenagers with skateboards. No one stared at the black Impala. Mary let go of the steering wheel with one hand, rested her fingers on the wide shift lever.

"Perfect, believe me," said Vladislav, before she could ask. "Not a dry eye."

Mary turned the rearview mirror so she could see all three of them in the back. N. sat in the middle with his eyes closed. Like the others, he had torn off his hood, but his eyes were closed and his breathing strained, as if he was fighting nausea.

"Or, what would you say—Bill?" Vladislav still had the submachine gun lying flat on his lap.

Adderloy, who sat next to Mary, only humphed in response.

"Sorry?" said Vladislav, pushing.

Adderloy smiled in a moment of delight that only Mary could

see. Then he pulled off the gloves for the second time that day, rolled them into a ball, and let them drop to the floor.

Reza stared at Vladislav, who avoided his gaze but kept track of the submachine gun sticking up between his knees.

"Did you secure it?"

No response. Vladislav pushed his hair to the side a little hesitantly and then leaned across N., grabbed Reza's weapon, secured it, and put it on top of the bag at his feet. Reza's jaw muscles pulsed stubbornly. Otherwise he was completely motionless, like a lizard on a wall. His and Vladislav's eyes had not yet met. N.'s eyes remained closed, his breathing still violent.

"My guess is three dead," began Vladislav, "and at least as many wounded."

Adderloy looked out on the street, as if he were amused by reading the signs, or thinking about the weather. As if nothing had happened, as if nothing was going on in the seat behind him. Mary sat with both hands on the wheel again.

Vladislav set his foot on Reza's submachine gun and turned so he could look him in the eye. "Who feels most alive now—them or us?"

Reza remained still as a lizard, only his jaws twitching.

"Them or us?"

N. didn't exist between them, only his panting that wouldn't stop. The car swayed on a curve. Music from somewhere outside came in and then faded away again. Reza drew his hand across his forehead and down over his face, a slow introspective gesture.

Then he whispered, almost hissed: "No one said anything about the guard, not anything about all this shooting." He glanced at Adderloy.

"I hadn't forgotten about the guard," said Vladislav.

177

"We just hadn't discussed what we would do about him."

Reza looked miserable. "I saw you . . . , " he said and tried to make a gesture, but his hand was too weak and fell down again.

"Welcome to America." Vladislav snorted. He struck his machine gun, making it jump on his lap. "Was it you or I, Reza? Nope . . . it was us, it was *us* who shot every motherfucker in there." He also gazed up at Adderloy, who remained silent.

N. was breathing normally again. For a few moments the air felt fresh. His ears still rang from the shots inside the bank. He looked at his hands. Alone at the door of the old warehouse, he was about to unlock the padlock again.

He fumbled with the gun before he went in, held it a little in front of him as he stepped sideways through the slit. His eyes had to adjust to the gloom. The dusty sunlight from the small skylights lit up holes in the gray-blackness. He peered in and kicked the gritty concrete to announce his arrival. It was completely quiet, the air damp and smelling of iron. He could make out a wall.

Then he saw the figure, stretched out across the floor right where they'd left him. N. lowered his gun and approached. At first, seeing no signs of life, he poked at Turnbull with his toe, as if looking for a small animal that had disappeared into a thicket. Then he saw the fabric hood move over the mouth and two fingers of one hand start to twitch. The brown-red stain on the bandage had reached the edges, but it would hold tight a little longer.

Minutes left. No sirens.

N. pulled off the hood. Then he stood and looked at Turnbull as he lay on his side, disheveled and pale. He blinked, began to move. His eyes were wild, faraway, as if demons rushed at him from the roof. He got up on one arm, his tongue moving erratically in his wide-open mouth. He rocked, fell back. His breathing was labored, hissing. As if he were drawing his last breath, over and over again.

You could feel the presence of death hovering in the room. No sirens outside.

N. remembered the head falling forward beside a desk in the bank. The hissing sound from the bullet that passed right by his own head. He remembered limbs sticking up from the rubble of a hotel. A pair of fish swimming around his legs. It was Adderloy who'd started it, the pointless violence that only he himself could explain. But it was this motherfucker on the floor who would have to pay, who would take the blame. Deep within, N. could feel, even though the price was high, that something within him had quieted. Soon it would be his turn, soon the fight would be over.

A sound, expected yet still a little too soon, got him to come to his senses, interrupting his thoughts.

He threw one last glance at the body on the floor and went out.

Vladislav had shouted, impatient. It was just him there, the others had already moved on. N. nodded without looking at him, took the lock off the door, and left it open a gap. Vladislav stood with a rag by the Impala he'd prepared: the doors and the trunk were wide open, it reeked of gasoline.

"They've woken up," he said and lit the rag with a lighter. Somewhere far away, they could hear sirens.

The flashover from the car was instantaneous. Vladislav shrank back from the heat, a black cloud rose straight up like a huge smoke signal. That was the idea.

N. felt the warmth right through his clothes when he threw the padlock in the flames. Soon the flames died down, but the fire only got hotter. Something black ran out from the car. Vladislav was already sitting in the red Nissan, engine running. He knocked on the window, then it came down.

"You win, but let's not go overboard." He smiled wryly. "I'd really like to get going now."

N. heard sirens again. They sounded much higher. Much closer. He thought he ought to be afraid.

# CHAPTER 23

### Diego Garcia, 2008

WAS WITH HIM, INSIDE HIS cell," Grip had told Shauna at dinner the night before. "Yet he says nothing."

Shauna just nodded. No questions. All the time in the world. The only thing she insisted on was that they go snorkeling together one day, she and Grip. She said she'd found a good beach.

One night's sleep and half a day later, it was almost time for lunch. But Grip would wait: on the TV monitor, he'd just seen the prisoner sit down to eat, and decided to make another attempt to speak to him.

The man's eyes were startled and hesitant when Grip walked in, as if his being released was as likely as getting a slap in the face. A state that lasted for a second. Grip had seen to it that there were two chairs in the cell—he took the other and sat down opposite. The man had food on his spoon, but it fell down on his plate. There was a hint of troubled breathing again. Grip saw the fear. He'd sat so that he was fully visible, not at the table, but a little distance away. Just at the edge of what at the moment seemed bearable.

"They don't allow knives or forks, I see," said Grip. There was some kind of brown mess on the man's spoon and on the plate, maybe chili. "Is it suicide or murder they're afraid of?"

The man didn't drop his gaze, let out a deep breath, and raised the spoon to his mouth.

"Child," the man said then, with contempt. "They want to make you feel like a child." He took a sip of water, and Grip did the math: no accent, not the Swedish taught to an immigrant, but clean. Not even a dialect. Educated?—probably. Age still unclear. The swelling had gone down, but the semi-long hair and beard made him difficult to assess.

"Do you know who I am?" asked the man and lowered his gaze.

"No," said Grip. "Should I?"

"You said you wouldn't lie to me."

"Yes."

"Is this being recorded?"

"I suppose."

"Are you alone?"

"I'm alone here from Sweden, yes."

The man shoved together food on the plate with his spoon. "I can't help it," he said tiredly, after he stopped coughing. Although he seemed calm, he wrestled with his breathing.

"Your reaction, you mean," said Grip. "The fact that you're scared shitless by strangers."

"The door opens at the wrong time. They have succeeded, I am a Pavlov's dog."

"I understand completely—"

"Sure," interrupted the man mildly. He tasted the tip of the spoon. "I'll tell you something that neither you nor they know." He nodded toward the cell door. "How many different cells I have been in—no idea. Flights here and there. No impression of the outside world, only the food, if there was any." He held his spoon as if it were a pointer. "The food becomes your compass. When it's finely chopped and you get this spoon nonsense, then you know who's in charge. The Americans. But they have their ways too, the Americans—they prefer to beat and choke when you don't tell them what they want. When you get those fucking flatbreads, then you know you're with someone else. The Arabs, they prefer to stab and cut."

"Where have you been?"

"Yemen, Bulgaria, Malaysia—I don't know. Not sure. You get injections, everything becomes foggy. Flights back and forth."

"How long has it been going on?"

The man glanced at one of the newspapers, then shrugged his shoulders.

"Several years?"

"It seems so." The man was struck by something, a wave of emotion. He seemed to hold back a sob. The next moment, he seemed indifferent again. "I don't remember much from when I arrived here—the syringes destroy and the hood blinds. But it was a warm wind, I felt it drag across my ankles." He pulled up the legs of his coverall slightly. "Maybe there was a salty smell too, maybe the sea. But I might be wrong."

"The Indian Ocean, we're in the middle of it," said Grip.

The man gestured toward the plate. "And it is Americans who run the show."

"Yes." Grip continued. "Where are the scars from?" He had seen the white streaks of scar tissue on his legs when the man pulled up his pants. Something similar also curled across his forearms. The damage wasn't of the same type as that on the face, or the swelling that appeared under the bandages on his feet. Although the scars looked bad, they were healed.

"These," replied the man, "they're old." He twisted and turned his arms as if he were showing a forgotten tattoo. "A swim, shall we say. There was a strong current, I got cut, the doctors didn't have the time they needed." Then he touched his face and added: "There are others that are newer." He looked Grip straight in the eyes, the defeated gaze suddenly full of rage. "They think I'm a Muslim. Some of them want so damn badly to believe it."

"So what are you?"

"What do you think?"

"Swedish," said Grip.

"Swedes can be Muslims."

"Yes, but not you."

"Why not?"

"You asked what I thought. This is getting ridiculous." Grip sighed loudly.

"I've spent years stuck in ridiculous discussions." The man cleared his throat. "Several days at a time, often with refreshing content. You never fall asleep during the inquisition."

"Have you admitted that you're a Muslim?"

"Many times."

"Other things too?"

"More than I can remember."

There was silence.

"You still don't know who I am?" asked the prisoner again.

"No."

"What are they saying about me?"

"They say they know nothing. They think you could possibly be Swedish."

The man gently ran his fingertips along the edge of the table. He looked down at his fingers, the nail stubs, and then whispered, "Call me N."

# CHAPTER 24

*Topeka, 2005*

T HERE WAS A RADIO AT the factory. Dozens of stations, all interrupting their oldies or Top 40s for the news.

The robbery was the lead story. The coverage short and sensational, at first mostly sirens and shouts from an emergency room or the square outside First Federal. Everything confused, very little said. A robbery, at least four dead, maybe seven, more being treated at a local hospital. The reporters sounded pretty worked up. One station said police had responded to a shooting at Waterstone High School; another reporter shouted about Topeka being under attack. The mayor couldn't be reached for comment. The police chief had been seen driving with an armed escort. Someone reported that at a downtown hotel, all doors had been blocked off and a SWAT team sent in. Witnesses saw people dragged out to waiting cars in handcuffs. Not until the afternoon did someone begin to put it all together. A pair of menacing and strange phone calls shortly before the bank robbery. Realizing that police response had taken too long because Topeka's officers had left the city to investigate a hoax.

A Republican who'd lost the recent state senate election criticized the city's response, always ending: "Had I been the one making decisions . . ." His speech merely filled time in the early-evening newscasts, when reporters at the bank and the hospitals still had little to go on. While everyone was still stumbling around.

That was before the police called a press conference.

By that time, Vladislav had long since ditched all the subma-chine guns in a pond and left the red Nissan in the woods. (They'd strewn empty beer cans and porn magazines inside the car, so the theft would look like a teenage prank.) In Mary's living room at the factory, the radio volume got cranked up with each new report and turned down in between. The noise of the generators drowned out a couple of updates. Under the stairway, the bags of money re-mained untouched. The atmosphere in the factory was cautious. Everyone kept to himself, except for Adderloy, who seemed to be constantly doing a head count. He kept sending Mary up to check on Reza, who had retreated to his room.

"Well?"

"He's still on the mattress," said Mary, and threw up her hands.

Back and forth she went. Same question, same answer.

Vladislav, lying stretched out on the couch, dozed off a few times. Occasionally he sat up, rubbed his face, pulled back his long hair, and then sank back again. He didn't seem interested in the news, but glared at the radio when someone turned up the volume. He gave an impression of completeness—what was done was done. Now he was finished, ready to go into hibernation.

Mary and Adderloy were the ones tied to the radio. Whatever they did, they did in wide circles around it. Mary was the most rest-less, kept herself constantly busy: made up lists (unclear of what), showered, sorted papers, changed her shoes. And each time the news came on, she'd stop as if she'd been caught doing something illicit.

"They're probably in surgery now," she'd say during breaks between newscasts.

Adderloy's conscience didn't seem much affected. He wanted details. What did they really know about the bank, who was the mayor's spokesperson? What was the death toll up to? The time between news reports was worthless to him—it only made him impatient. He puzzled, considered, counted. "Is Reza sleeping? Are the weapons in the shallow end of the pond? Did you catch what Turnbull said while he was delirious?"

It was after dark when the police press conference came on. Interrupting the music. The mayor, the police chief, and various other officials were introduced inside Topeka's echoing City Hall. Although many were in attendance, only the police chief spoke—Rudolph Oldenhall. He explained what everybody already knew about the robbery, adding that another person had died at the hospital.

"The investigation continues unabated," he concluded, and the room was strangely quiet. The silence was like a sudden paralysis, as if someone had choked. Just a short, short moment of anticipation.

"Thank you," the police chief said.

Then the storm broke. "How can you . . . ? Is it true that . . . ? Chief Oldenhall . . . Why . . . ? Apprehended . . . ?"

"Quiet!" yelled a voice into the microphone. "One at a time, one at a time."

Some held back, but a handful of journalists kept pressing: " . . . school . . . assault . . . the schools . . . police . . . ." The same words, in the same feedback loop. No one could hear the questions, yet obviously they were all disputing why the city had been emptied of police officers. As if they'd all agreed to hit where the police were most sensitive: their highest ranks had been thoroughly taken in.

187

"There were credible threats to our schools," began the police chief. He dragged out every word. "We had to act."

That was the chink in the wall; he was flooded by questions. The answers the reporters got back were somewhat random. "I consider it a terrorist act . . . a mass murder." "It was well-planned." "Yes, the threats were of a religious nature."

The pack sensed something; the thrust of the questions changed. Terrorists, fanatics, hordes of bearded men whose names they couldn't pronounce. "We know nothing about ethnicity," said the chief. "No, no Muslims have been arrested at the Century Hotel." Asked repeatedly about arrests, he chose to answer a different question: "The FBI is involved." Meant as a sign of action, but seen as the opposite. This was, after all, the Midwest.

"Topeka's own police are highly competent. It's not about that," he replied irritably.

Chief Oldenhall, Chief Oldenhall," repeated someone from the floor. An older voice, a tone that expected his colleagues to be quiet. A voice that also got what it wanted.

"Chief Oldenhall, so far you've only spoken about all the things that have *not* happened. Soon, ten hours will have gone by—you don't have any leads?"

"We—" The police chief choked back his anger. He was down for the count. Everyone had fallen silent, waiting for a response. At nine, he had to get to his feet. "Let's make one thing perfectly clear," he began, "the odds are totally on our side. Namely, we have arrested *one* man. He is being treated right now at a city hospital. He's one of them. Somewhat diminished, but once he recovers he will be held accountable. And before you ask—he is an American."

At the factory, Adderloy nodded approvingly, as if listening to a political speech. "There," he said quietly, "they had it coming."

When an ad for marriage counseling broke in, Adderloy turned down the volume and looked around.

Vladislav looked back, shrugged.

"Reza?" said Adderloy.

"Yeah, yeah," replied Mary, and started walking toward the stairs.

"I'll come with you," said Adderloy, and followed.

As they disappeared down the hall, N. turned to Vladislav.

"Why?" he said.

Vladislav muttered and then replied, "You know why. At least one person had to die inside the bank. You must have understood that calculation."

"But there were more—we hadn't agreed on that."

"We didn't agree on anything."

"And the guard, why didn't anyone check him out?"

"Fuck knows. This is Adderloy's cat-and-mouse game. And by the way, what does it matter? We had to shoot the guard, given what the dumb jerk was doing."

"I was lying down, didn't see anything, but Reza believes that what he saw—it wasn't done in self-defense."

Vladislav propped himself up on his elbow. "We've become subtle as hell, haven't we."

N. fell silent. Vladislav glanced toward the hallway above the stairs. "And," he added, "even if the guard hadn't done anything stupid, we would have shot him anyway. Or we, I—I would have done it. Reza is slow sometimes, but what the hell did you think?"

N. was still quiet.

"What did you think?" Vladislav repeated in staccato. "That

Adderloy believed a minor bank robbery would be enough to shake things up here in Kansas? Someone said you had to seize the opportunity, don't you remember? All five of us around a table, in the sand, on a beach. Survivors. Invisible. Someone said you had to seize the opportunity." He smiled. "Adderloy's vision. Didn't you understand? Come on. Or did you just close your eyes?"

"Is that what you are," said N., "a hired gun?"

"Now I am."

"All the dead—that doesn't bother you?"

"All the dead . . . hmm . . . The world is made up of mistakes. Don't you know that chance is everything? When my bus was filling with water, I pushed away people around me, everyone trying to get past. I rose to the surface, they didn't, but that doesn't seem to bother anyone. Guilt? No, I feel no guilt. Adderloy has his agenda. And this is a rotten country, it stinks." Vladislav sniffed. "We all need the money, but Adderloy wants to stir things up. Turnbull was a great scapegoat—but then someone had to die. They have the death penalty in Kansas, but not for everything. So we had to raise it to that level, to the death chamber. Only then would it make a difference."

N. shook his head.

Vladislav got angry. "Didn't you fucking understand that?"

"But we didn't talk about it."

"No, we didn't. For then the fragile beauty would have shattered—we were newly baptized by the wave, a bunch of pure white souls. Right?"

N. shrugged in a way that could have meant anything.

Vladislav leaned back again. "One thing Reza was damn right about, fate gave us new destinies. And another thing, I agree with Adderloy about this—you have to go all the way. Put someone on death row, only then will people listen."

"When did you decide?" said N.

"About the guard?"

"Yes."

"*We* didn't decide. Adderloy decided a long time ago. Someone would have to die. Then when we got here, Adderloy went inside the bank a few times, to choose. Naturally, it was the guard. The fact that more got hit—you have to chalk that up to Adderloy's mission."

"Last night, you and he went away to practice shooting. Afterward, when I stuck my finger in the barrels, they were clean. Not a shot."

"Yeah, pretty obvious, wasn't it?" Vladislav laughed and then became serious again. "He wanted to talk. Finally, it had to be said, after all. Who would actually do what."

"That you would shoot the guard?"

"Something like that."

"Something like that?"

"Yes, I guess I wanted to exchange a few words with him too. The part about someone having to die—I'd already figured it out—and that he thought I'd be the one to take care of it. So I took the opportunity to raise the ante. Doesn't Adderloy have a little more money than he pretends? I figured it'd be worth a million bucks, to shoot someone in front of the video cameras at a bank."

"Or else?"

"Or else I would have left this stinking factory and walked into the nearest police station. 'Here I am, call the Czech embassy and tell them they can scratch another name off the list of missing persons after the tsunami.' Poof, I'd be gone. Poof, another life."

"Did you get the money?"

Vladislav mimicked Adderloy's way of smoking. "He has constructed his little machine with utmost care, all the players and events, tinkered us together. I can't quite stomach it, so why not tinker a little myself?"

"Did you get it?"

"One million. He's not much into signing papers or even handshakes, Adderloy. He just nodded. Then if I don't get it . . ." Vladislav shrugged.

"For a nod? There isn't a police officer in Kansas who doesn't want to see you through a sight right now."

"They don't know who I am."

"And you think Adderloy will pay?"

"You know his type: seemingly smooth, and then that trimmed beard. If you pointed to the devil's messenger, it would be Adderloy, wouldn't it. But unless he's truly in the service of the supernatural, he knows very little about Vladislav Pilk. No more than that he's a hell of a shot. Or what do you think?" said Vladislav, throwing a new look at N. "If he doesn't pay up, what would you bet? That I'm the one who will find him and make his life a living hell—and that I'm not just trying to intimidate him when I say that? When I swear it before him, so that he feels the saliva on his face. What does he think about that?"

Vladislav waited a second, then said, "Adderloy nodded, and the guard is dead, right? Even though the guard shot the others, that does not diminish my effort."

They heard voices raised down the hallway, muffled by the distance, yet abruptly as if a door had opened for a second and then closed again. Vladislav and N. listened for more, but heard nothing. Only the old factory's diffuse murmuring.

"Hm . . . Reza," said Vladislav then. "I saw him when I came running around the corner. The idiot stood up. You never know

192

where you are with him, standing up when he should be sitting and vice versa. I like the type, they always take a different path. A blond Pakistani . . . gay, or whatever he is. You know what I mean, entirely his own person."

"He's angry now," said N.

"About the deaths—you really believe that? You've seen Reza, he's hot for weapons. Didn't quite know what we were doing, but wanted it to be real. Arm himself and make himself heard. Isn't there something about his part of the world, they want to stand there shaking their Kalashnikovs and denouncing the USA. Great fucking theater."

"When he yelled 'I saw you' to me in the car, he wasn't talking about the trigger-happy guard being dead. He screamed it at Adderloy. What he saw was the whole scheme: despite all the commotion, despite all the shots and screams—he realized he was just a pawn in something much bigger, something Adderloy had planned long before we got involved. Reza knows Adderloy is American. He doesn't trust him for a second."

Vladislav paused. "Haven't you thought about that? About what you're doing here? I—maybe I get a million, maybe I have to shoot Adderloy. I don't trust him either. And Mary, is she good in bed? Who does the giving, and who the taking?"

"Enough—not another word," said N.

"Her gaze devours more than just your lust."

"Shut it. Now."

"Goddamn it—you asked me *why*?"

"That's enough," snapped N., snarling.

"What did you think was the goal of all this? Sure, part of it was to make the Baptists pay for all the crap they spread. But just by shaking your fist and screaming a little? You shot Turnbull in

193

the leg, and the way I know you, whenever Topeka's Baptists come up . . ."

"Him, yes, him I would have shot in the groin . . . and in the head too." N. shook. "It is the right—"

"—the right you claim for yourself," Vladislav cut in, without looking at N.

They heard footsteps in the hallway. Mary glanced down the stairs. "Reza's sleeping," she said.

Vladislav laughed. "Oh, he does that."

Adderloy came up behind Mary and looked searchingly at N., who looked like he'd been caught. Adderloy started walking down the stairs and said something about a pair of searchlights that he'd seen light up the night sky outside the large windows.

Then Vladislav rolled off the couch and stood up. He passed right next to N. and whispered, "Now we just have to survive."

# CHAPTER 25

I N THE ABSENCE OF OTHER heroes, Stan Moneyhan became the man of the day. The dead security guard from First Federal's robbery was the media darling. He was the cop who, instead of retiring, chose to protect his fellow citizens. That was how reporters spun it, at least—in fact his meager pension had forced him to keep working. Old coworkers bowed to his memory, saying he'd never drawn a gun on anyone. At his second press conference, Chief Oldenhall announced that they should all be grateful to the security guard for his fine aim. The man they'd arrested could now be tied to the robbery, through his blood. The next day, blowups of Charles-Ray Turnbull's face appeared behind news anchors and on every front page. It was an unflattering picture, Turnbull lying on a sofa in a rumpled shirt, eyes half closed. The picture was obviously cropped, taken at some family gathering—an arm here and a leg there, from others sharing the couch. (Evidently a relative had been tempted by a photo agency to earn some extra cash.)

In news briefs the aged Turnbull Sr. repeated "We pray for him" with a stiff smile, while trying to hide his face with his hand. Already on the first day police had conducted a raid on Turnbull's home. Later, when white vans pulled up to Westhill Baptist Church and the plainclothes investigators with gun holsters on their backs carried out hard drives and document boxes, the church was no longer called "a congregation in shock" but instead "a hateful cult." At the hospital where Turnbull lay recovering, police stopped a man in greasy jeans who tried to enter the ward with a pipe wrench stuffed in his sleeve. As he was dragged away, he shouted to the cameras outside the hospital entrance, "That motherfucker will die soon anyway." The Republican politician from the last evening's news showed up, demanding that hanging be reinstated in Kansas, adding, "Nobody fears a syringe."

In the factory, Adderloy's gaze was sharp and clear as he went on and on about Turnbull's expected execution. Otherwise, he was noticeably silent. Reza remained in his room, and the money from the robbery remained untouched in bags below the stairs.

It was late morning. They were restless inside the factory, waiting, hidden, dutifully eating their stored food, quietly visiting the toilet. Vladislav, shirtless, complained constantly about the heat. The radio reports became background noise. Mary lived on chips and tried to start smoking. N. woke up every morning with a headache, had already consumed an entire bottle of pain pills, and wrestled with his feeling of powerlessness through long cold showers.

Still, the night before, they'd finally decided what to do next. Even Reza had stopped staring at the wall and come to sit with them. It was a short conversation. They would get to New York, then divide up the money and go their separate ways. Everyone agreed. Adderloy would buy a used van big enough for everyone.

He went out before eleven in the morning to check on some listings. As soon as Adderloy left, Mary got her appetite back. "I want food with taste," she said.

Vladislav suggested the Lebanese joint around the corner. Mary wanted to go farther, to a real restaurant, but when Reza predictably didn't want to come along, both Vladislav and N. thought they should stay close.

So Lebanese it was.

The place was almost empty, although lunch had just begun. A few customers made small talk by the cash register, waiting for takeout. One of the brothers said hello to Mary and waved them to a table. In the corner, a TV was switched to the news.

Vladislav looked skeptically at the chalkboard menu.

"No fish?"

"No, Vladislav," said N. "No fish in Kansas."

Vladislav threw up his hands.

"Shish kebab, you want shish kebab?" N. yelled, "Can we get two shish kebabs?"

"And a T-bone steak," said Mary. "So rare that it bleeds."

N. turned toward the kitchen and saw the large freezers. Kept his gaze there for a moment.

On TV, a fanfare announced the noon headlines. The new images caught their attention. In the boredom of the factory, they'd grown numb to the nuances, the reporters' angles, the latest witnesses. Now the story wasn't so much about Turnbull but the ones still at large. The bank had come up with a few grainy surveillance pictures: disorder, people lying on the ground. Suddenly Vladislav came into view: straight-backed and masked, a submachine gun at his hip.

"Quick as TV," he said quietly and squinted, unconcerned.

The news anchor pressed on. At the Houston airport, police had been swarming for hours. A flight to Cancun was canceled and the passengers taken off to be screened. Departure boards scrolled with delayed flights. Policemen in black ran in clusters. A federal police officer with a thick mustache said the men from the Kansas robbery had been trying to flee the country.

N. looked nervous. Mary fiddled with her cigarette.

The food arrived. The TV news was switched to sports. A basketball player shot a free throw before a cheering mob. In the street outside the restaurant, a jackhammer started pounding.

"This is good," said Mary mechanically after a few bites. Vladislav was lost in thought.

"To Cancun," she said, and laughed sharply.

"What?" said N.

"Where did they get Cancun from? People will fall for anything."

But N. wasn't listening; his question was aimed at Vladislav.

"Just going to get a little fresh air," said Vladislav, putting down his silverware. "Back in a minute."

He went out in the street and disappeared.

Mary kept going on about Cancun. "Is that what Turnbull told them?" She fiddled with her unlit cigarette, cut the steak, took a bite.

"Imagine, there he sits with a bullet hole in his leg and a sweaty lawyer by his side begging him to cooperate. He'll say everything, anything at all. Then maybe he'll avoid the gas chamber." The bloody juices made a red film on her plate.

She smiled again. N. had finished his beer; the last drops settled in his glass. He was watching TV. Images without sound: flashing blue lights, a reporter interviewing Chief Oldenhall, anonymous gray-brown city blocks viewed from above by a news helicopter.

"Obviously a mistake," said N. listlessly. "Cancun, the airport, all that. The police had an idea, someone ran through security control, a suitcase went astray." He saw one of the Lebanese open and shut a freezer in the kitchen. "Charles-Ray has nothing to say. He's just wondering what nightmare he woke up in."

They both turned around at the sound of the jackhammer when the front door opened. Vladislav came in and sat down.

"You feeling okay?" asked Mary.

He dismissed the question with a flip of his hand. "Do they often do street jobs like that around here?"

"I guess so. Why?"

"I went around the block and saw three gangs drilling. Awfully busy." He took a quick look out the window. "Removing old asphalt. Saw no lines marked for what they're doing. You know— sprayed. Seems pretty random."

"A gas leak, these neighborhoods, you know," said Mary, removing the cigarette from her mouth.

Vladislav bit his lip. "If you drew a circle on a map around the drillings, the factory would be right in the middle."

"Gas, sewer, there are always leaks around here," said Mary. "Eat!"

Vladislav took off his glasses and rubbed his eyes. N. glanced at the TV.

"Damn it," he said, getting up so fast that the plates jumped. Mary dropped her fork and recoiled. N. ran to the door and looked up at the sky through the glass. He glanced at the TV again, his gaze moving back and forth: TV, sky, TV.

Then he saw it. A news helicopter slowly circling above. The drilling outside the door had deadened the sound.

"Helicopter," he said, pointing at the TV. They could see their block from the air. Mary picked up her knife and fork as if nothing was happening.

"There you go," said Vladislav slowly.

N. continued looking out; the helicopter was out of sight. He twisted and turned and caught sight of it again. Lost it.

Then two black streaks passed overhead. So close that the muf-fled beats of the rotors broke through the drilling. The TV image shifted to the newsroom.

"I think there are two. Two black ones," said N.

Vladislav understood exactly.

N.'s cell phone rang. He looked at the TV before answering. It was Reza. At first N. heard only breathing.

"Someone's here."

"Reza . . . ," said N.

"Make sure he gets out," Vladislav hissed from the table. "He has to get out."

"Reza, you have to . . ."

But Reza had already hung up. Vladislav went for the door.


Inside the factory, Reza had heard the helicopters but didn't un-derstand. Their roar was lost in the din of jackhammers that had begun long before. It was the footsteps that scared him, the distant boots on metal stairs and wooden floors. Inside the empty factory, sounds carried far—echoes and resonances revealed every move-ment. People were coming.

At first the signs were small, vibrations from a door shut a bit carelessly, a banister's far-off shaking. But soon this rose to an audible tramping. Finally, as the response teams poured into the building, the sounds rose into a stampede. Down they came from helicopters on the roof, in through doors, smoke hatches and entryways in the street, smashing the windows for faster access.

A surgical intervention, striking with precision. But the bowels of the factory were far too treacherous and confusing for them to actually get where they wanted. Walls had been demolished and others added later, doors welded shut and corridors made dead ends. The police couldn't know any of this from the city's outdated blueprints.

Reza heard them, like hordes of rats forcing their way inside. He stood in the open space above the stairway, the steel door on one side, the endless hallway on the other. A few guns were stashed at the bottom of the stairs, along with the money. In a few seconds, he could be armed. He looked at the bags, the instinct to defend himself surging inside. He stood and considered; the sounds approaching. Alone and abandoned, amid the machinery of hidden agendas. A futile resistance—wasn't that what they wanted, the slightest excuse to fire at him? In a rage, he crushed his cell phone against the brick wall.

He would not arm himself. Simply stand, take it. He would explain. Someone would understand. He would never be given a chance to talk if he armed himself. The ones who came rushing in would set him free.

Reza thought they'd bust in through the metal door, so he was surprised to hear sounds coming from the hallway. Past the row of rooms that ended who-knows-where. The yellow-white beams of a few flashlights moved in the darkness, dancing in step to the same swaying tempo of the stampeding boots. First sound and light, then figures. Reza took a step—they would understand.

Someone was shouting.

Reza raised his hand to show he was unarmed and at the same time hold back anyone approaching too urgently.

A force of six men arrived first. Like all other units, they'd been lost too long inside the factory's labyrinth. "The terrorists" would get their guns, prime, arm, and wait in ambush. The element of surprise was gone—now they themselves were potential victims. Weighed down by equipment, numbed by lactic acid, they ran blindly down a never-ending hallway. The commanders broke radio silence and screamed into their earpieces. Everyone knew that at any moment one of their own would fall. Adrenaline-drained resignation took over. Everyone ran, just ran. In tight, drilled groups they swept the darkness.

Then one of them was standing there.

Shouts into the earpieces. At any moment an ambush would strike or the whole building explode. Was he alone, was he carrying? Two or three police officers screamed for him to lie down. Six men and an entire arsenal came running: weapons, shock grenades, helmets, body armor. The man before them did not appear to have anything, only a gaze that never wavered.

And then he raised his hand. Just as they screamed. Just before they threw themselves on him. The second-in-command's view was blocked by an elbow. Or so he said afterward, anyway. "I thought he was lifting a . . ."

He had already drawn his pistol. From the moment he entered the building, he'd seen everything through the red point in his sight. His legs were stiff, his shoulders aching from holding the weapon in front of him.

Perhaps he didn't even mean to, only an unfortunate reflex that traveled straight to the trigger.

Reza Khan got a 9mm bullet through his frontal lobe. A pink mist shot out of his head upon impact. Mostly skin and bone, but not only.

He never closed his eyes. From the floor, on his back, he looked at them, at the man who had shot him and at those who were trying to stop the pool of blood that was flowing from his head.

Inside the Lebanese restaurant, N. caught the onrushing Vladislav in a rough embrace.

"No." N. snorted. "They'd like nothing better."

Vladislav stepped back, then pressed his fingers to his temple as if his head was about to explode. "The passport . . . damn it!"

"Here, it's cool!" said N., patting his coat pocket. "I forgot to tell you."

N. had been the last to leave the factory. Vladislav, half dressed when they decided to go for lunch, had dug around for his clothes, debated, thrown aside a tracksuit, then grabbed his jacket instead. And when N. was about to leave, he saw Vladislav's wallet on a table. He stuffed it in his pocket and ran after the others.


Vladislav took the wallet in both hands and pulled out the edge of his passport to make sure that it was still there. He closed his eyes and nodded.

Back in the kitchen someone had noticed the running and agitation. One of the brothers looked out from the doorway.

Vladislav smiled broadly, gave a clueless look. "Yes?"

"Is everything all right?" said the Lebanese, nervously drying one hand on his apron.

"Absolutely," Vladislav replied.

"We should pay," said N., returning to the table. The Lebanese nodded but stayed put. N. pulled out some bills. Mary sat motionless, while the TV showed photos from above: the two black helicopters flew out of the picture, and a swarm of red and blue lights flashed in the streets.

Then the sound of the jackhammers stopped. There was a moment of silence.

"I'll call Adderloy," said Mary, reaching for her phone.

"Wait," said Vladislav like a thunderclap, without taking his gaze off the Lebanese. The tone of his voice, Vladislav's relentless expression. The Lebanese excused himself with a hand over his heart and returned to the kitchen.

An ambulance raced past the restaurant with sirens wailing.

"Reza, or one of *them*," said Vladislav. He stood straight-backed with his creaking leather jacket wide open. "No one calls anybody. Let's go."

N. changed the TV channel before placing a salt shaker over the bills on the table.

They walked toward downtown Topeka, avoiding the busy streets. Heard sirens in waves. N. made them turn their cell phones off: "They've got Reza's, they can check and start tracking us."

At the first ATM machine Vladislav said, "Make a couple of substantial withdrawals, then we won't touch the cards again."

Several news helicopters were moving in a restless swarm over the city. Each time the helicopters picked up something new and moved in their direction, Mary stared at her toes and Vladislav muttered oaths. Downtown, more people were around, and there were more ways to disappear. But there were also more lingering glances and cars passing too slowly.

N. observed Vladislav, his long, wavy hair and sturdy eyeglasses, the gaze that caused people on the sidewalk to avoid him. If someone who saw him had heard a police description, there would be no doubt. And Mary, still black from head to toe.

N. was afraid now, truly afraid. He wanted them to take seats in the back of an empty café and wait for dark.

"No!" said Vladislav, uneasy. Mary said nothing.

"So meaningless," Vladislav repeated at regular intervals.

Then, "Wait here," and ducked into a hardware store. He came out five minutes later with a couple of screwdrivers and pliers in a bag.

N. understood immediately. They continued walking. Vladislav was searching the cross streets.

"We'll go this way, just a sec," he said. After a few blocks, he took off alone again.

N. pulled Mary inside a Laundromat and waited, watching for him through the steamed-up windows.

Half an hour later, Vladislav pulled up in a stolen Ford, honked, and drove halfway onto the sidewalk. Mary and N. ran out and threw themselves into the backseat as if it were the only taxi in a rainstorm.

On the highway they settled down a notch. Being on the road, with the factory and helicopters behind them, was enough for N.

Mary was still searching for helicopters, pressing her cheek against the window so she could look straight up and then turning to see the saw-toothed skyline through the rear window's gray haze.

"We can't leave Topeka quite yet," said Vladislav all of a sudden.

"So when?" Mary asked.

"Tomorrow."

"Not tonight?"

"No, tomorrow." Vladislav drummed a screwdriver against the dashboard. From the broken ignition switch, cables hung like colored spaghetti. "You should never flee in haste."

"Overnight at a motel then?"

N. caught his gaze in the rearview mirror. Looked at him for a while. "One night," he said. "Cash payment, but only if I get to choose the motel."

"Sure."

"Good." N. sat up. They passed a few exits before he pointed to the side at an orange sign on a pole. "There! Looks like the kind of place that prefers cash."

Tumbleweed Motel. Not the tallest in the forest of signs standing beside the exit ramp. A few bulbs framing the name blinked uncertainly, as if they would fail at any moment. Vladislav braked and took the exit. Mary looked at N. in disbelief.

They rented two rooms, made a mess of the linens in one, and then all three of them settled into the other. A quiet agreement was made to do everything together. Two queen-size beds. N. and Mary would share the bed farthest in.

Mary went into the bathroom.

"One more night in Topeka?" N. asked Vladislav. "Give me *one* good reason."

"We won't get anywhere without money."

N. glared at him.

Vladislav weighed his wallet in his hand. "What do we have, a couple of thousand? We have to disappear again, completely disappear. It's not enough."

The toilet flushed.

"For Christ's sake Vladislav, didn't you see—helicopters and God knows what, a whole fucking posse. This is Kansas. They hang people from trees here. And we stay another night to, to do . . . what? To rob another bank?"

"No more robberies," said Vladislav.

The bathroom door opened again. Mary had been crying; she didn't try to hide it. "I hate this place, but if we have to stay one more night, I want clean clothes. I want to feel clean when I leave."

They drove to a shopping center, bought clothes. Mary found more black. Vladislav stood a long time, feeling the sleeves of silk shirts between his fingers. N. bought everything he needed in fifteen minutes in a jeans store. Then they raided Walmart for shampoo and toothbrushes. As they closed the trunk, Vladislav decided he wanted something to read.

They stopped at the mall bookstore, and Vladislav headed to the back. Mary searched the headlines in the daily papers, while N. scanned the shiny faces on the magazine covers. Row upon row in racks—a grandstand of smiles. *Time* had a special issue on Pakistan. Vladislav approached from the checkout counter with a couple of travel guides under his arm.

They drove back to the motel, showered. The sun went down and died, deep red at the horizon. Car headlights and neon lights dimmed the stars.

It was impossible to resist TV: yet another person arrested, a massive effort, gunfire. Yet another person held in isolation at a hospital. They saw the factory from every conceivable angle, police cars, breathless reporters. Someone shouted accusingly on a street corner: "Why are all the suspects being shot?"

Vladislav browsed through his travel guides. Mary ate the beef jerky she'd bought, while N. made instant coffee and tore the labels off his new clothes.

Police Chief Oldenhall called another press conference. For the first time, they saw his gray eyes and pockmarked cheeks up close. Oldenhall confirmed the arrest—a foreign citizen—and said they now believed the crime involved religious terrorism.

"An unholy alliance here in the heart of Kansas."

Vladislav looked up from a guide to Hong Kong. "Masterful, isn't it?"

N. couldn't make sense of the police chief's statement. "What the—"

"It's brilliant, throwing in a Pakistani."

"No . . . Reza." N. moaned as the idea sank in. As if it were a death notice.

A Muslim in a factory full of firearms and money from a robbery. Turnbull already linked to the deed. Westhill Baptist Church and the Pakistani hordes. This was the unholy alliance Adderloy had created. If enough people bought it, there were no rules anymore. Not for anything.

Mary was already asleep. N. lay next to her, watching a black-and-white movie on TV: Cary Grant in sunglasses, winding roads on the Riviera, a beautiful actress at his side with wavy curls. N. watched the scenery, unable to follow the plot, too preoccupied by other thoughts. He got up and filled the electric kettle for a cup of instant coffee he didn't really want. Vladislav lay with his arms across his face, sleeping deeply with his mouth wide open, hissing. It was long past midnight.

N. got hit with the stale coffee odor of his own breath as he lifted the blanket to lie back down on the bed. He felt hot. He pulled back the blanket again and saw Mary's bare back. Lying down on his side behind her, he felt carefully with his fingertips across one of her vertebrae. She was motionless. In the dark he could sense the black cat staring back. He tried to touch its bushy tail.

At St. Francis Health Center, as federal agents filled the hallways, Reza Khan spent the whole night in surgery. An impatient, red-eyed senior doctor kept telling the dark suits that he still didn't know. It was possible the patient might make it.

# CHAPTER 26

*Diego Garcia, 2008*

**M**AYBE IT BOTHERS *you?*"

Grip sat as before, in the cell opposite the man who called himself N., at the small table. He'd told N. that not only were the Americans likely recording their conversations, but they might also be getting them translated. Grip had asked if it bothered him.

N. hadn't responded, and they began to talk about other things. Only much later did he lean forward to Grip and say, "Maybe it bothers *you?*"

It was his eyes that made Grip react, because the look was direct and immediate. Their meetings in the cell had passed through different stages: pure fear, compliance, outbursts of defiance alternating with moments of obsequiousness. But never anything followed by a look of understanding, of insight into Grip. Suddenly the situation was reversed—N. held a split-second advantage.

The idea that the Americans probably recorded and translated everything that was said bothered Grip enormously. He hadn't felt that way the first time he came into the cell. Then it would have been natural—even expected. But the staged show had started to shift. For diffuse reasons, Grip felt forced to stay on Garcia. And from what was said in the cell, were the Americans really only interested in the unidentified man's side of the conversation? "Is he Swedish?" was no longer the only issue.

"Doesn't bother me at all," replied Grip in an offhand way. "It's standard procedure to record interrogations." They looked at each other.

"I've been through all kinds," said the man who called himself N. Someone had seen to his battered feet, which were wrapped with new white bandages. He was shaven, but his hair hadn't yet been cut. He reminded Grip of someone who had been in a coma for several years and had now woken up. His movements were tentative, as if he was not yet master of his own body. His hair was neater; someone had washed it. (Grip couldn't imagine he could do a thing like that for himself.)

"You homesick?" said Grip.

N. seemed unmoved by the issue, only gave a slight shrug.

"Where did you live?" No reaction. Grip got the impression that N. was thinking. Grip continued: "You know I can take a hair and search you through the DNA registry, if anyone reported you missing."

Grip didn't know himself what he was looking for. What did he want to know about this man?

"Would you like help from Sweden? The embassy—" Grip paused at the absurdity: Which embassy would that be? That was the whole point of the place where they were sitting. An island without a country.

The man's gaze was absent again, gone. You wouldn't see that in Sweden anymore, the gaze of someone held incommunicado for years. The silence in the room briefly reminded Grip of other interrogations, when he was younger and questioned juvenile offenders. Some car thief wouldn't talk, had thrown away his wallet—they demanded a name and only got shrugs. But they could scare the wits out of those types, just by using a gentle voice, honeyed. Grip looked at the white bandages on N.'s feet. Cudgels, he thought, on the soles. Apparently destroys the nerve endings. They never really could walk properly again, and what they'd endured was said to be unbearable. So which drew the most useful confessions, the cudgels or the honeyed voice? Grip truly wondered.

"What's your name?" he asked, dropping the thought.


Grip waited. The man's gaze floated. His hands were always folded, resting on his knee. Grip closed the notebook in which he'd written only the day's date.

"I have no more questions. Nothing more is coming to me. I'll be back again tomorrow—"

The man—N.—closed his eyes. "Imagine that you wake up, and everything is floating. The ocean is now where you usually walk, you see fish in the streets."

"Fish?"

"Yes," the man said, and opened his eyes. "Two, I saw two fish swim past me, next to a car."

Grip was quiet, feeling more than he wanted to admit. "You were traveling?" he asked at last.

"Yes, an eternity ago. Everything was different then. I was different. Now you'll have to settle for N. Now I'm just Anybody. The fish swam past me, and I began to walk up the mountain."

Grip opened the notebook again. For the first time he heard about Weejay's and Topeka, eventually about First Federal United and Charles-Ray Turnbull. And Adderloy appeared, along with the others. The guard at the bank, the helicopters, the Lebanese restaurant, the escape, and the night at the Tumbleweed Motel. For three days, Grip took notes while N. talked.

# CHAPTER 27

I N THE MORNING, VLADISLAV AND N. went down to eat while
Mary showered. On a little corner table in the lobby stood the
minimal offering the motel could get away with calling breakfast:
a pot of coffee, milk, little boxes of cornflakes, and a pile of pale
muffins that had no doubt been there all week. It didn't take long
to eat.

When they got back to the room, Mary was sitting on the end
of the bed, looking as if she were waiting for something. She was
dressed, her hair smooth and glistening with moisture.

"Want some?" said N., holding out a cereal box.

She shook her head almost imperceptibly. Leaned back slightly
with her hands on either side, over the quilt.

"What?" said Vladislav.

"No, no. I'm fine. . . . They have coffee?"

"Can I borrow your phone?" asked Vladislav.

Mary shrugged. "Why?"

"Where is it?"

"In my bag." She pointed to her new canvas tote.

N., who'd just turned on the television, switched it off again.

Vladislav dug out her phone. "Turn it on."

"You going to make a call?"

He didn't answer. Mary turned on the phone, entered her password, and Vladislav took it again.

He went to her menus and then held up the screen: "Last call dialed . . . just five minutes ago."

"He deserves a chance——"

"——to Adderloy." Vladislav whipped the phone across the desk.

N. sighed in frustration and snorted as if he'd been punched.

"We can't just abandon him," said Mary defiantly.

"No, absolutely not." Vladislav nodded. He stood with his hands in his pockets, with that ominous calm that N. always found intimidating.

"Adderloy will be here in half an hour." Mary turned her gaze from Vladislav and looked out the window. Vladislav stood close, no more than an arm's length from her. She closed her eyes, the sunlight reflecting on her face. She looked up again.

N. had never felt more like a stranger to her.

"Before Adderloy took off yesterday, didn't he tell you to go out and get something to eat?" said Vladislav.

"Yes, he suggested that," Mary replied.

"Knowing full well that Reza would say no."

She sat quietly, cool.

"So you——" N. was furious, but Vladislav stopped him.

"Shhhh." He crouched down next to Mary, with one hand on the bed just behind her back. She still wasn't looking at him. He said quietly, "You're playing, Mary. You're good at setting up challenges for others to finish." Mary didn't flinch. Vladislav edged closer. "You know full well that Adderloy nailed Reza, that he had the police raid the factory—and then you do this."

Silence, only the muffled sound of traffic outside.

"About half an hour, you say," Vladislav started again. "Before Adderloy shows up here." He stood up. "What I should do now is take my passport and go—just go." He glanced out the window, grinning. "But I don't want to treat him to losing the two of you as well. I don't want to give him that satisfaction."

"But he saved us, made sure we weren't in the factory. He just wants us back together again, and then we can all get out of here."

"Is that really what you think? I say, what we need is to get out of his web, and for once get a few steps ahead of him."

Vladislav took Mary's phone off the desk, dialed a number, and looked in the mirror while he waited.

"The police, please . . . Main number . . . Connect me." A few seconds of silence again. "The robbery at First Federal United . . . No, not the tip line, I want to talk to someone in charge, an inspector, investigator, whatever the hell you call it." He was transferred again, and after saying yes and no a few times, he raised his voice: "Stop typing and start listening. In the raid on the factory yesterday, you got three Glock 19 pistols and four black bags filled with cash. Also you took a Pakistani . . . That's right, a Pakistani. No, I realize you can't confirm that, I'm saying it so you understand that I know a few things. Quiet now—the rest of the group you're looking for is currently at the Tumbleweed Motel, in"—Vladislav fished his room key out of his pocket—"room 230. What my name is . . . Adderloy, Bill Adderloy."

Vladislav turned off the phone.

N. had already begun stuffing his belongings into a plastic bag. Vladislav looked at Mary. "They'll be here in fifteen minutes, that's my guess. Are you coming?"

Vladislav walked over to the bedside table where his stuff was lying. "At least we can give the police a hasty departure. Distract them a bit, give them a little more of what they thirst for." He moved quickly, tore random pages from a backpackers' guide to the Arabian Peninsula, which went sailing out over the floor. Mary looked around in disbelief. N. pushed more clothes into his bag. In a guidebook to Los Angeles, Vladislav dog-eared a few pages and drew a line with a hotel pen under the address of an Arabic bookstore before he threw it down.

When Vladislav and N. were done fiddling around, Mary stood up from the bed and took her bag. She was last to go out the door. Their dirty clothes lay in a mess with the sheets and wet towels, Vladislav's torn-out pages, the travel guide, and their new toothbrushes.

They paid, got into their stolen Ford, and drove away.

Within just a few blocks they passed white police vans, and when Vladislav turned off onto a side street, two identical Buicks rushed by, each with two men wearing sunglasses. But not until they were on the highway did N. see the news helicopters swarming to the strip of motels and fast-food places that were disappearing out their back window.

Vladislav saw a helicopter pass in the rearview mirror. "That was fast," he said at first, and then a little quieter: "Those fuckers are really on the ball."

He pulled off the highway and stopped the car next to a concrete ditch where the water flowed slow and brown. He rolled down the window, weighing his cell phone in his hand. "Because we need to trust each other," he said. And then he threw it.

It bubbled on impact.

"Yours also, both of them."

Next they stopped at the square in front of First Federal United. They got out of the car and started walking.

"This is idiotic!" repeated N. He'd realized that the whole reason they'd spent another night in Topeka was so they could return once more to the bank. Mary's indifferent look was gone; her eyes were alive again.

They crossed the square. N. watched for police while Vladislav went first, making empty observations all the way to the entrance: "Money, we must have money. Everything stops and starts with that." His jacket was unbuttoned, his hair blowing around him. "Wasn't that why we did it? Anyway, it was why *I* did it."

In the car, N. had come around, after they said it wouldn't be violent. He also knew that without money, they were doomed. He wanted to finish this his own way, not be thrown at the mercy of the justice system. But now that he was on the square, saw the sign for First Federal. Hesitation. He remembered the shots and screams, and his own confusion.

"Those two," he said, nodding toward a pair of dark-clothed men with square caps and stitched creases on their pants.

"Guards, they don't matter, come on."

N. had stopped but caught up again. Mary ran her hand along the police cordon tape, set up between some cones even though the bank was once again open. Around the bank entrance, temporary glass panels had been glued over the web of cracks and bullet holes.

"What the hell," said Vladislav, elated. And they entered.

The atmosphere inside was one of almost blunted calm. There were far fewer people both in front of and behind the counters than the last time they were there.

"Wait here, the system is old-fashioned." Vladislav went alone to a counter, exchanged a few words, wrote a name on the signature card. He beckoned to Mary and N. as he went on toward the vault. With all its mechanisms and bolts, the open door looked like clock-works made of steel.

"I ran in here," said Vladislav, passing through the round opening to the vault. He stopped, made sure that they were alone, and then took out some thin plastic bags he'd taken from a cleaning trolley at the motel. Mary looked intrigued.

"Safe-deposit boxes," said N. "Get to the point, I want out of here."

"Yes, I rented one, a few days before. . . . Every time you come, they check your identification and make you sign, then you go in and open it with your own key. Look around, no cameras." He'd already taken a key out of his wallet and opened one of the larger compartments.

"Twenty seconds alone—it was my little addition to Adderloy's plan." He pulled the box out of its slot. "I was alone at the bank counters around the corner, alone with everything they had. I took a little detour on the way back—didn't have to bother with IDs or signatures to get into the vault. Twenty seconds, maybe fifteen." Vladislav lifted the lid and showed the bundles of money. "Most of what I took from there went in here."

N. looked annoyed, but Vladislav saw it coming. Grabbed his neck tight and pulled him close. "You're right. While I was back here, there was an idiot out there, shooting wildly. I could have just run past the vault and nailed that fucker, done it right away. Saved a few bastards." He shook N.'s head. "And we'd have been standing here completely broke." He let go.

"It—"

Vladislav put his finger on N.'s chest as soon as he opened his mouth. "Watch it. A shot from you through the guard's skull could have saved everyone. But instead, you huddled under a desk.

A woman walked into the vault with a key in her hand.

"One moment," growled Vladislav, as if he'd been surprised naked in a fitting room. She turned, frightened, and disappeared.

"We've got money, and we're getting out of here. That's it," he said, holding up the first bag.

N. and Mary stacked it.

They carried the money in double bags, not so much worried about weight as that the print from the bundles would show through the thin plastic. Two bags each for Vladislav and N., as if they'd been out shopping. Mary put on her sunglasses and, carrying her little tote bag, went first out of the vault. Vladislav followed, giving a smile of recognition to the woman who stood outside and waited.

An estate changing hands, or a family suddenly deciding to leave town—there was something sad about the woman in black wearing sunglasses who walked through the bank, followed by two men carrying what appeared to belong to her. The newly hired guard nodded as she passed. From their ladders, a couple of glaziers looked over their shoulders, before they went back to taking down one of the shattered windows.


Nearly nine hundred thousand dollars. Vladislav split it down the middle without asking—one half for him, the other for Mary and N.

"Not a whole life, but a beginning," he said, and tied a knot on the last bag.

He sat in the backseat, Mary drove. Interstate 70 east: Kansas City, St. Louis. Then I-55 heading south with N. at the wheel: Missouri, Arkansas. He kept going all the way to Winona, Mississippi. It was late, but all the motels' neon signs still said VACANCY, so they took time to eat before getting a room. A clattery diner with booths, at midnight, where everything served was roasted or deep-fried, iced tea in pitchers and menus with items crossed out or added in marker. The familiar confusion: Vladislav who flipped and asked questions, until finally N. ordered for them both.

But now everything was happening for the last time. The very last.

Mary had gone up to the glass counter to choose a pie for dessert when Vladislav said: "It's only a few hours to Jackson. You can drop me off there tomorrow."

"And then?" said N., not sounding particularly surprised.

"That I'll decide later." Vladislav glanced toward Mary, who was leaning over the dessert counter. He seemed anxious about something. "You know it too," he began, "that this is only borrowed time. Senseless escape, by a few who shared only their own downfall."

"A stolen car from Topeka—nobody's going to be looking for it down here in Mississippi," N. tried.

"It's not the car that's important. And as I said, I'll be on my own after Jackson." Vladislav glanced over his shoulder. "I'm good at this, at banks, at weapons, at stashing money and getting away. I'm going to stick with it."

"You're going to live like this?"

"The world's already full of it. Won't hurt for someone to do it right."

"But what did you do, before we—"

"Before the tsunami?" Vladislav laughed. "Well, and you?"

N. just lifted his glass and drank.

"No, exactly," continued Vladislav. "As for me, I swam out of that bus and then—then I was another person. Shooting, I knew how to do that before, just hadn't done it this way."

Mary stood at the counter. A waitress had gone into the kitchen to find something for her.

"Adderloy?" reminded N.

"Adderloy still owes me a million." Vladislav looked at N. "He sacrificed Reza. God knows what he has in mind for the rest of us. He knows that I'm alive, and he knows he owes me money."

Mary had gotten a slice of pie slid onto a plate. She looked at it a little quizzically, then stretched back over the counter to get whipped cream sprayed on top.

Vladislav fished a pen out of his jacket and pulled a napkin from the holder. "Whatever you do, remember this address." He wrote down something and spun the piece of paper. It was an e-mail address. "A life for a life," he said, tapping with his index finger on the text.

"Huh?" said N., puzzled.

"You got my wallet and my passport out of Mary's goddamn dungeon. That saved me, and also you put yourself in the doorway of the Lebanese. Remember the address, it will be the way to reach me. You can expect me to do anything for you—once."

N. leaned forward and read it again.

"A life for a life," repeated Vladislav.

Mary was back. "Blackberry," she said, and licked a dollop of cream dyed blood red from the juice. She slid into the booth while Vladislav dried his hands with the napkin and stuffed it into his pocket.

Yet another motel room with paths worn in the carpet. After the whine of the concrete highway through three states and all the fried food, a syrupy fatigue overtook them. They were slow to get ready for what was left of the night. They didn't even turn on the TV and the news. The atmosphere was somewhat aimless—sitting, lying down, picking up things, as if by not actually going to bed they could manage to escape something.

N. opened his bag of money and looked down. "You can't just deposit it."

"You could," said Vladislav, lying on his back and looking at the ceiling. He was silent for a few seconds, as if chewing on something. "Go to Florida," he said, and sighed as if he felt a little nauseous, "take a cruise to the Cayman Islands. . . . While the others run ashore to shop for cheap jewelry, take your bag and pick a bank."

"Any?"

"There are hundreds to choose from."

"And what do you say?"

"Poker, you won at poker." He sighed again. "That's what people do nowadays."

"Poker," said Mary. "So that's your tip for the two of us." She lay on the side of the bed. "I get the feeling that—" She didn't finish the sentence.

"That I'm not following you there, no. I'll leave you in the morning."

N. tied his bag and closed his eyes for a few seconds.


At a bus terminal in Jackson, Vladislav disappeared. He got out to take his bag. His palm twice on the roof, like a hitchhiker saying thanks, and then he was gone.

The sun shone brightly. N. and Mary drove on, among the trucks and motor homes heading south. Louisiana, wetlands on both sides of the road, then east, Pensacola, insects smeared over the windshield. They lived on bright red hot dogs from gas stations and cinnamon rolls that glistened with syrup. They saw the first signs indicating the distance to Miami.

Last-minute tickets for a cruise, that was the idea. The Caribbean, maybe South America.

When they arrived in Florida, their motel was all white. A pine forest surrounded the parking lot, where a warm breeze swept through the darkness. One last night before Miami. A clean place, wall-to-wall carpeting so thick that you swayed. N. showered; Mary said she would go down to reception and pick up cruise catalogs.

When he came out of the bathroom with a towel around his hips, the room was dark. He seesawed on the carpet, trying to see where she was.

A movement to the left.

And then a hand from the right, like a blow across his shoulder, and at once more hands that wrestled him down. The men in the dark were quiet, and he himself made not the slightest sound. Just gave up.

Life as he knew it had once again come to an end. Apprehended and abducted. Days, weeks, months. Never any formal charges. Years would go by, float away.

Of everything they subjected him to, the hardest to resist was a man who one day walked into his last cell, speaking his mother tongue.

# CHAPTER 28

*Diego Garcia, 2008*

SHAUNA FRIEDMAN HAD A TRUE swimmer's body. With just a slight movement of her hips, she took off through the water. The first time they'd eaten together in New York, the way she'd pecked with her chopsticks said something about who she was. Beach and water proved to be just as much a part of her nature.

It was she who'd arranged for the masks and snorkels, it was she who drove when they set out. Alone, she and Grip on a private beach, first the sandy-bottomed shallows, then a reef. The remote little beach lay on the far side of the atoll. It was morning, without a breeze, yet not unbearably hot. No ships in sight, an unbroken horizon. The water enveloped her hair and stretched it into a billowing veil down her back as she left the surface and dived down to the corals. She descended faster, deeper, even though they had no flippers and she only used her legs. It was she who found the fish, pointed, made explanatory gestures Grip didn't always understand. He nodded. At one point she took him by the arm and led him a few feet deeper, to see a moray eel that lay pulsing with half-bared teeth in its den.

As she walked out of the water, she pulled the mask down under her chin, and then, where the shoreline lapped, she stopped to sweep the water droplets from her arms and legs with the same fast, barely conscious movements as someone expertly peeling the skin off a fruit. As she climbed out, the white coral sand clung like pearl sugar to her feet.

Shauna Friedman wore a one-piece black bathing suit. Few people look good in black swimsuits, Grip thought. Friedman did, although the swimsuit wasn't at all daringly cut and looked like something designed for competition. Color and fit, both right, without making an effort to be noticed, although she usually was. Likely there were men who for years after remembered exactly when they'd caught sight of her, without knowing anything about who she was. Not because of any single detail—the poor guys who wanted only slender legs or shapely breasts fell for other women. With Friedman, it was something else. Her body played a part, that was true, but even more her gaze, which never looked anxious.

"It's said they can bite right through a man's thigh."

"Who says what about what?" said Grip, who had just sat down, and now pushed the wet hair from his forehead.

"About moray eels," said Shauna. "That they can bite through a man's thigh. How come they always talk about men's thighs?"

Grip looked down at his own, which were stronger than hers. "Only men are stupid enough to approach them—or maybe moray eels only bite men."

"No," she replied, and held up her hand to him. The root of her thumb, two white dots in her tan.

"There you go," said Grip and put on sunglasses. "Men's thighs and women's hands." He leaned back. She was still sitting upright on her towel.

"The man in the cell has started talking," said Shauna, her gaze somewhere in the distance.

"Yes, he's talking, and I'm taking notes," said Grip.

"Two whole days now?"

"Three actually, counting yesterday."

"Stackhouse says you lied to him," continued Shauna.

"Oh."

"When he asked whether the man is Swedish."

"Lied, I don't know—I probably avoided the issue. But if you want to be absolutely accurate, I told him that I've drawn that conclusion, though the man has never confirmed it."

"But Stackhouse asked you."

"True. It was a few days ago, and yes, I lied." Grip lay on his back and looked straight up into the sky behind his sunglasses, only seeing Shauna's back at the periphery. "And," he continued, "I can conclude from this that someone has started translating my conversations inside the cell."

"They flew someone in the day before yesterday. And if you're wondering, I get to see their copies."

"Very much us and them in this—*they* flew in, *their* copies."

"Yes," said Shauna, "that's what this has become."

Grip felt a drop of water run down his stomach. He was almost dry; only the damp bathing suit still refreshed him.

Shauna looked at him over her shoulder, head to toe, then turned out toward the sea again. "There are incarcerated people scattered throughout the world, it's no secret," she began. "Everyone knows it, everyone is trying to deal with it. But often the big picture gets lost. Information surfaces, confessions are made, it's used, yet kept half hidden. You're handed a folder—intelligence. But what it contains is short and lacks all nuance, as if it were a law of nature. Never where it comes from, never any names, never places. Will it ultimately be worth anything? Within different organizations we draw different conclusions, it's inevitable."

"Who's we?"

"Stackhouse is one side of the story."

"CIA?"

"If you want to bundle them like that, then fine."

"And who are you?"

"I've said—FBI. Does that simplify things?"

"A black-and-white world always makes everything easier. Stackhouse believes that the end justifies the means, while you have to take laws into account. Or?" There was no missing Grip's irony.

"You're Swedish, you sit on the sidelines."

"Exactly. It's pleasant being the one who always knows what's right." Grip shaded his eyes and raised his head. Shauna mumbled something in response. She pinched sand between her fingertips and threw it in front of her, impatiently.

"The handling of these detainees poses several problems," she continued. "Once you've placed someone outside the law, you can't get him back inside it."

"You mean, confessions made with electrodes attached to your scrotum can't be used in a regular court. You can't ever get a conviction, the evidence isn't admissible."

"Something like that."

"Do Stackhouse and his gang even want them convicted?"

Shauna didn't answer.

Grip continued: "Don't they just want a little revenge—some general statements, and then the next names they should capture, drug, and fly around the world?" Always, he had a hard time resisting the chance to give Americans a taste of themselves.

Shauna had stopped her hand midway, then tossed once more, releasing the sand. "The general turban hunt doesn't interest me," she said. "I want to know how things actually stand." There was silence for a few seconds.

"The man in the cell, is he what you'd call an ethnic Swede?" she said later.

"You mean—he is after all quite dark."

"He is dark-haired."

"I'm also dark," said Grip. "Beat me enough to blur my features, keep me from getting a haircut or shave for a while, and—"

"Stackhouse's team thinks he may have foreign ancestry," interrupted Shauna.

"They think he's a Muslim."

"They think that about everyone who doesn't look like Jesus Christ himself."

"Wasn't he a Jew?"

"Exactly," said Shauna emphatically, and the joke fell flat.

"He's Swedish," said Grip after a sigh, "meaning he's not a lot of other things as well. Swedish—it's the only thing I'm quite sure of right now."

"The only thing?" She seemed surprised.

"How many more lost souls are sitting there in that building?" countered Grip. "Scarred, shaking little heaps. Doing a tour of your coalition of willing torturers and hangmen."

"Keep battering away—feeling any better?"

"Maybe. Whatever you keep yourselves busy with, we on the sidelines always seem to maintain moral superiority."

"You can beat the answers out of them," countered Shauna, "or wait for the next wave of hijackers headed to Manhattan."

Grip didn't know what to say, laughed, and Shauna gave him a forced smile over her shoulder.

"That's one way of looking at it," she said then. "You know what they call Garcia, by the way? I mean here, what the military itself calls the island—'The Footprint of Freedom.'"

Grip had seen the stacks of stickers in shops on the base: the atoll's stylized shoreline in the shape of a footprint.

"A practical little footprint in the world's backyard," she continued. "A springboard. From here, B-52s can thread their way throughout Asia and Africa."

"A pack of raging dogs, on a very long leash," said Grip. "To sic on all the bastards who need to know their place."

"That's the whole point. Out here on Garcia, no one sees when they take off and land, no one looks at who comes and goes. So much better than Guantánamo. Here, there isn't even anything to deny." She rustled in a bag for a can of soda. A diet cola—she handed him one.

"B-52s can be seen in satellite images," he said after the first sip. "Prisoners are more difficult to count."

"What's your estimate?"

"More than two, less than a hundred."

"Correct."

"How many cells?"

"Stop fishing," said Shauna, unmoved. "I don't even know the answer myself. I'm FBI, you know, not CIA."

"But we're dealing with delicate goods."

"Those who may not exist. Those who may not be seen."

"Final disposal?"

It was the first time since they came to the beach that she thought carefully about her response.

"I guess so," she said finally.

Grip was impressed by her. By the whole thing, the swimming excursion. She was no risk taker. "Come—now," she'd said. "If you don't want to swim naked, grab a bathing suit, the rest I'll take care of. Even got extra towels from the maid." It seemed so spontaneous—now we're off. As if just minutes before, the thought hadn't crossed her mind that they'd be going right then. Out to the beach, alone, into the water, even quite deep. All constructed with the best intentions, as insurance for them both. A bit excessive perhaps, but still. She was thinking he could hide something. A little equipment, some type of microphone, stuff that could eventually compromise and trap. Salt water, the depth—no surveillance technician would guarantee function after that. Did she think that about him—microphones? At any rate, no one could listen in or record, not between them, not from the outside, not now. So apart from the hotel towels and his sunglasses (which he'd bought on the way, when they stopped to get cold sodas at one of the base supermarkets), everything they had with them had been soaked in deep water, and now they sat as unclothed as they could be without breaking taboos. The ideal form of conversation for the paranoid—or how the matter was solved on Diego Garcia. The island of hypocrisy and secrets.

She needed confidentiality, that he too would feel it. That nothing could be reproduced later. What was said, was here and now.

Shauna stroked sand off her feet. "Our man," she said, "your Swede. Stackhouse would have it that he fits the usual profile—they've concocted something about religious extremism. I think he's something else."

"Our man calls himself N.," said Grip.

"N.," said Shauna thoughtfully. She tossed aside a thought. "He has been responsible for many deaths."

"Says who?"

"Not least his own statements. Then there's a thin, thin thread of barely viable evidence, and a Pakistani who has a hole in his skull where he should have a memory."

"Impressive."

"Not particularly. But I believe the Pakistani."

"Where is he now?"

"He sits, waiting to be executed in Kansas."

"Quite a collection of characters."

"If you only knew." Shauna took a sip of soda. "For me, I got started on this while investigating art thefts. Not small stuff—it was pretty big-time, and people lost their lives. I was on the main guy's trail, couldn't tie him to it, but knew it was him. The name that came up was Adderloy, Bill Adderloy." She let the name sink in, continued: "Yes, exactly—the one N. told you about. And pretty soon after I had a name, we realized that art thefts were only a part of his story, more of a hobby. The real game was that he had a couple of rebel movements in Asia under his belt. You know, a few hundred godforsaken men in a jungle in Indonesia, with foreign money to back them up. They always need an intermediary, someone to run the game: arrange weapons and ammunition, spread money around, all kinds of stuff. There's a hell of a lot of illegality involved, and the FBI was on Adderloy's trail. I had two agents on him, two who got close. Do you understand what the job entails?"

"Living undercover?" said Grip.

"Yes. Have you ever done it?"

"As it happens."

"For more than a year? They spent more than a year at it. Long periods abroad: Indonesia and Thailand. My agents' thing was that they played a couple, that was what worked. Theater on a tightrope—walking hand in hand through a minefield. But step-by-step they won Adderloy's confidence. He was difficult, one smart mother. Didn't leave a paper trail and employed only useful idiots to handle the merchandise. My two agents were arranging a weapons deal. Adderloy himself would come and inspect, that was the idea. His fingers in the cookie jar—then the handcuffs. Cooperation with the police in Bangkok worked brilliantly, but then . . . You never know how it goes with these things. Adderloy suspected mischief, maybe got a tip from inside. Alex and Brooke, my agents—yes, you already understand the rest. How the Thai police could then call what had happened attempted robbery." Shauna shook her head. "They were shot, two shots in the neck. But first they were tortured for a few hours. I was the one who had to fly out there and identify the bodies, at a Bangkok morgue. And Adderloy left a clear message on those stainless-steel tables: Don't you fucking come after me! Brooke had two sons, three and five years old. Alex's first kid was on the way. How many agents back home do you think wanted to take their place? Well, right after the funeral, obviously everyone wants to bust ass. But actually getting someone to go back in, when the whole arrangement stank of insider tips. Although we tried to run it, even though I hate to admit it, the whole operation ran out of steam. Never got out of neutral.

"But then, all of a sudden on death row in Kansas, a Pakistani starts babbling about Bill Adderloy, and the lights go on again. There were several repercussions when Reza Khan began to remember things. For the first few days, the bank robbery in Topeka was considered simply a bank robbery. When it happened, the police were out chasing around, just like after any violent bank robbery, and we at the bureau helped. When Reza was arrested, it blew . . . wide open. Media circus, TV, the whole shebang. As soon as they realized he was Pakistani—you know the thing with Al-Qaeda—then Stackhouse and his people went nuts. They immediately fell on N. like starving wolves. And they've kept him ever since. Fortunately, at least they report to someone higher up, and a few years later when the Pakistani started talking, a guy in Washington connected the dots: Adderloy, Reza, and N." Shauna turned to Grip. "It was about that time that I got called in."

"Hang on, back up a little," said Grip. "There's a hole."

"You mean—Topeka."

"Why would Adderloy want to organize a bank robbery in Topeka?"

"It was to punish Turnbull and his Southern Baptists for the way they behaved after the tsunami—but most of all, the group needed money."

"Sure, that's how Adderloy sold it at Weejay's. And at least N. went for it, maybe Reza too. But what was the game really about?"

"You mean, why did Adderloy enter in?"

"Adderloy steals art and plays with rebel movements, you said so yourself. He wasn't the type to get upset over some Baptists' moral backwardness."

Shauna sat silent for a few seconds. "It's both harder and easier than that," she said then. "Adderloy actually cares a great deal about Southern Baptists. Before he inherited a small fortune from a childless uncle, he spent a few years in intelligence during the Reagan era—early eighties, it was a long time ago. But people got to know him, contacts were made. I didn't know that two weeks ago, but I know that now." Shauna rubbed her calf. "If you piece together rumors and actual events, you end up with this: in the early nineties, Adderloy began freelancing. What I was talking about before, the rebel movements, a salesman trading in violence and power. He wanted more action and less talk. It wasn't his convictions that mattered to him, but the money he got to play around with. Greed rules, and I'd thought until recently that it was all about foreign capital supporting him—I completely bought it. But in the South and Midwest, the churches out there, do you have any idea how much money they have? And what they're willing to spend it on? Small character-building projects around the world—the crusades of our era. Adderloy made it happen. He was the intermediary from the donors in Texas and Mississippi to rebel movements and strange opposition leaders across the Middle East and throughout Asia. Everything from weapons to rallies to buying candidates that pretended to support democracy—with Adderloy pulling the strings. Business wasn't hurt by

234

September 11. Of course he pulled in fat commissions, while satisfied people in Washington watched, looking through their fingers. Adderloy made things happen that can't be aired in committee hearings.

"But then . . . should we call it international developments? Everything that went wrong in Iraq and the whole mess that followed, the value of the United States' stock in the world. Those with the money began to hesitate when simple crusades didn't work. The fact that Bush's agenda wouldn't last forever, even if he'd just been reelected, yes, that was felt right down to the Bible Belt. Belatedly, people got cold feet. Although they had a few years left, there were many who understood that they'd be swept out with the Bush clan. And they, they wanted to make sure they wouldn't fall too hard. *Summa summarum*, fewer and fewer checks got written. Adderloy paid no attention to the fate of the rebels or the jackals—it was the drying-up of his income that got to him, cutting into the life he lived, his extravagance. He was furious when he no longer got invited into the inner sanctums. If southern ministers at least believe that they follow the Ten Commandments, Adderloy has no such scruples. His plan B was blackmail and revenge by example. Turnbull's fanatics weren't major players in all this, even though they coughed up a little money—really no one cared. But they were, after all, a church like all the others. 'Look at this,' said Adderloy to those who'd turned their backs on him—he picked up Turnbull and crushed his nasty little sect in front of everybody. Adderloy made sure everyone who was supposed to see got the message. And you have to admit, see how brilliantly he always plays multiple strings? He made sure to get Reza Khan on board, and then saw to it that he got busted. The nightmare—Pakistani Islamists in America's heartland—came true. Now the churches could start giving him money again without losing face."

"As good Christians," said Grip.

"They're all good Christians, except Turnbull's defunct church."

"But now?"

"Now, absolutely nothing will change. Business as usual," said Shauna. "I can't prove it. All of this, what I'm saying here, it dies in the sea breeze of Diego Garcia. What I know is from confidential conversations and a couple of tips in repayment of old debts. Nothing of the slightest value in a court of law. None of the good old boys want to be reminded of Adderloy, especially not those who watched silently from Washington. Hush-hush, lips sealed. The executions of Reza and Turnbull are just the final touches."

"So, good," said Grip, sitting up on his towel. "For you, I mean—that you're back on Adderloy's trail again." Shauna looked incredulously at him. And it was true, Grip wasn't going to be led astray. Not going to let her confuse the main event with the sideshow. "You know, Adderloy isn't my business," he said. "I'm on a completely different side of things."

"Are you?"

"Yes, I have every reason to believe that a Swedish citizen is being illegally held in custody, here on Diego Garcia." He said it in a loud voice, a little formally. He wanted to call her on it.

Shauna tilted her head. Knew exactly how to pose so as to exude total confidence. So well that you could easily believe that she'd never given it a thought. Sun and skin. Swimsuit, salt water, and deep ocean. She knew her shit. There was no one around to hear them, no one who'd ever remember. Who was he squawking for? It was just the two of them there. There was only here and now.

"Oh, before you go on about formal charges and extradition," she began, "why not enjoy yourself a little. A day like this, how often do you get one?" She turned her face toward the sun. "You're not even here. You're in New York, no one knows anything different. Right?"

She looked up, expecting an answer, as greedily as someone who'd accused a lover of infidelity. A sound in the distance rose and disappeared just as quickly, the whistling throttle of a distant jet engine.

"New York, yes," she said later. "Of course, you like art. Did you see . . . when you were in New York, did you see Christo's *Gates?*"

"Well, as it happened," he replied after a few seconds, "I walked by." She couldn't possibly know that he hated to be reminded of it.

"Imagine, more than twenty-five years before New York City said yes. When you first read about it, the project sounded so over the top, almost vulgar. Over seven thousand gates in Central Park. Why?" She laughed. "But then, think of Central Park in February: gray trees, frozen lawns. And then one morning, well, you saw the orange trail. The slightest breeze visible in the banners, which moved like slowly falling dominoes."

"It was beautiful," Grip managed to get out. "A beautiful spectacle."

There was at least one coincidence too many. First at the officers' club the other night when she'd gone on about Jean Arp, his sculptures. And now—Christo and Central Park. It was as if she'd drawn two cards from a deck—it was these two cards you thought about, the ones you least of all wanted to see. What would the odds be? Sure there are coincidences, there are always coincidences. Chance. But he had also seen a slightly too-thick folder with his name on it in one of the FBI's offices in New York City.

"N. was what we were talking about, yes," said Shauna, "his legal status. You know, my only privilege on Garcia is to question him, the man who we now know is Swedish. It's the only thing I can do. Everything else is off limits. No questions about anything else to anyone else, just him. But you know as well as I do, I'm an American, he'll never speak to me. Not a word. It's only you who can get anything out of him, your presence. Help me out."

"Sure, I can keep interviewing him," said Grip. It was like admitting guilt, even if he just wanted to buy time.

"I appreciate that," said Shauna. "Let's find out who he is. Who actually did what, and then we'll solve the formal process."

Grip felt he had to take back some control, regain steering. "Make sure that someone looks at his feet, then. A real doctor. And that he gets a haircut. I want to see what he looks like."

Shauna nodded. "The newspapers," she said, "we'll continue with them?"

Grip sat silent, sunglasses hiding his uncertainty. He groped for a moment, thinking.

"Sure," he replied abruptly, and turned to her. "N.—whatever we should call him—he solved the crossword puzzle in one of the papers I gave him. Maybe he likes crosswords. Maybe they make him relax."

Grip looked at the waterline, splashing a short distance away, then at the sand on Shauna's feet. Her hands, her hair, her eyes. The black swimsuit.

"I'll make a new list of papers for you tonight," he added, to say something. She shrugged.

Whose useful idiot was he now? Shauna Friedman's, Sweden's—or just his own?

# CHAPTER 29

WHEN GRIP ENTERED THE CELL, N. looked at him defiantly. N. had gotten a haircut, not the typical prison crew cut, but short.

"I guess this is your work," he said.

"They bandaged you up, so I thought they might as well give you a haircut too. Yes, at my suggestion."

"So as to become more myself?"

"The tangled mess that hung there before couldn't have been you." Grip opened to a new page in his notebook. "Is the hair a problem?"

"I didn't look like this before."

"Is that so." Grip wasn't particularly interested.

"They've cut my hair to be like yours. Was that also your idea?"

Grip glanced, seeing the possible similarity. "No," he said. "Maybe they think all Swedes have the same haircut, what do I know." He shrugged. "Can we—"

"Go ahead," interjected N.

"Yes."

"You've read my entire statement: Weejay's, Topeka, that fat fuck Charles-Ray, and all the rest, maybe you found some contradictions. Maybe you have a list of additional questions."

Grip nodded. "Something like that. But first I simply want to know who you are."

N. straightened up. "For whose sake?" Since Grip had no immediate answer, N. continued: "I know who I am, and I sit where I sit. So for whose sake?"

"Mine. Is that enough?"

"What does it matter?" said N., while Grip rolled the pen between his fingers. "At home, I'm sure there are lists of everyone who's still missing. Taken by the Wave. I must be on there, the person I was must be on the lists. You could figure it out, among the entire families that never came back. But that's no longer valid. You'll only find the person who is no longer me."

An emotion made him tremble, his fingers clenched above his knees to hold them steady. He'd decided to go for something.

"I worked with a Pole once," he said then. "A Polish Jew who retired a year after I started the job. He said that when he was a kid, he didn't even know he was a Jew, it was the Nazis that made him one. And now he was. Couldn't be anything else." N. gasped. "In the same way . . . in the same way, I've become someone I was not. Arab, maybe. They got that idea, and now I am one. Tortured to it. In every location, every step of the way here, they pounded, beat, and stabbed every single one of my convictions." He tried to ignore the tears that rose in his eyes. "You know," he said, and swallowed. "You know, when you're being tortured, you become a child. There sit Mother and Father, watching as everything you are and were gets demolished. At the end, in the hole that's left, sits someone else. Ask them out there, they'll say that I hate the world. Now I do—they were right. And they need me. Evil must be given a face."

"And you're just a victim?"

"I've told my story. Guilt and innocence are now rather uninteresting."

"You think so?"

"Listen to what I'm saying. Guilt and innocence are of no importance. I know what I've done, and I know that I'm sitting here. Right now, we share this cell. And you should listen to me."

Grip became uncomfortable, self-conscious, and felt, at a stroke, all too exposed.

"Since they arrested me, and the whole way here," continued N., "for several years—a fucking eternity—they let all the races on earth come at me: Arabs, Asians, Africans. The worst is always when they do it themselves, when the Americans make an appearance. Then it's not just reckless. Then it gets very thorough."

Grip glanced at the camera in the wall.

"Don't worry, they can stand to hear what they already know," said N. "Oh, they're inventive, but it's not their methods that we're going to talk about, it's the result. I guess I've confessed to everything."

"Everything?"

"Everything they wanted—signed, crawled, and prayed." N. ran his hands over his legs. "Talk about pawn sacrifice—I had to pay twice for Mary, Vladislav, and Adderloy to get away. And now you're here, for what?" He almost smiled. "They don't beat me, at least not anymore." He took a long look at Grip, too long.

"I like to do crossword puzzles," he said then. "Can you arrange to get some magazines with crosswords in them?"

"Might be . . ."

"That's all I want. They're not beating me anymore, and I want to do crossword puzzles."

Grip understood very well that they were bargaining over something, he just didn't know what. "It's time for a break. I'll see." He stood up.

As he left the cell and came out into the corridor, he saw a back vanish behind a corner. In the surveillance room, Stackhouse sat as usual at the monitors. He turned around shortly after Grip arrived.

"It's not true," said Stackhouse. The chair next to him was pulled out; there were some papers on the table.

"What's not true?" said Grip while looking through some old stacks of magazines.

Stackhouse hesitated. "The torture," he said, "that we would have . . . participated."

"No, you knew perfectly well and did nothing, everyone knows that."

"You don't believe me."

Grip looked up. "What would you think?" he said, and in that same moment, he realized the significance of the empty chair and the man's back in the hallway. They'd decided not to give him any kind of head start—after all, he and N. spoke Swedish with each other. Now on Diego Garcia, there was at least one simultaneous interpreter.

Grip held out some papers. "Give these to him, and he needs a pen too. I'll be back after lunch."

"No pen," said Stackhouse. "He can't be alone with a pen. The risk is—"

"Then give him a fucking crayon," said Grip, and walked out.

He got a hamburger at one of Garcia's sleepy lunch joints. The rest of the base seemed to be busy driving trucks. Dusty convoys passed by incessantly in the heat. He got a second coffee in a Styrofoam cup, saw bomb bodies go by without tarps covering the loads. Why did N.'s cell suddenly feel so frightening?

N. was sitting at the table solving crossword puzzles with a short, blunt pencil when Grip came back. He opened his notebook again, started asking questions. Details of how they'd crossed the border between Canada and the United States, an ambiguity about the time in Topeka, if he knew where Adderloy found his weapons. N. answered, but continued doing his crossword puzzle in the newspaper. Grip ignored his impulse to tell N. to put down the newspaper. N. was scribbling, Grip thought.

What was it N. had tried to say before lunch? Something as simple as protecting the memory of a lost family? Not clearing up the matter of his identity, allowing all the dead to remain dead. Certainly, but there was something more.

"First mother," said N., in the middle of a statement about something in Topeka. "Three letters—Eve—don't you think?"

Grip sat silent, eventually asked another question. N. replied mechanically; Grip noted the answer.

Obviously, Stackhouse's minions would never release N., both because of what they'd done to him and what they'd found out. What the hell am I doing here? wondered Grip. For whose sake? No more questions. What he ought to do was go home. He closed the notebook.

N. saw that he was about to leave. He turned the magazine around on the table. "First mother—mustn't that be Eve, here?"

Grip, already standing up, sighed.

"Not with a W, right?" N. continued, and pointed with his pencil. Grip looked and read. He'd written ARP in pencil in the three boxes.

"Obviously, with a V," said N., and erased the whole word. "Here also, yes, it must be Shakespeare and Macbeth, but is Banquo the third word?" He pointed to the line of words that ran all the way across the puzzle. "Banquo, the one whose ghost dogs Macbeth?"

Grip didn't make the connection at first; then he read the long line again. N. had written: THEY INTERROGATED ME LAST NIGHT.


Grip slept badly, and his view from the hotel room window that night was appalling. He'd grown accustomed to the sound of planes and proximity to the runway, those didn't bother him anymore. In the mornings, he woke up to the weather reconnaissance and courier aircraft that landed early. But that night, after he finally fell asleep, he was awakened by a deafening roar. Got up sleepily to look through the blinds. The engines, they seemed to be coming from every direction.

Then he saw them, flashing anticollision lights and white navigation lights, constellations moving like a string of pearls across the sky. He saw the silhouettes ease off the runway, high-winged and bulging from their heavy loads in slowly rising trajectories. It was B-52s, bombers in waves. He thought he heard cheers from outside. A new wave of planes rolled out. They seemed to go on without end.

# CHAPTER 30

THE GAME OF HINTS WAS repeated the next day. A nonsense conversation of questions and answers inside the cell, while N. sat doing crossword puzzles. Grip's issues with the time sequence at Weejay's meant nothing, and N.'s little interruptions of half-mumbled five-letter words and garden flowers meant everything. The newspaper crosswords went back and forth across the table a few times, while Stackhouse and his simultaneous interpreter heard all about Vladislav's swims and Reza's excitable moods.

For Grip, it was like juggling hand grenades. What had they interrogated N. about the day before? And Arp, what did N. know about Jean Arp? Grip wrote: NEW YORK? one time and spun back the newspaper. N. nodded, but what did it mean? Nothing in N.'s earlier story touched on New York. Why had N. asked him about it? Meanwhile, Grip filled the air with words and questions about the other stuff, keeping all the plates spinning. N. tried in turn to have something to say, but held his cards close. He wrote: MAUREEN. Twice he faintly penciled in the name, then erased it each time. On Grip's list of every name that N. had mentioned, he couldn't find a Maureen.

A LIFE FOR A LIFE also appeared in the crossword, and PAWN SACRIFICE was some sort of call to action. It was a game with too many possible associations, Grip knew it. The human longing to connect, to see patterns no matter how the dots are scattered. You want to so badly. Was N. like a fortune-teller, cleverly tricking someone into seeing their own hopes and hidden fears? Plant a seed, and the mind does the rest. A couple of years of torture and interrogation, yet still he gave the Americans headaches. There was cunning embedded in that—what to say and when. N. knew all about the laws of nature in a universe that consisted only of a cell with four walls. The game with the Americans would have been one thing. What was it now: Did N. want to give, or just take?

When Grip wrote CHRISTO, N. seemed not to understand. After taking it in for a long time, Grip finally spelled THE GATES. It seemed to strike N. as vaguely familiar, but nothing more. No hidden nod, no new word back. They danced around each other, Grip deeply puzzled and juggling everything.

He decided to switch tactics. Convinced that N. still held the strongest hand, he had to rush him.

"I'm leaving the day after tomorrow," he said—a lie—and shifted on the chair so that it would be clear that he was about to be done for the day.

N. quickly wrote down his last two words: TORTURE and MAUREEN, and then wiped them out again.


A life for a life" was what Vladislav had said to N., about saving him from going back into the factory when the police showed up. Promising to repay a debt.

Thoughts of those words came and went, while Grip looked around inside the door of the officers' club. It was full of people—a party. Flight suits, beer, and backslapping. Grip tried to find Shauna, who'd left a message at the hotel saying she wanted to meet him there. For the past several days, they'd eaten dinner alone.

He saw her up at a table where they used to sit, surrounded by a half dozen pilots, with a deck of cards in her hand. A couple of them laughed, while the others watched the cards that ran through her hands like water. Among the beer glasses and drinks, she laid down, flipped over, and sorted the cards. Her fingers and the deck flickered, while the rest of her was stillness itself. The queen of spades was the only card that flashed like lightning as it came into view. The black lady constantly disappeared and showed up again, as the crowd tried to pick her out. The stack of banknotes at Shauna's side said something about how well the pilots had succeeded. They swore and laughed, completely seduced.

Grip watched another few rounds from a distance, more notes added to the pile. Shauna's hair was down and hung over her back, and her eyes wore more makeup than usual. He thought she did it well, that game about her age. He couldn't quite put his finger on it, but somehow she floated—certain small details that couldn't be pinned down. Most of the aviators around her were younger, yet she fit right in. Was she younger or older than he was? Grip thought it was something he should ask her.

Around them, the party was going full swing. The volume of the music went in waves, while sweaty aviators and a stressed-out mess manager argued about volume control down by the bar.

Shauna neatened up the bill pile and then saw Grip.

"Thanks," she said to the men around her when he arrived. They hesitated, wanted more, to have their rights. But Grip looked at them as if they were out of line, touching something they shouldn't get involved with. They stood up one by one and disappeared.

"A beer?" said Shauna. "Nine seventeenth is buying. The squadrons are celebrating."

"All those B-52s last night—I had a hunch."

247

"They're buying, all night."

"Obviously they returned unscathed, all of them." Grip caught a waitress's attention, gestured toward a glass on the table, and sat down.

Shauna smiled, victorious.

"So what have you given yourself up to today?" said Grip. She didn't reply. "Are you still getting copies of what N. says?"

"Short summaries. Stackhouse knows I can get to you directly, so I guess he sticks to what is actually being said. Right now, not much. However, he said the fucking crossword puzzling has to come to an end, he intends to take the papers away. He thinks he doesn't have control over what actually takes place in the cell."

"He sees us the whole time. What does he think we do, speak through the crosswords? The newspapers get him to relax, wasn't that what you wanted?"

"In part."

The beer came. Grip took a sip and then asked: "So what more do you want?"

Shauna thought for a moment. "You realize that I, as FBI, interpret his answers in different ways than Stackhouse's minions?"

Grip shrugged.

Shauna rolled a peanut between her fingertips as if beginning a new trick. "I'm very interested in when and where he was arrested."

"He says he was arrested at a motel in Florida."

Shauna closed her hand and opened it again. The nut was gone. "Stackhouse claims they arrested him on a ship off the coast of Florida. It's a very important legal detail—otherwise N. could not be sitting here. The CIA is not allowed to arrest people on American territory." She paused. Grip let her be.

"If Stackhouse says he was arrested on a ship," she continued, "then of course that's the way it is. The fact that I have every reason to distrust what he says doesn't matter. But let's imagine for a moment that Stackhouse is playing it straight, and that N. has cooked something up."

"He's hiding something?"

"We'll see. N.'s story ends in a motel in Florida. It's easy to pinpoint the date by counting the days after the police raided the factory in Topeka. That would make it February 21, 2005—while Stackhouse argues that N. was arrested on board a ship on March 15. If it is as he says, those three weeks are not accounted for. Stackhouse's and the CIA's version takes more time. What was N. doing during that period, before he left on that ship?" The peanut appeared in her hand again. She put it in the bowl and then looked around at the bomber crews, the uniforms. Less for dramatic effect than to gather her thoughts. "Truth is," she said then, "as we both know, a relative term."

"Why are you telling me this?" Her game of insinuations, of intimate ties. She'd pushed it too far. "What are you saying?"

"Nothing in particular. You are Sweden's representative. It is you we are talking to." Her obsequiousness was worse than that of a cheap conference hostess.

"This man who still wants to call himself N.," said Grip angrily. "After everything that—" He put down his beer glass. "You will never release him, never even acknowledge his existence. The arrest, the torture—pure, fucking illegal."

"Now you have—"

Grip interrupted her. "No, Shauna. Who is it you want me to represent—Sweden, or just myself?"

Shauna was unmoved. "How many passports do you possess, Ernst?"

"They interrogated him last night—not a word was said to me about it. Is Stackhouse questioning him?"

"I'm sure he sits and listens. No, it's one of my own, I flew him here a couple of days ago. How many passports do you have?"

"What, why have you started questioning him? And I only have one passport. Why?"

"You yourself said that he has opened up. So one must seize the opportunity."

"What are you talking to him about, what does he say?"

"He says enough."

"What about?" repeated Grip.

"Do you celebrate Christmas with your family?"

"You're changing the subject."

"Yes, I am. Do you celebrate Christmas with them?"

"No, not my thing, all the damn trees and elves. I travel, it suits me." Anger made him bite off his sentences.

"Your Christmas habits are more interesting than you might think." Shauna reached into her bag and took out something. It proved to be a passport; she held it out to him. "Where were you when you heard about the tsunami?"

"Since it was Christmas, I was on the road. A diving trip in Thailand." It was a Swedish passport he had in his hand. Grip opened to the middle of the stamped pages. "I was diving, noticed nothing out of the ordinary. Not until the boat was bringing us back did we see the devastation. Personally, I suffered not at all."

"And the passport?"

"What a question. Like many other beach hotels, mine was completely demolished. My passport disappeared." He leafed through the one he held in his hand.

And got to the picture of himself.

"Why—"

"—are we sitting on Diego Garcia and discussing your lost passport." Shauna looked at him, considering the moment. Then she said: "Have you introduced yourself to N.?"

"By name?"

"Yes."

"Under the rules of conduct, Stackhouse made me promise not to. So no, I haven't."

Shauna nodded. "Regardless of where N. was arrested"—she gave him the briefest hint of a smile—"one thing is quite clear: with him was a passport that identified him as Ernst Grip."

A second, it took him a second to grasp the concept, and then the express train hit him head on. Yet Grip did not drop his gaze; he managed to keep looking at her.

"He had your passport. Can you imagine that, Ernst?"

# CHAPTER 31

T
HERE WERE—"

"I know," said Shauna. "Tens of thousands of Swedes at those beaches."

"Someone found my passport, then left it at one of those hospitals that so many passed through."

"Exactly."

"And that was where he got hold of it."

Shauna Friedman nodded.

Somewhere in the back of his head, Grip asked himself why he was trying to appear innocent. He wasn't guilty of anything. His trip hadn't been the least bit strange. The tsunami—it was a natural disaster. And his passport had ended up in the wrong hands. There was nothing that needed to be defended.

But still.

"You, both of you, Stackhouse—" Grip threw up his hands. "You asked for me specifically. It was me and no one else you wanted to make the trip from Sweden, here to Garcia."

"Not both—I was the one who called you."

"Because of the passport?"

"Yes." Shauna nodded. "I suggested there were questions that only you could answer."

"Namely, how my passport ended up where it did?"

"Yes, and I know that now. But then there's the question of all those trips to New York."

It was the second blow of the evening, and it fell just as hard. In the midst of the bomber pilots yelling and screaming sat Ernst Grip, raw. He was still holding his passport in his hand, his old passport, which, like his new one, was filled with stamps from trips to New York. Another insight stung even more: when Grip met Shauna for the first time—when they went to lunch and he noticed her hair, her hands pecking so skillfully with chopsticks, a simple detail like the way she listened to Django Reinhardt in the car—even then she had those questions ready for him. Why was there a man in a cell at Diego Garcia who carried the passport of a member of the Swedish security police? And what was that police officer doing, constantly going to New York?

"As I assume you already know," he replied, "I have belonged for some years to the bodyguard detachment. The royal family travels a lot, the princesses, their daughters . . . their studies, friends, UN visits, Christmas shopping . . . how many reasons do you want? Besides, I like the city a lot."

"Whatever it is, you hide it well."

"Who is really hiding what?" Grip grinned. An intimate moment, because everything was at stake.

"You know there are many strands to this knot," Shauna began. "We're running several parallel investigations. The interconnections that haunt us, we can get to later. But the case involves an art theft and a woman. No one special, just a schoolteacher, but she was shot to death in Central Park."

It was time to get out of there. Time to go. He'd been set up, and she kept firing. He couldn't just sit there and take it.

The break came, quite naturally. One of the pilots stopped and unzipped the top of his flight suit for Shauna to see. On the T-shirt underneath was the silhouette of a B-52 above the words ROCK THE PLANET. He was dripping with sweat, or maybe someone had poured alcohol over him. He nodded proudly in time with the music, then someone pulled him along, farther away.

"Rock the Planet." Grip savored the words.

"He released his first full cargo of bombs," said Shauna. "That's what they call it."

"He looks young, and now, having popped it, he's officially initiated. And how do you know these things anyway?"

"They explained it to me."

Grip turned in his chair toward the jerking sea of rolled-up and unbuttoned flight suits, bottles of beer, cigars, and the roar of self-congratulations. "I'm sure they've tried to explain all kinds of things."

"What?"

Grip had hoped for it, that slightly offended reaction. "Your blouse and your tan," he said, turning back slowly. "And if I could imagine a purple bra strap while you were doing your clever tricks, then certainly a hundred combat-drunk bomber pilots in here have done the same. If you've just released ten thousand tons of bombs onto somebody's head, then no doubt you want to end the day by shooting off the last of your manliness."

"I know," she replied. "And there are twenty tons of bombs per aircraft."

He smiled ingratiatingly. "Is that a lot?"

"Yes, that's a lot."

"Then I'm sure they have a perfect right to empty themselves of testosterone, after such a contribution to peace. By the way, who do you think was braver, these gentlemen or the ones who flew into the Twin Towers?"

"Is it courage we're measuring?"

"Men always measure courage."

"I think it's time—"

"—to go, yes."

And they stood up.

The floor was sticky the entire way. Once they'd made it through the sweaty, noisy crowd and come out into the hall, a lonely old airman appeared who immediately puffed up when he saw Shauna. She didn't seem either concerned or interested when he started saying, "No, not yet," and "Come here, baby." And then he saw Grip. It was his eyes—*Who the fuck do you think you are?*—that made Grip take an extra step between them, blocking Shauna so she couldn't see anything more than his back. He put his hand on the man's shoulder, smiled, and just when the crew cut with the stubby forearms was about to react, Grip squeezed. No fancy Asian moves, just a pure, relentless hold on his throat. In one second, or not even that—taken by surprise, drunk in the heat—he was nothing more than a hundred and eighty pounds of cells fighting for oxygen. He tugged, couldn't get loose, his legs buckled in fear. Then Grip released him.

"What happened?" said Shauna, looking up.

The major squatted with his hands on his throat, as if surprised that everything was still attached. He stared vacantly, coughed, and dry-wheezed. Looked ready to vomit.

"It's the heat," said Grip. "Too much to drink, too much emotion. Come."

After they got back to the officers' hotel, Grip went to his room, lay fully clothed on his bed, and waited about an hour. Then he went out again, just a few hundred yards. He'd seen it before, the recreation area. A bit apart, with a row of trees screening it from the rest of the base. There was a neglected tennis court, brown grass, and some picnic areas with fire pits and cinder-block grills. Embers were still smoldering in one, and he blew life into them and started tearing pages out of his notebook. When the flames came to life and began to lick the papers, he added the notebook cover and the small folder he collected his papers in. From now on, he would keep everything in his head.

It burned slowly. He prodded and poked with a leftover skewer to make sure everything would be gone. Watching the glow, he let his thoughts drift.

Back home, the Boss had certainly spoken the truth. He'd thought the Ministry of Foreign Affairs was the one asking Grip to go; he hadn't realized that the request came directly from the American side. Had he known it, he wouldn't have given the nod, Grip was confident of that—they went back far enough not to sacrifice each other. But now Grip was where he was. He'd accepted the fucking ticket and was in for the ride. He'd have to fend for himself. Those were the rules.

And Shauna, what was she doing? Shauna had to figure things out, that was her job—right? Into her lap had fallen N., who couldn't be shown to anyone, a beat-up remnant who wouldn't talk. And the bastard had been arrested with a Swedish security police passport in his inside pocket. Grip's passport. Among all the possibilities, one twisting thread led to another: a robbery in Topeka and a dead woman in Central Park. And that led to—what did it lead to? It led to N.'s cell now holding them both.

However unlikely it seemed, the connection—Topeka and New York—he shouldn't be blinded by its having been made. There were other elusive threads: Stackhouse had a different agenda than Shauna did, and N. persisted with Maureen, a name that didn't

fit. Trails and blind alleys that could be useful. Shauna had asked
him about New York, straight out. About why he went there so
often. But if Shauna knew what Grip knew, she wouldn't be fishing,
throwing out hooks and implying threats, the way she had. That
revealed something. And it was too blatant not to be conscious. She
was waiting for a reaction. The interrogations of N. she'd arranged
during the night—those weren't about Topeka and the time at
Weejay's. Shauna was wrestling with something. Something unclear. But what? Grip moved the embers, where a few small blue
flames still flickered among the burned pages. His thoughts spun
once more.

Half an hour later, only a few bright spots remained of the fire.
He crushed the last charred pages of the notebook to powder, blew
the ashes so they rose in a cloud, and left. The ashes hung for a moment like a gray ghost in the night.

There were two things he could cling to. Shauna Friedman
wasn't sure where the line between him and N. really stood, what
actually happened after the passport got lost. Who had been where,
when? Grip knew it. And he'd figured out the math. At the same
time that N. claimed he'd been arrested at a motel in Florida, Grip
had entered New York as himself. *The Gates*, the woman getting
shot, all within the space of a few days. Stackhouse said N. was
arrested later—it was a lie, but that was the time frame the CIA
needed to make the arrest legal. They probably had dates that
needed to match up, in case someone checked. And those turned
out to be the weeks missing from N.'s life. Shauna wondered
whether it was he or N. who had been in New York. That was the
first thing he could hold on to. The second was N.'s nighttime interrogations. Shauna had tried to give the impression that N. had told
her something, but that wasn't true. He'd maneuvered and wrig-

gled while Shauna tried to tie him to New York. Grip had never used his name inside the cell, but N. had nonetheless made the connection. After several years of hell, suddenly a Swedish security police officer turns up. The air-conditioning is turned on, he gets bandaged up, and he's given a haircut. The old tormentors are lying low. Of course he knows something is going on. Then the last bit, it had probably been gnawing at him—where have I seen that fucker before? Maybe he'd simply recalled the picture in the passport, or maybe someone from the FBI had said too much one night. And then questions about New York and questions about art. Clearly, N. realized that someone would get the blame for something. And Grip himself didn't understand anything, like a fucking sheep all the way—until Shauna threw everything in his face. How similar were they really, the two faces on either side of the table in the cell? Apparently enough to cause confusion. N.'s face, which had been badly beaten, was now reasonably healed up. Except for the scars, it was true, they were starting to look increasingly alike. Especially now that they'd given him Grip's hairstyle. And he himself had told them they should give N. a haircut. Then they'd taken the opportunity. He had missed it, but N. had understood—the Americans knew whose identity was shared by two. And now N. was picking up cards. Shauna was skilled, but against N. she had nothing of value to put on the table. N. figured the only bet worth making was on Grip. He had to trust it.

It was the only way out.

# CHAPTER 32

N. SLOWLY PULLED HIS FINGER across his throat. What was at stake—*a life for a life*—meant that someone had to die. If you'd only seen his finger move, you would have missed it; you had to catch his gaze as well. It was there that the death sentence lay.

And now they had an agreement.

Grip left the cell as usual and entered the monitoring room. He lingered, made small talk with Stackhouse, got him to lower his guard. Said they were done with the crossword-puzzle thing, showed some understanding. Asked about the waters off the reef, and if he'd ever been out fishing in Garcia. He had. They talked lures, hooks, and a huge yellowfin Stackhouse had reeled in one time off the Florida coast, or maybe it was the Red Sea. Memories of the outside world—and then Stackhouse decided to send for some coffee. And soon he was the only one talking, polite conversation about how fine Stockholm was in the summer and how fucking ruined everything was in Beirut.

Grip just nodded.

He had to search for a while for a way to get back into the conversation and regain control. But through a sensitive deportation case he made Stackhouse recall, and an imaginary meeting in London, Grip finally had an opening to say, "Yes, and she was there. Maureen . . ."

As if he was racking his brain for the rest of her name.

Impossible to say whether it was curiosity or discomfort that made Stackhouse delay his answer.

Grip put his hand on his cheek, as if to draw out details from his memory about the woman's appearance.

"Birthmark?" said Stackhouse.

"Yes."

"Whipple, Maureen Whipple."

"Whipple, that was her name, yes," said Grip. "Tell her I said hello."

Of course Stackhouse never would.

Maureen Whipple—so that was her name. According to N., she was the worst, that much Grip understood. During the worst of the torture, Maureen had turned up in different parts of the world. They couldn't possibly have been introduced, her first name something N. had picked up when he wasn't supposed to hear, and he'd seen the odd mark on her cheek. MAUREEN. BIRTHMARK. Two words in the crossword, and a finger across his throat.

Stackhouse had spilled enough. It was late afternoon, and Grip sat at the Internet computer in the hotel lobby. The first e-mail he sent was a short, informal intelligence inquiry. The kind you can only ask if sender and receiver know each other well. "What you got on Maureen Whipple?" He appended a list of keywords: interrogation, CIA, birthmark, Guantánamo, torture . . . Grip fed in a long list. The woman who got the e-mail—an old analyst from the security police who collected comic books and who'd reportedly made a fortune in Bulgarian pyramid schemes—wouldn't find the question particularly strange, and wouldn't need to tell the whole world that he'd asked. Grip must be in a tight spot, she'd think, and need it fast.

That was the easier e-mail.

Since the crossword puzzles ended, Grip and N. had developed a more subtle language, but now that they understood each other, there wasn't much they needed to say. It could be woven in. The idea was to remain low key, not go into overdrive—and therefore the method didn't allow for many details.

But there was enough for Grip to gather a few things. It was obvious that Shauna kept up the nightly interrogations of N. because the FBI was trying to solve the art theft and murder in Central Park. One fact they seemed to know with unshakable certainty was that a Swede had been involved—the question was just which one. The evidence was complicated by the fact that there were two passports circulating under a single name.

What N. had conveyed to Grip was this: he was willing to take the blame. Take the blame for everything. But it would cost him.

And then Vladislav's name came up. N. had torn a piece from one of the newspapers and written down an e-mail address that he'd apparently kept clear in his memory through it all. He poked the scrap in between a couple of pages, the day Grip told him that there'd be no more newspapers or crosswords. After that, Grip left the cell.

Being able to come home and walk in Ben's door, to have something resembling a life. That would cost him. Grip wrote his second e-mail of the evening—to Vladislav, who was at large, as free as he was dangerous, somewhere in the world.

He wrote:

I represent an old friend of yours. A friend who, like you, survived the tsunami. A friend who had the habit of ordering for you, whenever you ate together at restaurants. You last saw each other in a car driving out of Kansas. Your friend is now in indefinite detention. He wants to exercise his option—a life for a life. Does it still apply?

Grip stayed away from the officers' club that night. He wasn't particularly hungry, and he had no desire to engage in another matchup with Shauna. He'd give her this last day's round as a walkover.

Already the next morning, Grip had a reply, signed V. All it said was:

First I want to know, who said we should shoot the pelicans?

Grip did nothing, just logged out and left. The rest of the day he kept to himself, let the hours pass. Sat on a deserted beach with a few cans of beer in a cooler in the morning, then slept through a violent downpour in his hotel room until evening.

At dusk he sat down at the computer again and wrote, "It was Mary."

He got a hamburger, extra-large fries, and a much too frozen milkshake at a fast-food place not far from the hotel. From there, he went to the gym for noncommissioned officers and enlisted men. It wasn't the best-equipped gym on the base, but it was the most lived-in. It had the heaviest weights on the bars, the most laughter and crude jokes, no staff majors to turn down the loud music—and views of only the best-built naked torsos. Grip lifted for an hour and watched a marine platoon holding its own bench-press competition. He would have done fine, but could never have beaten the Puerto Rican medic who howled like an animal when he lifted the last bar and took the pot. Estevez, his name was.

When regular business hours were over for the security police in Stockholm, and it was almost midnight in the middle of the Indian Ocean, Grip tapped on a mouse to bring the hotel lobby computer to life, and logged in.

Maureen Whipple. A day's work. Grip's pyramid-scheming analyst had sent him everything she'd found. Mostly excerpts and quotes taken out of context, single sentences from here and there, Swedish and English, something in French. Connecting the scattered dots, it wasn't hard to see that Maureen Whipple lived her life in the seams between the major US covert organizations. She'd been seen out in the world, and at times certainly devoted herself to interrogation. There was a picture too, a highly enlarged grainy clipping from a group photo. With someone's shoulder on the right, and another's on the left, a uniformed chest behind and a face at the center. Short-haired, ruddy, middle-aged. She tried to smile. And there was something on her right cheek. Was it a birthmark? Or just an incidental shadow? At any rate, her address had been traced to an office complex in Charlestown, West Virginia. The kind of office you put in a bland place, so no one will notice.

Grip wrote up a summary in English and saved it in Drafts.

Just as he finished, his in-box showed he'd gotten a message. It was from V. Apparently, Vladislav now trusted the person who'd become his friend's acquaintance.

I'm ready.

Nothing more. The words were like a whispered destiny, the last words spoken before the soldiers stormed from their trenches. As they mounted their bayonets, everyone still alive. In the last quiet moment.

# CHAPTER 33

'VE STAYED HERE ON THE island much longer than I was supposed to," Grip said.

"You're not the only one," said Lance Corporal Estevez, laughing. "Garcia," he said meaningfully and shrugged. He had chalked hands, two hundred and eighty pounds on the bar behind him, and a sweaty bandana across his forehead.

"And now I've run out of pills, didn't bring enough."

"Don't need 'em, no malaria on the island," said the medic from the Marine Corps.

They spoke for a while, Grip congratulating him on winning the title the night before.

"It's true," said Grip, about the malaria. "But you know the rules, we have to take them when we're out here."

"Like us with nerve-gas pills. Any time there are minarets and muezzins around, we fucking have to eat that shit."

"The hospital here, the doctor is only available . . ."

"It's just awkward, fuck him. You can't need very much."

"Chloroquine . . . what's the word?"

"Chloroquine phosphate. Also called 'fucking malaria pills.' How many d'ya need?"

"For a week or two. One pack, whatever that is, maybe thirty or forty tablets."

"No problem. I can get 'em from the platoon pharmacy. Stop by when you're done."

Grip nodded. Estevez beat his fists on his chest to bring the muscles back to life and leaned back on the bench under the barbell.


In his cell, N., introspective, slowly rocked back and forth in the chair. He was lost in his own world, while Grip wrestled with his usual dilemma of having to find something to wrap their case in. Although N. didn't reply, he had to convey the impression he was still conducting an interrogation.

"Did you ever contact the consulate . . . ? Did you perform your actions under threat . . . ? Where did the money come from . . . ? Did you feel your life was at stake?"

The cell was so air-conditioned that it felt cold. Grip had goose bumps, and the more he repeated his nonsense questions, the more he felt the eyes watching them from outside. N. rocked and hummed vaguely, like someone who needed electroshock therapy and psychiatric drugs, not more questioning. It wasn't fatigue but hopelessness that characterized him now. He could no longer play the game. He showed none of his usual provocativeness or nonchalance but only gave terse replies for the sake of the television monitor and the invisible translator. When N. completely stopped talking, Grip kept going, as monotonously as someone reading stock market quotes.

Through certain hints, Grip managed to get across that he was in contact with Vladislav. And that Vladislav was the type who remembered old promises. N.'s eyes flickered and then said to the wall, "He'll give it to her, right, get her good . . . for all her savagery?"

Grip didn't let on, only tried to cover the words by raising his voice and pulling some new question from his exhausted supply.

N. turned so that their eyes met, fought with defeat, then automatically uttered a familiar and irrelevant answer. Just a few words, while his shining eyes looked toward the real question.

Grip closed his eyes and nodded as inconspicuously as he could. Afterward, N. sat lost in his own world again. Grip ground on monotonously, gave the appearance of finding new questions in some loose papers, and finally just went over his notes when it became all too obvious that N. wasn't there at all.

He waited.

Until N.'s eyes moved, and Grip sensed a fleeting moment of consciousness. He leaned forward.

"You know . . . ," he said, and caught N.'s hand as it moved across the table. They'd never come close to touching each other, and now it lasted not even a second. Just a tender hold on the wrist, which he released again. "I think you need a new pencil. Take this." Grip pulled a pen from his breast pocket.

"A new one?" said N. slowly and looked at the pencil on the table.

"Yours is worn down," said Grip. "I'll sharpen it tomorrow." He tapped once as he put the pen down on the table. "If there's any detail you remember that you want to tell me, use this to write it down."

"I'll go now," he said then. He stood up.

"By the way," he continued, "you asked me about a crossword-puzzle clue the other day: Masada. Where the Jews defended themselves against the Romans, remember? When all hope was gone, they threw themselves on their own swords."

N. gazed straight ahead. "Thanks," he said after a moment, and looked at him for a long time, before Grip turned and went.

The afternoon cloudbursts had continued late into the evening, but now the puddles reflected flatly in the dark, the rain and thunder having stopped. Grip sat with his coffee in one of the base's all-night hangouts, a combination convenience store and fast-food restaurant. The shelves held mostly chips, cookies, and wrapped magazines flashing bare breasts; grilled hot dogs and glazed doughnuts sweated in the warming oven. Grip sat at a counter made of scratched imitation marble, entirely bare and immensely long. A few black guys sat at the far end, dressed in evening civvies: sports jerseys and basketball shoes. They seemed just as restless as they were at home in the place, with nowhere else to go. Here at least they got away from the barracks' crowds and their own uniforms. Music played from small speakers in the ceiling.

The woman behind the counter offered Grip sugar for the second time, and he turned it down again. The front door banged.

"I thought so . . ." The sound of steps. "That it was you, Ernst."

He turned around—Shauna.

"I drove by," she said, and waved her hand. "It looked like you through the window." She looked a little tired and at the same time very happy. Grip pointed to the chair next to him, which she was already settling into. She refastened the hair clip behind her neck and pointed at Grip's cup to the waitress.

"Well?" she said then, as if it had been several weeks since the last time.

"Just killing time," said Grip with a shrug.

Shauna waited for her coffee. "He admits to it now," she began. "N. admits it, says he was present when the woman was shot in Central Park." She rubbed her eyes. "We've pieced it together. What he told you is only part of the story. N. wasn't arrested in Florida, he

270

was free for several weeks. Went up to New York, joined in there. Thought he could make some money."

"So much to do," said Grip.

"It makes everything fall into place."

"If N. says that it was so, then it was so. Is it that simple?" Grip couldn't resist.

"Of course not. But we have Romeo."

At first, Grip didn't understand.

"We have a driver who was involved, a slippery bastard with a clever lawyer," Shauna explained. "It was around the time that Reza began to piece together memories in his cell in Kansas. He had the idea that one of them was Swedish. Meanwhile, as I said, we arrested a driver for participating in a little operation in Brooklyn. I wasn't connected to it, but pretty soon he demanded to talk to someone about—" She stopped, dug something out of her bag. "Here, read for yourself," she said, handing him a clear plastic sleeve containing a few pages.

### Transcript of Hearing. Tape: 1 (1), D432811

**Date:** March 1, 2008
**Location:** Nassau County Jail, East Meadow, New York

#### Appearing:

Examining Officer Shauna Friedman (SF), FBI
Defendant Romeo Lupone (RL), detained on suspicion of complicity to commit forgery

**RL:** Do we have to record this?

**SF:** It won't be worth much otherwise.

**RL:** But I'm not testifying now, we agree on that?

**SF:** We don't agree on anything. It was you who wanted to talk to us. I don't know what this is about.

**RL:** I don't like tape recorders.

**SF:** Should I leave?

**RL:** No, wait. [*Silence.*] You know how it works. Some dudes in Brooklyn run a print shop in the evenings, extra income. It was good notes, the paper was only so-so, but the notes looked good. I would have fallen for it if someone shoved one in my hand, but you don't give a shit."

**SF:** Maybe not.

**RL:** So maybe I drove a little extra for that printer in the evenings, I didn't know what they were loading into that truck. I just drove, some addresses here and there. But now some goddamn feds are trying to nail me, said I knew more than I did. They fucking tapped some phones.

[*Silence.*]

**SF:** I'm listening.

**RL:** I'm on probation, for an old thing. If I take the rap for this shit, I'm going in for at least eight years. [Silence.] What would you say if I told you about Angelico and Metro's loading dock on October 25?

**SF:** Four years ago?

**RL:** For example.

**SF:** You'll have to say more than that.

**RL:** Hell if I know the name of the guy who made some statues worth a shitload, but two of them were stolen. Nobody has gotten fingered.

**SF:** Jean Arp, the artist.

272

**RL:** Maybe. And the statues never turned up, huh?

**SF:** No, it's still unsolved.

**RL:** There you go.

**SF:** So what?

**RL:** Never mind. So finally we get to this week's big lottery prize, Central Park on the night of February 27, a few years ago. Should we say at the top of 96th Street?

**SF:** We can say. What happened there?

**RL:** Come on, you know.

**SF:** You tell me, I don't have a probation violation hanging over my head.

**RL:** Okay, putting on the screws. Can we at least agree that a woman was injured around there that night?

**SF:** She died eventually.

**RL:** Oh fuck.

**SF:** You could say that—it changes the crime a little. It's called murder now. What were you saying?

**RL:** Is the fucking tape recorder still on?

**SF:** Still on.

**RL:** Who knows where the fuck this will end up.

**SF:** I'm the one who decides what the tape gets used for. Come on.

**RL:** Let's say those two were the same crew, the statues and Central Park.

**SF:** Well, anyone could walk off the street and claim that.

**RL:** Okay, let's imagine, then, let's say . . . I knew someone who drove for them. Who was part of it, saw a lot, met a lot of people.

**SF:** Even in Central Park?

**RL:** Maybe.

**SF:** What do you want?

**RL:** What the hell do you think—someone to correct the feds on what they did and did not hear in those telephone calls. And protection from being prosecuted for what I'm going to talk about, in black and white.
**SF:** I don't think we need this anymore.
[*Tape recording ends.*]

Grip slipped the papers back into the plastic sleeve. Romeo Lupone—so the fucker had surfaced again. A little threat of a decade in prison and the chickenshit starts talking. A little buying and selling of his prosecution, the kind of thing they like, the Americans.

"I've talked to Romeo since then," Shauna said.

"I'm sure," said Grip.

" 'The Swede,' he repeats constantly. Surely he means N., with your passport?" She wasn't provoking, she was reasoning.

"Or me," said Grip. "Wasn't that the obvious reason why you brought me here?"

"N.'s mumbling provides sufficient detail for him to have been involved. It's him, and that's easiest for everyone, isn't it?" Her nail clinked against the cup.

Maybe he ought to thank his lucky stars, Grip thought. Completely unknowingly, Romeo and N. had vouched for each other.


At the far end, a palm hit the counter and the guy laughed out loud. Shauna turned and gazed at the young men as if something interested her.

"Shouldn't we try the officers' club?" she said later.

"It's late."

"A few will still be there cleaning up—they can pour us a drink."

Grip muttered that he was fine where they were. Shauna reached for the sugar shaker. There was silence for a moment.

It was as if Shauna was speaking to her own cup when she finally said, "Reza, N., Romeo Lupone—of course, they don't mean anything, not anymore. The one I really want to get to is Adderloy." She turned to Grip, a short, tired smile. "There you have the real destroyer, the black soul." She stirred, poured in more sugar, stirred again. She let the cup be confessor again. "I want to look into a cell and see Adderloy alone with four walls. So that it's not the final word, his sending two of my agents, two of my best friends, to the morgue. To gaze inside there, when he knows that I know, and look him in the eye. I need to have that moment." She drank the coffee.

Grip glanced at the clock on the wall. Past midnight. The waitress and the young men at the other end were arguing about something. It finished with their questions about what time she'd be off for the night. She giggled nervously.

"What do you have then?" said Shauna.

"What I have?" Grip balanced the edge of his empty cup on the table and let it go again. "All I know is that there's a badly tortured man on Diego Garcia who speaks Swedish. That's a report of scarcely a page, to someone back home."

"Don't you want him back?"

Grip continued as if he hadn't heard her: "Papers will go back and forth, until finally, someone at the Foreign Office—" He looked at her.

"—shrugs his shoulders," she suggested. "Because no one actually misses him?"

He glanced at the clock again.

"Something like that," Grip said finally.

They went back to the hotel in the car. The empty stillness was broken only by the patter of insects against the lights in the stairwell. They were standing in the hallway outside their rooms. Shauna undid the clip from her hair, her shoes already hung from one hand. Grip stroked a finger over a sleepy moth on the wall.

"Are you married?" he asked.

"If I'm married?" Shauna said, stretching up. "What is it the airmen say, here at Garcia—"

"Two stopovers from home, and you're good to go. I've heard that too."

She laughed, a little wary. "So why do you ask?"

"Because I wondered."

"No, you didn't. You pay far too much attention to details, and you've seen the wedding ring."

"It comes on and off."

"No, I had it on until we got to San Diego. Then somewhere along the way, it came off. So you're wondering to whom?"

"We're getting there."

"He's a member of the House of Representatives in Washington, from North Carolina. Impressive, huh?"

"Doesn't say much."

"We have no children."

"That says more."

"Sometimes the ring performs its function, sometimes not. At the office in New York, I'm married, and not to just anyone, and he needs a wife. But he knows more about the lower back of his speechwriter than he does about mine. There is nothing we pretend about, at least not to each other. And here on Garcia, there's no point in being married." She pushed her hip toward one side, and her hand with the shoes toward the other. "If you're wondering," she said then, "I had one of those pilots up in the room here the other night. Not when they were all drunk, I mean a few evenings before. But he hesitated too much, so he had to go." The hand holding the shoes sank. "And you? Are you as free as you appear to be, in all your guises?"

"Completely. Or yes, I also live with someone who doesn't particularly care what I do with strange women."

"Who would lose the most if I invited you into the shower?"

"You'd do that?"

"So you think. Are you good?"

"You'd be shouting yourself hoarse."

He smiled, she laughed it off. They parted.


But Grip didn't go into his room. He went downstairs again and out into the parking lot. There he stood leaning against a wooden post with his hands in his pockets until the last light in Shauna's window went out, and then he went back into the lobby and sat down at the computer. He had everything nearly ready. It would only take a minute. To the fact file on Maureen Whipple, he added a few lines about what the woman had actually engaged in, her trail of screams and tormented souls. He clicked send, and the screen blinked. The rest was up to Vladislav.

He logged off, but remained seated. Dragged his fingers along the leaves of an artificial flower that stood next to him and broke out in a cold sweat. Conscience, anxiety, the flimsy hope: everything converged on him at once, and drops fell slowly down his back and his neck. He felt himself go pale. Someone seeing him would have thought he'd suddenly fallen ill. He hung over his knees on his elbows, completely exhausted. Soon enough, he thought, his breathing would be calm again, and he'd have only the dry mouth left. He just had to wait it out. A few more breaths, and he'd be able to pull himself together.

Later, as soon as he got back upstairs, he pulled off a long strip of toilet paper and dampened it in the sink. Inside the room, he'd left everything from his desk on the floor—now it was a quick thing to wipe down the shiny surface. He did it thoroughly, the edges too. Making the last traces of white powder disappear. Earlier in the day, he'd sat there and crushed forty chloroquine phosphate tablets by hand, between two spoons, which he then used to fill the cavity of a ballpoint pen. He'd spilled some, he'd been in a hurry to get out of there, but now it was clean. Grip opened the window and threw the paper ball into the bushes. Put his desk back in order, and lay down, naked.

# CHAPTER 34

GRIP HAD HIS USUAL APPOINTMENT, went dutifully to the white cell block. Just as expected, he was stopped before he got to the monitoring room.

"Not today," said the young, unfamiliar face who cut him off, while another man thoroughly studied Grip's ID card. The atmosphere was edgy, nervous.

"Where's Stackhouse?"

"Not today, we said."

Grip grabbed his ID card and turned on his heels. No one said anything as he opened the front door and disappeared again. In other words, he wasn't yet suspected of anything.

Because someone had in all likelihood been found dead in his cell. No wounds, no ropes, simply cardiac arrest. A weakened man, years of isolation and torture, it happened all the time. One could think.

Chloroquine phosphate. Thirty malaria pills killed most perfectly healthy people, forty was foolproof. Possibly in under an hour. The hard part was not the nausea or cramps, but the anxiety. Even if the soul wants to die, the body never does. He just hoped that N. had gone through with it. That he'd kept himself from making noise when his heart rhythm grew irregular, when the beats flip-flopped, and that he'd screwed the top back on the pen. If so, it would be a hard one to trace. A life that ends with a period. Cardiac arrest.

Sooner or later, someone would come looking for Grip—that would determine his future. He sat alone under the faded advertising parasols on the officers' club terrace.

It took a couple of hours.

"Out there," he heard someone say from within the club, and then heard the determined steps of a familiar pair of shoes, heading for the terrace doors. Shauna Friedman sat down opposite him with folded arms and glared. She took off her sunglasses, rocked a few times in her chair but didn't say a word, just stared straight at him.

"So then you know," she said at last. Her tone was hard, her skin pale, her eyes sharp.

"I know nothing, but I can imagine."

"He's dead."

"They didn't let me in earlier."

"Flat on his fucking bunk, staring straight up at the ceiling." Shauna looked around. Farther down on the terrace sat two young officers who'd come out just before, each with a beer. "You two," she said, raising her voice, "you can go."

They disappeared without a word.

"One guess," said Grip when their backs disappeared into the house: "cardiac arrest." With obvious irony in his voice, he added: "Given everything the man has gone through."

"Hey, I've heard that shit so many times before. It was the first thing Stackhouse said. His crew has left such a trail of crap that they immediately started burning their bridges. Hard to know if they did something, or were just surprised. And here you sit, seemingly untouchable, in the sun."

"Imagine that."

"Did you deal under the table with Stackhouse?"

"Stackhouse hated me from day one. It was you who brought

me here, remember? If you think something stinks, get an autopsy done on N."

"Hell yes, it stinks. But you know as well as I do that the moment he's no longer alive, no one wants to know him, not even us obviously, except as ashes scattered far out to sea."

"You can keep fighting your windmills," continued Grip. "I'm going home now."

"There are no flights. And even if there were, you will leave when I say so."

"Are you keeping me here?"

She didn't pay attention to his question. "Windmills—what do you mean by that? A stupid idealist in a purple bra—is that it?"

"So you're holding me hostage?"

"A Swedish citizen has died under unclear circumstances."

"A person who spoke Swedish will soon be burned into ashes, dissolved in lime, or simply thrown into the sea. After that, the man, the body, or even the designation N., never existed."

"You're their messenger boy."

"You're wrong."

"And you'll stay here."

"I'll contact my superiors. They'll send a plane."

"Give me something. I have a thousand reasons to keep you."

"I'm from Sweden. We remain neutral."

"Give me something!"

Not much more was said.

The next day Grip didn't go to the cell block. Instead he borrowed a beach chair from the hotel and sat on an inhospitable patch of grass overlooking the harbor.

Time passed. The sun burned over his arms. Shauna, he hadn't seen her since the day before. What did that mean?

What did Stackhouse believe about N.'s death? Or did he simply think he had one less problem weighing on him? Did anyone understand? Was the pen being analyzed, or had it simply been thrown out?

He sat and drank beer out of his cooler, waiting to be arrested at any time. Light beer; he didn't want to cloud his thinking. Shauna or Stackhouse would come. Come walking down the road, that's the way he saw it. With one or two men, like when the police have located a lost child. It mattered, whether it was Stackhouse or Shauna who came. He just couldn't make up his mind which way. But whichever it was, he would . . . It was the picture of Ben that came to him. Always the picture of Ben, looking over his shoulder when Grip came home to him, the skewed, easy smile. The few real moments. That was the life he had to protect. No matter what.

Evening came. Grip felt dehydrated despite all the beer. Were they keeping him under surveillance? He wasn't being paranoid, he was just surprised that nothing had happened. Were they expecting something from him? He folded up the chair, took his cooler, and started walking.

At the officers' hotel, he wrote a note and asked the man at reception to make sure that Shauna Friedman got it. He wrote that the Swedish security police and the Ministry of Foreign Affairs wanted to know immediately when he could be expected to leave Diego Garcia. It was nonsense. He hadn't even been in contact with them. Had he tried, he probably would have been told that he had to travel on whatever flights the Americans made available.

Perhaps his bluff nevertheless got him home. The next day he received a note in reply, saying he should be at the airport with his bags no later than six o'clock that evening. His sunburned arms smarting from the day before, he packed up, and reception said his room bill was already taken care of.


On the tarmac were a half-dozen black B-52s lined up and a single off-white passenger plane from the US Navy, the same kind he'd flown in on the way to Garcia.

"Mr. Grip?"

He nodded, and a crew member helped him aboard. A few more uniforms arrived and took seats in the large cabin.

Last came Shauna.

"Here," she said, handing him a bunch of tickets and reservation confirmations. She avoided looking at him. "You'll take the same route back, ending up in San Diego. Then you'll fly domestic. They couldn't find you anything direct to New York, so you'll have to go through Atlanta. A night in a hotel out by Newark, and from there, SAS to Stockholm. Then you'll be home."

Grip thumbed through the stack, then nodded and waited for her to say something more. Around them, empty rows of seats. Shauna sat on the outer armrest in the row opposite.

"No," she said. "I won't be coming with." Behind her, a crew member checked off the few passengers on a clipboard and gave it to the cockpit.

"The first thing you said inside N.'s cell," she began then, "was something about not lying."

Grip looked out the window and gave the impression of searching his memory. "I said I wouldn't lie or make false promises," he said, looking up at her.

"And did you hold to that?"

"Yes."

"And now I say the same. No lies, no false promises. We have maybe five minutes left before they throw me off. No matter what is said, I will leave, and you will get to go home. All the way home."

Grip didn't move a muscle.

"I'll start," she continued. "N. no longer exists. His body, everything, is gone."

"There you go," said Grip. He fingered the ticket for New York to Stockholm. At any moment, Shauna could terminate all flight preparations, he knew that. Through the window, he saw the fuel truck pull away from the airplane.

"Stackhouse," said Shauna, "is busy making a smokescreen, suggesting that N. could have come from anywhere. His being Swedish didn't fit into the picture, not for Stackhouse. Everything around N. is disappearing, there's nothing I can get to."

"Does it matter?" said Grip. "We have no interest in resurrecting him, not in this way. For us, he was already dead."

"But he was tortured . . ."

"Thoroughly and long."

"The CIA regrets it, claiming that others were at fault. That in other countries, things got out of control."

"You mean that's what they tell you, when you have to investigate the matter?"

"Something like that." Shauna was silent, moved some debris on the floor with the tip of her shoe. Then she asked, "Did Americans torture him?"

"You want to know what I think?"

"What you know."

Grip looked at the clock.

Shauna continued: "Don't we have a common interest in solving this kind of puzzle?" She waited a moment. "Do you like names? We can play names. One that turns up occasionally is Maureen Whipple."

"Is that so."

"Yes, she has been seen where she shouldn't be." Shauna gave a quick nod. "Do you know anything about her?"

"Not much."

"Not much—still, that's a start. During your weeks with N., of course you learned more than what we overheard. You found a way to talk to him."

"Hey, time to go," shouted the crewman in the aisle. Shauna raised a sympathetic hand but remained seated.

"Stackhouse," she continued, "wanted to keep you here. As of yesterday, he became quite forceful about it. That's why I'm sending you off. The heat's on Garcia, it fuels all kinds of desperation. Stackhouse's world teems with terrorists, and he's willing to go quite far to keep his machinery operating." She let it sink in for a second. "I received a report from Washington yesterday concerning Maureen Whipple. For Christ's sake, if you know anything about her . . . You get to leave, but I have to have something, to hold off Stackhouse."

"Maureen . . . ," began Grip.

"Now you damn well . . . ," cried the crewman to Shauna.

"One second."

There was a roar as an engine started up.

"Maureen Whipple," Grip began again, "is one of N.'s torturers."

"He was able to identify her?"

Grip nodded. "The shit is yours to dig in. She belongs to you. Clearly, it's her assignment to drown people or let them be raped by dogs."

"Not is—perhaps was—her assignment. She was found murdered yesterday morning, in the woods outside her home, somewhere in West Virginia." Shauna pushed a finger into her own chest. "Someone drove a stake straight through her. Like a vampire. Fat headlines, a thousand questions."

Grip couldn't bring himself to give more than a surprised nod.

"Now means *now*, we're closing," roared a face sticking through the doorway at the front of the cabin.

Shauna stood up.

"Had N. himself had the chance to do it," said Grip then, "he wouldn't have hesitated for a second."

"Someone obviously took his chance for him. The stake was pierced through a piece of paper quoting the White House's assurances that torture does not occur"—Shauna looked toward the door and added absently—"in the war on terror." She nodded, to herself, making a decision. "Yes," she said then, "N. is dead. I only wish that you and I had had the chance to sit down and talk about the others as well."

"About Adderloy and Mary?"

"About them and Vladislav. Especially Vladislav." Then she left, didn't look back once as she disappeared down the aisle and out the door.

The plane rocked, began to taxi. Eventually, they came to the end of the runway, turned around. Sat there. The waiting that followed was excruciating. To get away from the island—Grip could have pushed the airplane himself.

Then came the engines powering up, and the brakes released.

# CHAPTER 35

U P AT ALTITUDE, THE PEACEFULNESS of the evening sun made his eyelids heavy. Still, Grip couldn't fall asleep.

The stake. It wasn't the mental image of the woman in the woods that disturbed him, but the thought of what he'd unleashed. Vladislav—after only a few days, he'd already done the job. It was like an incantation, a demon. Why did Grip feel drawn to him? As if an aching nerve had been exposed.

Grip squirmed in his seat, tried to close his eyes. No luck, squirmed again. The setting sun shimmered like melting glass over the horizon. He pulled out Shauna's pile of tickets and documents, began leafing through them to give himself something to do. Among the papers, he found an unmarked envelope. The flap wasn't licked, just tucked in. Inside the envelope was a pair of double-folded, blurry photocopies. Grip unfolded them.

**Transcript of Hearing. Tape: 1 (2), K921314**

**Date:**     April 21, 2008
**Location:**  Nassau County Correctional Center, East Meadow,
            New York

Appearing:

Examining Officer Shauna Friedman (SF), FBI
Defendant Romeo Lupone (RL), detained on suspicion of
complicity to commit forgery

**RL:** Why this time? You never needed to record us before.
**SF:** All our previous little dates can remain a matter between you and me. But now we have an agreement, what you say must be official, and so it has to be on tape.
**RL:** For fuck's sake, people will say I snitch.
**SF:** Call it whatever you want, this is the deal, if you want to walk out of here a free man.
**RL:** When do I get out? Today?
**SF:** Give me something to convince the prosecutor that you are worth his time, that you actually have something to offer. Then we'll see. Withdrawal of prosecution is no trifle, there are many people involved. Two or three weeks, I would think, before a judge will let you go free on bail.
**RL:** Three weeks in this fucking hole.
**SF:** That's the game. Do you want to play or not?
**RL:** Go to hell.
**SF:** I didn't hear you. Try again.
[*Silence.*]
**SF:** This won't take long, we'll start with this.
**RL:** That's a fucking passport photo, right?
**SF:** Yes, it is.
**RL:** I've said that I can tell you how it happened, how they did it . . .
**SF:** How *you* did it.

**RL:** Yeah, how we did it, then. Both the sculptures and the thing in Central Park. But no names. If anyone finds out . . .

**SF:** We don't give a damn. And right now, we don't care how you did it either. We need names!

[*Silence.*]

**SF:** Look at the picture. You've talked about "the Swede," that the one who did the planning was called the Swede. Is that him?

**RL:** Maybe.

**SF:** Maybe?

**RL:** Shit, that was years ago now. A single fucking picture.

**SF:** *Maybe* isn't good enough. You're having trouble understanding? Right now, I see a prosecutor turning his back on you when he hears this. I see a driver from Brooklyn in his freezing cell in upstate New York.

[*Silence.*]

**SF:** A hell of a lot of years in Sing Sing.

[*Silence.*]

**SF:** I see that things are sinking in. That you're getting it.

**RL:** That's him. I think it's him.

**SF:** Oh no, it's not that easy, just saying you think it's him. You have to be certain.

**RL:** Please, I need . . . give me. Give me better pictures.

**SF:** Let's leave the Swede. We'll go on to this one instead. Him, I have more photos of. Take a look!

[*Silence.*]

**SF:** Look at all the photos. You can't miss this one, if you've seen him. Really try to concentrate now.

**RL:** Bill.

**SF:** Bill, yes, but many people are named Bill.

**RL:** Adderloy, Bill Adderloy.

**SF:** So he was with you, Adderloy was with you?

**RL:** No. [*Clears throat.*] Adderloy wasn't with us, it was Adderloy we worked for. I was there when he inspected the goods afterward in a warehouse, both times, both statues and the fucking thing from Central Park.

**SF:** Bill Adderloy?

**RL:** Yes.

**SF:** Now that's more like it. Maybe it won't be that cell in Sing Sing, after all.

**RL:** Do I have to testify? I mean, testify in front of people?

**SF:** One thing at a time. If you can identify Adderloy, you will go free on bail, I'll see to that. But the judge won't let you off completely until you've given your final word about the Swede. I will get hold of better photos, and in the meantime, you make sure to put your memories in order. Then if you're lucky, you can avoid both the cell and the witness stand.

Grip sat still. Completely still with the pages in his hand, maybe a minute. Maybe ten.

Had . . .

Below him passed the Indian Ocean, or perhaps they were already over the Pacific. It was night in any case; he had one night to shield him. Before him lay the ticket that would take him all the way home, and with it, a blurry transcript. Grip dismissed the idea that he had a choice—the easy world would last only as long as his flight. One night, then the wheels would touch the ground again.

Had . . . ?

The hearing transcript left him with both clarity and fog. Why had Shauna Friedman done him the favor of tying N. to New York?

It didn't fit, not with Topeka and the quintet from Weejay's—all it did was give Grip a chance. Just like with Romeo Lupone, who'd do anything to avoid a few decades behind the limestone of Sing Sing for accessory to murder. Grip had been picking around in Shauna's puzzle before, but it was only now that he saw *all* the pieces. The way it truly was. In Kansas, Reza had babbled on about Adderloy and "the Swede" in his cell. Shauna had already trailed Adderloy for art theft and collaborating with terrorists, and then she got hold of N., who had Grip's passport in his pocket. A passport with too many entrance stamps for New York. And sure enough, someone busts a petty thief in Brooklyn who snitches when it gets too hot. Once again a lot of vague talk about "the Swede." Conveniently enough, N. was the one who could be blamed for everyone's sins. N. as bank robber in Topeka, and then as art thief in New York. Shauna trimmed the edges to make it fit: Adderloy, the art theft, the crazy orgy in Topeka. She assumed that N. and Adderloy went way back. This made things easier, the idea that they'd worked together at least since the theft of the Arp sculptures. That came first, then Topeka and finally Central Park. Among all the marionettes, N. was the lead puppet, the common link. Of course, you wanted to believe that. Anything would do.

But what about reality then? The reality was Adderloy. Bill Adderloy made money off Baptists and Methodists, who wanted to Christianize and poke in all the world's abscesses—and with that money he bought and stole art. For fuck's sake. Had . . . had Grip then worked for Adderloy? The thought made a steel band tighten around his heart. It was chance, had to be chance. He twisted and turned every circumstance. So much had been going on in his head as he stood in that workshop in Brooklyn, when he looked over the plans, rewrote them. Among the maps of the robbers, the prospective art thieves. The same went for the hit in Central Park. Who cared about the unknown client? Grip had just made sure that nothing linked him to the one ultimately behind it all. At both jobs, Ben had been the only link. That's how it was. Conspiracy was an impossibility, a twisted tale. Grip didn't doubt it for a moment.

Chance, he had to find a way to accept it. Shauna had even said so herself. Adderloy had sought out the forbidden long before the tsunami. And Grip had been sucked right in. But it was chance, and now he had to free himself from it. For one night, he could keep it at bay, as long as there was air under the wings. The robbery in Topeka, and N. in his cell. It was like he was held by a thin, thin wire that could pull him back to Garcia any time. And there was another wire in his chest, reeling him toward the American continent at five hundred miles per hour. Toward Central Park and Romeo Lupone.

The hearing transcript disappeared into the envelope. A crew cut in a suit who'd just been to the bathroom passed by. Their eyes met, and Grip felt it, the thin wire pulling him back to Garcia. Shauna Friedman, she wouldn't simply release him outright. He knew that, he did, but now he thought it through: even if she didn't have people on the airplane, she'd no doubt have him followed as soon as he set foot in the States.

Shauna Friedman's intimacy, the drinks, the day at the beach. Beauty always weakens you, inevitably, no matter what your orientation. If there's ever a thought of caressing what her kind radiates, if only to touch the soap bubble and see if it lasts, then other things fall away. Then you let down your guard. You start to underestimate, and you guess wrong. Grip knew all about that. Everything. And yet. He was a primitive animal, his responses all too ingrained.

The Pacific, all black. Still a few hours left.

Shauna Friedman had shown the passport to Lupone. Grip's

passport, Grip's picture. Grip had noted the date of the hearing: April 21. It was just over three weeks ago, or exactly three days before Grip was called by the Boss in Stockholm and handed his tickets. Lupone had hesitated, and Shauna had decided to put Grip and N. in the same room. Which was which? Lupone was still uncertain, and three weeks later, still no decision had been made. Suddenly, Grip was the only one left.

And now what?

Now Shauna Friedman wasn't just trying to keep an eye on him. The envelope, the copy of the hearing with Lupone—it was a call to action.

# CHAPTER 36

N SAN DIEGO, GRIP WAS picked up by a bleary-eyed driver, after his plane landed in the dawn mist on North Island.

"Welcome, Ernest Grip!" The mistake was repeated at the hotel reception in Coronado. Shauna's stack of prepaid reservations was getting used up, one by one. Grip's next flight wouldn't leave until after lunch, so he went up to the room and slept for an hour, then took a walk.

Getting onto the Internet was easy enough. At a café with huge windows, he paid a few extra dollars to log on to the flat-screen monitor at a bar overlooking the sea. Two short e-mails. First to the Boss, saying he'd be on his way home soon. No dates, just that. For a while, he considered how to word the second one. Drank his coffee, looked out over the sea, and decided to be blunt.

He wrote: "What about Adderloy?"

He left it that way, and looked out to sea again. Sunny, no wind, but the breaking waves roared even inside the café. A few surfers, mostly lounging around on their boards. They lay there for a while, swaying, like lethargic seals. But when a big wave rolled in, like a flock of birds on a sudden whim, they all began to paddle—and then rose to a crouch. They shot out fast, the white surf breaking over them from the towering wave behind. It lasted only a few seconds, then nearly all of them fell headfirst. Only one managed the turns at the top of the crest and back. As the foam from the dying wave formed a white mat around him, he threw a lazy glance over his shoulder and dove in.

When the surfer's head rose to the surface, Grip looked down at the computer again, read: "What about Adderloy?" He clicked send.

The e-mail went out to Vladislav.


At the hotel, Grip began to repack his bags; he would only take a carry-on. All the dirty laundry he'd amassed now filled the large suitcase, along with one of his two suits—it couldn't be helped. He took the elevator down and walked out the back of the building. Near Deliveries, he found a Dumpster and hoisted his bag over with a crash into the garbage. Then he went back to his room, showered and changed.

A new car with a driver showed up at the appointed time. The dry concrete whined under the tires, and they shot like a plane at takeoff over Coronado Bay Bridge, with views of the aircraft carriers in the harbor and the bay in all its glory. It took a full hour, crossing the city, to get to San Diego International.

"Only one carry-on." The woman with glittering gold nails and raven hair nodded. "Through to New York via Atlanta, checked into business class with window seats on both routes."

Grip took the two boarding cards from her hand.

In business, the flight attendant was obviously gay, had a nice tan, and served pepper steak. Grip stopped him and mentioned extra wine. He also had his second radar on—going back and forth to the bathroom, he instinctively looked for eyes keeping track of him for Shauna. But he found no obvious feds. Maybe they'd just lie low, be content to watch him once he checked into the hotel in New York? Maybe not.

Then his thoughts slipped away to other things. *What about Adderloy?* And so Grip went back there, thought about Vladislav. Examined his own mental picture of him. The long, swept-back hair, the big outlandish glasses. The bus that was drowned in the tsunami, the guard on the floor of the bank in Topeka, everything that N. described. How he always got away. Even that stake in West Virginia—Vladislav would get away with it. Napoleon always stayed close to his generals who'd survived the most battles. Some are born with that kind of luck. Or that kind of instinct.

Grip chewed ice from his empty cup and looked at the flight attendant. He was reminded of nights and clubs a long time ago. Of something unrestrained and raw.

He stopped for a moment at the monitors when he got off the flight in Atlanta. Barely a half-hour layover, people streaming past him from every direction. On his way to the new gate, Grip went to an ATM and maxed out the card, putting the bankroll in his inside pocket. Among the seats where they waited for the New York flight were faces that had become vaguely familiar since the pepper steak. Grip found a spot and sat down; at the counter, someone got agitated over a booking error. The general atmosphere was impatient, newspapers and bags rustling. Then the flight was announced, and people immediately lined up.

Boarding cards got fed into the machine for Delta Airlines' evening flight to New York, and people walked onboard. With maybe five to go before Grip, he leaned forward to a flight agent behind the counter with a phone to her ear. "Restrooms?" he asked.

She pointed lazily.

He broke from the line.

In the reflection of a kiosk window, he saw that no one was following him. He turned the corner, no hurry, and then another corner.

As he went by, the boarding pass disappeared into the bag of a cleaning cart, a pair of glass doors slid apart with a whisper, and he felt evening air. The taxi driver hadn't even gotten out of the car before Grip sat down in the back.

"Yes?" said the driver, as he accelerated onto the highway ramp and still didn't know where they were going.

"You choose. The best place to buy a cheap used car."


At Ed's Motorcar Gallery, they probably hadn't expected any more customers that day. An office hut under a canopy of silver streamers, hundreds of cars in rows, with prices painted in rainbow colors across the windshields. Grip paid for the taxi while a single salesman, sitting on a hood, cautiously stood up and looked him over.

But then it was done in five minutes, even a quick wash for the sake of it. A black Ford Taurus with anti-rust paint across the rear bumper. Grip stood in the office holding an instant coffee and looking at a shelf of motocross trophies while the salesman feverishly rooted for the documents that required signatures. The quick handshake had stressed him out. He tried to tell stories about the trophies, but descended into profanity when he kept looking in the wrong folders. Finally they got a couple of signatures down, a cash payment, and the seller turned out the light behind him before he went out to rub off the price on the windshield with a rag.

And Grip drove off.

The gauge was on empty, so he tanked up on the next block

before heading back out to the highway. Northward, he'd gone through the first tank by midnight, left Georgia behind for South Carolina—and by then his eyelids were closing too often. He checked into a motel, threw his little bag into the room, turned on the air conditioner, went back down to the night clerk, and asked for the Internet. The man showed him to a computer in the office behind the desk.

"No kiddie porn now," said the clerk, and went out again.

Grip was tired, his mind a blank. He rubbed his eyes for a while and tried to remember the temporary account password.

Then he logged in. Vladislav had replied.

"I found Adderloy down in Houston. It took me three years, but I found him."

Vladislav had found Adderloy. Grip thought about Maureen Whipple in West Virginia, about the stake. What did he mean by *found*?

"Is he alive?" he wrote, and sent. He wasn't sure which answer he actually wanted. Couldn't feel the different weights on the scales, blamed it on being too tired. Adderloy, Vladislav, Central Park, Shauna, Ben. Vladislav wanted revenge on Adderloy—that part had to play a role, no?

Then his in-box blinked. A new message.

"He's still alive" was Vladislav's reply. Reading him so directly felt like having a séance with a ghost.

"Be careful," wrote Grip. Mostly just to hold on to Vladislav, a quick answer to show that he too was sitting there.

"Why?" came next.

Why? Grip ate sugar cubes out of a bowl on the desk. Why? Wasn't that the ten-thousand-dollar question? Why? Because! Because if Vladislav got caught, so much else would go down with him. Can't get busted now. Not a single one of them.

"There are more people looking, FBI looking," Grip typed in.

He got the answer right away: "Do you work for them?"

Grip sensed it, how the ghost was about to fade away. No bluffing now; he had to hold on to Vladislav.

"Among other things," he replied.

Grip remained seated, one, two, he looked at the clock, five minutes.

Took the last sugar cube, peeled off the paper, and sucked on it until it fell apart in his mouth.

"Excellent," said the e-mail, when Vladislav had decided. Then a second followed: "If you want to earn gold stars from the feds, get in touch again in exactly one day."


Grip slept, got back into the car before the sun rose. After a couple of hours, he stopped for breakfast—eggs, sausage, and bacon—at a truck stop outside Greensboro, North Carolina, then relied on doughnuts and burgers all the way up to New York. He could have gotten there a day earlier, on the flight from Atlanta. But now no one knew where he was. No one. It was late, he had an hour to go, yet the calm decisiveness had begun to spread inside him. He passed the clock tower in Brooklyn, and at that exact moment felt at once totally anonymous and completely at home. He checked into a hotel, where he could see a piece of the East River from his room, as a reminder. Only a corner of Manhattan, but still: there on the other side of the water, Ben probably held court with a small circle at a bar—stubbly, smiling.

When Grip logged in, his in-box was empty.

"I'm here," he wrote and sent. Waited.

"That makes two of us," came soon.

"Well—the gold stars?" wrote Grip.

"Tell the feds to go see what's at the bottom of Adderloy's freezer."

Grip read the sentence twice, and thought of a few stuffed plastic bags. A "?" was all he wrote.

"It's in the basement." There was an address that apparently belonged to Adderloy.

"?" he wrote again.

"It's not Adderloy lying in there, but let them find out. It's enough."

"They'll be looking for you."

"Everyone is looking for me. That's just part of life now."

Nothing more was said.

Adderloy's freezer—that and a couple of days in New York before Grip had to show a sign of life. A balance of terror with Shauna. A quid pro quo. He'd have to stay steady along the slackline, the whole way.

The next day he bought a prepaid phone card and started calling: got to the haulers, checked addresses, moving in a slow spiral toward his goal. He was an old investigator at heart—locating people, that he could do. Crisscrossing Brooklyn in the black Taurus: offering someone a cigarette with a flick of his wrist, having pastrami with mustard for lunch with the drivers at Delvecchio's Deli, doing a scratch card with a bored cashier in a convenience store. Asking little questions, sometimes getting little responses back. Finding him wasn't particularly difficult, Romeo Lupone. Even the guy who turned out to be his lawyer had spilled over the phone, said something about a judge allowing him to go free on bail until further notice. He needed to quickly master his habits. Grip predicted there would be a bar. Lupone was the type—a stool at a counter that no bastard sat on if he was nearby.

It took Grip those two nights to find the hangout. At last he saw Lupone leave a neighborhood bar; Grip already knew where the apartment was, so he didn't follow. Instead he went in. It smelled of sweat. A topless dancer with a worn-out body was gyrating in a corner without an audience, otherwise mostly leather jackets, slicked-back hair, and silicone bustlines.

"Romeo?"

The bartender said he'd just left. A shabby-looking guy with a girl on his knee nodded in agreement. The seat next to him, swung out, empty. Good enough. Lupone would be back, free on bail with a probation violation hanging over his head—the snitch would claim his territory to the bitter end. It was only a question of tomorrow night, or at most, the night after.

The next day Grip went into a hardware store and bought some screwdrivers for show, and a sharp awl. On Kent Avenue, there was an Army Surplus with uniform overcoats and Marine Corps T-shirts from floor to ceiling. Above the rows of hangers hung naked mannequins wearing only gas masks. A hand-written sign at the counter said RAPE SPRAY. Grip fingered one of the containers.

"My wife wants something stronger than pepper spray," he said, and put the container back.

The bearded clerk looked incredulously at him. Finally decided with a smack of his tongue, and bent down to the shelves behind the counter.

"Two," added Grip, laying bills on the counter.

"Be careful," murmured the clerk and gave him a brown paper bag. No change, no receipt.

Grip ran back toward Williamsburg, stopped at a FedEx office, wrote a note by hand, and stuffed it into a large envelope made of stiff cardboard. Got help with the address, paid. Then he called FBI's general tips line from his car.

Once he reached a live voice, he said, "An item will be delivered to your office on Kew Gardens Road during the afternoon. It's addressed to Shauna Friedman—make sure that she gets it."

"I can't guarantee—"

"I know you can."

"There are thousands here who—"

"She's a special agent with you, with her own secretary and a pretty office here in New York."

"Who may I say it's from?"

"Forget it—the item is for Shauna Friedman. And if she's not there, someone has to call and read her the message."

"We'll see."

"I'm sure we will. And tell her that starting tomorrow night, I'm staying"—Grip pulled the note from his pocket and read—"at the Best Western in Newark." It was the hotel she had originally booked him into.

"But?"

"She knows who I am."

# CHAPTER 37

THE CLOCK SAID NOT EVEN two in the afternoon. Grip was back in place, with his views of the East River. He was starting to get restless. Not nervous, not afraid, just restless. It was the night that mattered. In a few hours he would become his opposite, the type a bodyguard would never manage to spot when he looked over oceans of people. Not the man with the stare, not the obvious threat, but the fish in the water. The invisible, the deadly. The facades and the river outside the window looked mostly like dead scenery, nothing worth a gaze. Grip squeezed one of his own shoulders. Reassuring—he could strike as hard as anybody. But it wasn't about that.

He lay in only his underwear on the narrow bed, felt himself above the arms and then down across the stomach. Slid his hand into his underwear; his sex was cool and unperturbed. He got up, got dressed. When he pulled on the heavy jacket, he was standing by the bed again. A second of hesitation, but then he had full control of himself. It wasn't his life that mattered. It was Ben's.

So he left.

He drove out and parked near the power plant by the Brooklyn Bridge. He still had a few hours to kill, so he walked to the subway station and rode into Manhattan. The tools, the paper bag with the spray, were all that he left in the car. This was a detour, his ritual. One way to become a fish in the water, his way of harnessing his own restlessness. No fuck-ups, not like in Central Park—he depended on no one.

Given the situation, it was obvious he'd head to the Whitney Museum. A late weekday afternoon, not many people there. Not deserted—that wouldn't have been good—but sparse. He had the rooms to himself a few minutes at a time.

Grip bought his ticket, glanced into the café at the inside table where he and Ben usually sat, and took the stairs, not the elevator.

He passed a couple on the way out of the room, and then he was alone.

There was no painting calmer than this one. Hopper's *Seven A.M.*, so still. Another hung next to it, *South Carolina Morning*: a woman in a red dress and hat, waiting. Morning light, that's what the two had in common. But Grip's favorite painting didn't contain a single figure. *Seven A.M.* showed distant trees on one side, and on the other a storefront that time had passed by. So still. Some kind of story could probably be told, but one refrained from asking questions. The light and shadows convinced the viewer to exist in the moment. Hopper had drawn sharp lines where the sun cast shadows on the white walls inside the window, while outside the ground gleamed like warm sand. The hands of an old wall clock suggested that the time was seven. Someone who should have been there was somewhere else. Yet nothing was missing. With the morning light streaming down on the ground and in through the window, time might as well have stopped—so the clock always stood at seven.

Just like that, a place where nothing ever changes.


Romeo Lupone didn't even flinch but turned slowly around. Grip had kept watch outside the bar and then hurried ahead when

Lupone came out. At a corner piled with garbage bags next to a basement stairway, Grip had stepped forward. The sudden sound of someone nearby made Lupone turn around. But before they made eye contact, he was hit, completely unprepared by the tear gas, his scream half smothered by the surprise and stinging pain. Grip threw himself forward with a swift knee straight to the thigh, making Lupone crumple down among the garbage bags. Then Grip straddled him, with one hand clutching his jacket and the tear gas spray ready in the other. Held still, while Lupone yelped and cramped. Blinded, he'd emptied his lungs, and once he was gasping for air like a drowning man, Grip emptied the spray bottle into the gap. He inhaled everything.

Mucus like from a dog foaming at the mouth, vomit in convulsed waves, but no screams to attract attention from the neighborhood. When the second spray can was empty, all that could be heard were little peeps. Grip was grimacing, coughing, his own eyes filling with tears. He wrenched Lupone up to kneeling and dragged him along like a package, bouncing him down the basement stairs beside them. At the bottom was a cramped concrete chamber they barely fit inside. Empty plastic containers and cans bounced up against the walls as they made impact, like two wrestlers. Lupone's legs kicked feebly around him. Grip blew snot from his nose and wiped his eyes on his sleeves to see in the murky cellar hole.

Then he pulled out the awl.

# CHAPTER 38

J UST AS HE'D SAID HE would, Grip checked into the hotel in Newark. After he'd left the Atlanta airport, there were four days that didn't exist. The clothes were new, the car was sold. He was walking without any luggage through the evening darkness.

"How long?" asked the desk clerk.

Grip shrugged. "One night, unless you charge by the hour."

The receptionist laughed uncertainly. Grip let him put an advance on his credit card before he went up to the room, turned on a pay TV channel, and sat down to wait.

The final scene of the movie was approaching when the phone rang. It was from reception. There was a message for him to pick up.

An envelope.

A note with an address and a time. He could make it, of course he could. Everything always so orderly. Grip went out and got into the first taxi. He'd put in his appearance—round trip to Newark—and now headed back toward the Holland Tunnel and the Manhattan skyline.

T he address was in Gramercy, the entrance behind a row of well-tended trees. Perhaps he'd passed through the neighborhood before, but in any case Grip had never noticed the discreet location.

The buildings mostly older. No sign that suggested anything to him, either on the street or inside the gate.

"Mr. Grip, welcome," said a man in a black-and-white-striped tie behind an old-fashioned wooden desk. There were moisture cracks in the walls, and the air smelled of chlorine.

Ten minutes later Grip stood in a borrowed bathing suit, tried to regulate a shower with separate handles for hot and cold.

"Locker forty-seven, then head directly into the baths," the man had said.

Tile, slightly yellowed, with black-and-white mosaics: a diffuse pattern of shields and emblems on the floors, ancient gods posing naked along the walls. In the locker room, all the furnishings were dark wood, with polished edges, solid. The few other men he saw inside moved remarkably slowly; someone carried a racket. He got the feeling that the place was about to empty. It was after all quite late. Grip showered off and continued inside.

"Well, here you are," she said quietly.

Shauna Friedman sat with her arms outstretched along the edge of a quiet Jacuzzi. She was alone. The air bubbles made silver beads around her.

"Salt water," she said, "and it shouldn't bubble more than this, they say."

They were above the pool and inside a row of columns in the hall's covered arcade. The light was pleasantly dusky. The pool's glimmers danced across the walls and reflected on the ceiling, while the Jacuzzi's blue-gray water seemed almost bottomless.

"Are you a member of this . . . temple?" said Grip.

"No, but I know someone who is."

"How convenient." He looked around. "Through your politician husband, one may assume?"

"Maybe."

Grip nodded.

"As you see, not many people take a dip at this time of evening," she explained.

"Members with both money and packed schedules?"

"They come here in the morning or right after work. This late, they're at the opera or eating dinner with their auditors."

In the pool below, only two heads glided back and forth. Of their conversation, no more was heard than an echoing murmur.

"Come in, it's just warm enough."

"Salt water?"

"Like the sea."

Grip put down his towel.

The Jacuzzi's pleasant warmth had reached up to his knees when Shauna said, "There was an empty seat on the flight from Atlanta—you disappeared."

"Yes," said Grip, "a whim," and sank completely.

"Whim?"

"I realized that I was in the American South. The Civil War, you know, Gettysburg, it wasn't far. I've always wanted to see . . . the battlefield."

She smiled a prosecutor's smile. "Gettysburg?"

"Yes."

"How did you get there?"

"I bought a car."

"There you go. General Lee and Pickett's Charge—why don't you tell me a little about them?"

Grip swept his hand through the water, ignoring the question.

"You can never prove it," she continued.

"I don't feel that anything needs proving." Grip looked at her again. Soaking with Shauna Friedman, trust hanging in the balance.

"The Civil War . . ."

"We can let it go," he interjected.

"I just wanted to say about the Civil War," she continued, "that some would argue America is returning to it. The same kind of destructive atmosphere, the same kind of—"

"Unholy alliances?"

"Adderloy's freezer—someone deserves thanks for the tip."

"So you went after him."

"Someone sent an envelope with the address." She nodded approvingly. "In the end, we found his fucking hole—a big house, I swear to you, all in old-plantation style. It was a raid with God's good grace."

Grip sat silent. Light off the water and murmurs from the pool washed over them.

"You have no idea what we found, do you?" said Shauna then.

"No. What? Adderloy himself?"

"Adderloy." She snorted. "Adderloy, yes, we got him. Doesn't say a word, but we have him. We found a lot of stolen art, those sculptures by Jean Arp, among others. Sooner or later we would have nailed him for it, but how long would he have stayed in? A battery of lawyers, and he'd have escaped with a few years, if that. But then . . ." Shauna looked in wonder at Grip. "No, you really have no idea. The freezer. What does someone like Adderloy have in his freezer? Something that took him all the way back to Topeka. You remember, the bank, N. said they'd poured the blood all over the floor of the bank. Turnbull's blood. They stole two bags in the hospital, but used only one at the bank. The second bag, there it lay, fat and red as frozen cranberry sauce, right in Adderloy's home freezer. Couldn't be better—the hand completely buried in the cookie jar. Fuck knows why he saved it. *Complicity*, half a dozen prosecutions attached to that—bank robbery, murder, kidnapping, you name it. Anything less than life would surprise me. His lawyers argue that there had very recently been a burglary at his house, that anyone could have gone inside to plant the blood. . . . But unfortunately the burglary was never reported to the police. Do you know anything about a burglary?"

Grip shook his head almost imperceptibly.

"No, exactly."

He sat with his eyes closed, thinking of Vladislav. So Vladislav had taken the second bag they'd left with the Lebanese. Grip sank farther, so that the hot water came up over his chin.

"Turnbull?" he said then. "Is he still awaiting death?"

"Not for long." Shauna raised her hand so that the water flowed between her fingers. "The Kansas governor has been informed. A little paperwork, and Charles-Ray Turnbull will get pardoned within a few days. His wife has already divorced him, but still."

"And Reza," said Grip, closing his eyes again.

"Would this change his situation?"

"He's innocent."

"According to whose goddamn yardstick?"

"Mine."

"He was in the bank," said Shauna.

"He was just a pawn, you know that."

"Reza Khan sits where he sits. The CIA's prestige, the train of prosecutors, the police chief in Topeka, yes, the whole fucking state of Kansas, demands it—of course he must die. Especially once that bizarre connection is gone—terrorists and Baptists. Everyone down there was deceived, and Charles-Ray was such an easy person to hate. Now he's free, but the debt is there, the air must be cleared. And they only have Reza left."

"Not even a new investigation?"

"No."

Grip didn't move, and Shauna grabbed his arm under the water so he looked up again.

"It's just you and me here now, remember that," she said. "Those who haven't been deceived in this are few and far between."

"And you let them take Reza, because you have Adderloy?"

"Someone poked out Romeo Lupone's eyes last night," she replied.

Grip sat silent for a second. "You're changing the subject."

"Am I? Adderloy—art—Lupone. Lupone lay screaming bloody murder at the Wyckoff Heights emergency room. The nurses complained that they couldn't even stand to look in his direction. A well-built man was seen standing and washing himself off down the river about the same time. While you were . . . in Gettysburg."

"Lupone, remind me?"

"Don't be ridiculous."

"The driver."

"Yes, the driver who said there'd been a Swede involved in Central Park. Why don't you ask me how he's doing?"

"Who?"

"Lupone."

"How is the poor fellow?"

"Thank you, he's going to make it. But my agents wanted to show him pictures of N. again, and now his eyesight . . .

"Listen," she said then, "we found more interesting things at Adderloy's." She paused, watching an air bubble rise up through the water. "Can you believe that in the middle of one room was one of Christo's orange arches? Arch, gate, whatever you call them. Among all the oils and sculptures, it looked like something from outer space. In the middle of the room, like a religious object. You know, all the gates were supposed to be destroyed, every single one. And none had been reported missing. But I checked the documentation, the locations of all the gates, and where the murder took place . . ."

"I think I understand where you're heading."

"A gate disappeared unnoticed. And in that very place—nobody thought it was anything more than an ordinary robbery. The poor woman must have surprised them."

"The fact that people want to steal art, I can understand that," said Grip. "They want to possess what's beautiful, and for someone like Adderloy, there's the added challenge of obtaining it. But then we have Topeka."

"You mean that something about Topeka would change because we have Adderloy?"

"That's reasonable."

"Well, in Topeka they like thinking about terrorists, and they even got to catch one. Jihadists in Kansas. Turnbull now being free just confirms that image. The police chief in Topeka thinks he has managed to uncover a diabolical conspiracy against good Christians."

"But Adderloy is American and white," said Grip.

"Adderloy doesn't say a word."

"He had a bag of blood in his freezer, it connects him to Reza."

"Yes, but nobody is particularly happy to hear that. Adderloy had friends in high places in Washington before. Now they're deadly to him. Nobody is going to let themselves get caught up in Adderloy's case, neither the Southern Baptists nor the shadowy figures in Washington. And right now, Adderloy himself isn't saying a word. My guess"—Shauna nodded a few times—"my guess is that someone shot a little message under the door of Adderloy's cell. He understands that silence is his ticket to a life sentence—if he divulges even the slightest bit of information, he'll get a last meal, a priest, and a needle in the arm. That's the hand he's been dealt, because we've got him. Reza has identified him—that was the only thing the man ever uttered of legal value. The evidence would be pretty thin if the bag with Turnbull's blood hadn't been saved."

"Have you seen Reza lately?"

"Just a few days ago."

"How's he doing?"

Shauna smiled. "A conscience white as snow, and half his brain somewhere else. He's trying to gain time, says he remembers more and more. He talks a lot about the big birds flying in a line. Pelicans. More and more details are coming out about the others who were with him. Agency psychologists say they need at least a few months to build a case that would hold up. But that time doesn't exist."

"Is it soon?"

"They give him the injection in three weeks."

"America is wonderful."

"Better than that," she countered. "America is for real."

"Is that the answer to all questions?"

"As much or as little as Gettysburg is the answer to mine."

"Lupone . . ."

"Lupone," interrupted Shauna, "is the one who ensures that Adderloy gets locked up for eternity. If I can't manage to tie him to Topeka, I'll compensate by nailing him for art theft and murder in Central Park, and various other mysterious dealings."

"I would just say that—"

"Even without his eyes, Lupone has given me Adderloy?"

"Pretty much. As you already know, on the flight from Garcia, I read through the interview where Lupone implicated Adderloy."

Shauna looked unashamedly at Grip. "Look, I have every reason to question who you are. The passport, N., and all trips we both know you have made to New York."

"Unfortunate circumstances, accidental coincidences."

"The bag of blood in Adderloy's freezer."

"Not a coincidence." Grip sat silent for a moment and then added, "And you would never have gotten Adderloy if it weren't for me."

"And you want something in exchange. Your lost innocence, perhaps? For Lupone's eyes?"

"I was looking at rusty bayonets in Gettysburg."

"For a cardiac arrest, in a cell on Diego Garcia?"

"A word of advice. Don't fire all your ammunition before the war is over."

Shauna stopped with a smile. "Advice, for me?"

"Yes. You fire and fire away, and yet you need me."

"What is this, a guessing game?"

"It was you who wanted me to come here, right?"

"So why are we here?"

"We're sitting in this Jacuzzi because you want to make sure that I'm caught on all your hooks. N., Lupone, and whatever else. Imaginary bargaining within silent walls."

"Watch it," said Shauna, "investigations are ongoing."

"And out of pure gratitude, I should maintain polite silence."

Down in the swimming pool, no more voices were heard.

Grip moved his hand through the water. "I'm deadly curious about one thing. What is it you don't want me to see?"

A door slammed. The light and the silence of the swimming pool gave a sense of the surrounding night.

"You Swedes can still afford to play dollhouse with the world."

"Said by a harmless woman from the Justice Department. For most in the FBI, no more than two gorgeous tits and tail."

"Most people can at least handle not saying it out loud."

"In a bathing suit, you can seduce a Swede."

"Around here, you get fired for saying stuff like that in the service."

"I think we've both qualified ourselves for suspension of service, but on completely different grounds."

"That's enough." Shauna stood up. "And so . . . shall we go?"

"Surely there's someone we haven't touched on?"

Shauna turned around with the water at her waist. "Must you really?"

"Mary," said Grip firmly. "She's missing."

"And Vladislav, by all means." Shauna ran her hand across the rippled surface of the water. She didn't seem surprised by the turnaround.

"Mary first."

"Yes, it's simple." Shauna blew in her hand and then opened it, as if something had gone up in smoke. "Mary got away. Mary as we know, through, yes, what do we know of her? We know her only through N."

"But she was . . ." Grip closed his eyes thoughtfully.

"She was not on the surveillance tapes from the bank," Shauna filled in.

"She waited in the car."

"Exactly—according to N. And when they were in Toronto, before they crossed the border. They gathered at a bar, but according to the receipt, they paid for only four drinks."

"Mary drank water," recalled Grip.

"N. said that, yes. He wasn't stupid. He wove it together well, he had explanations for everything we could verify."

"That she'll be erased, turned to smoke? Is that what I should believe?"

"N.'s history is essentially correct. But Mary, she was entirely his own invention."

"How many people have been working on this? Checked up? The police in Kansas, FBI?"

"Hundreds of police officers and agents. Take the factory hall. N. said she'd lived there for several years, right? But the rent was only paid a couple of weeks before they got there. The transactions can be traced to Adderloy. And at the hospital, where they took the blood." Shauna shook her head. "No one that fits her description has ever worked there. It's a dead end. They stole the blood from there, but Mary, N.'s Mary, never set foot in the place. That Turnbull was a blood donor, anyone could find that out."

Grip looked long at her. "So all of it was but the mirage of a mangled soul?"

Shauna gestured that it was obvious. "Everything, the whole story works without her. Who knows, maybe on Weejay's, while at the beach, there was someone, Jane Smith. But not since. When they came into the States, they were only four. Four men."

Grip sank completely beneath the surface, blew air out for a few short bursts, and rose again. When the water had run off his face, he said, "But you forget one thing—the pelicans. You've heard of them—Reza spoke clearly about them pretty recently, and so did N. They flew in a line, until someone started shooting at them."

"I know."

"And it's still just you and me here in the bathhouse. The walls here are old and deaf."

"Do you mind if we go down and swim in the pool?" suggested Shauna.

"Not at all."

They walked with their towels around them through the covered arcade. The stairs to the pool were at the far end. All the little echoes off the tiles were their own.

First, only quiet, wet steps, then Shauna said, "Do you remember Chung Ling Soo?"

"Mm, your father's posters."

"Exactly, the posters. Actually Soo was an American named Robinson. As a magician, he never had much success until he put on a pigtail, made himself up to look Chinese, and went off to Europe as Chung Ling Soo. From that moment on, he became Chinese, both on and off the stage. Never spoke with journalists except through an interpreter, and during performances, he said not a word, just waddled around like an old man. Enthralled, amazed, fooled everyone. The trick was greater than anything he did on stage. He lived it."

They walked down the stairs.

"Some people get away with everything," Shauna said, picking up a lost thread again. "Vladislav is wanted in all fifty states, and the rest of the civilized world. Dozens of my agents, they say they're on his tracks. That it's only a matter of time. Vladislav can't even order food in a restaurant without people noticing him."

Shauna stopped at the landing and turned around. "No, don't say anything," she said, and put a finger to Grip's lips. "Nothing." She eased her finger a quarter inch, but still kept it as an exclamation point in front of him. "I don't believe them—they won't get him. Vladislav is a human exception. He's the one who enters the elevator at the last second, turns the corner, misses the train that gets stopped by the police. It's unintentional, but a true talent. A kind of law of nature he became aware of only when he escaped from that bus, after the tsunami. He went his own way at the right moment after Topeka, and now he supports himself on contracts. Lives as a hit man. Fearless, unstoppable, starting to get a certain reputation. Four months ago in New Orleans, five bodies were found in a luxury suite at the top of the Crowne Plaza Hotel. A showdown, and someone down there seems to have hired our Vladislav. Apparently he checked into the same hotel days before, was a nuisance when he ordered food, talked back, everyone who worked in the restaurant recognized him. And then he disappeared from the picture, as only he can."

She touched Grips lips again, stroking them. "If I ever, if I could in the slightest way, say to myself that I was in contact with someone like Vladislav, then I would be very careful about him. You know, once you've lost your virginity . . . having the power to summon a demon, imagine being able to do that. Sooner or later it will come in handy."

The pool water was so still that it felt illicit to go in. Shauna shot out first from the ladder. Grip dove in silently behind her. On the far end stood a huge statue, a bare-breasted woman with a vacant marble gaze. In the stillness, with the pillars surrounding the arcades and the glow that filtered up from a few lights on the bottom of the pool, it was like swimming in a temple, or an abandoned banker's palace by night.

They glided side by side.

"The pelicans . . . ," said Shauna. She swam first, didn't look back.

"Vladislav," Grip filled in, "he asked me who said they should shoot the pelicans. You know what I replied. So if you found a bag of blood in Adderloy's freezer, then once again Mary exists. She was much more than just N.'s imaginary creation." That Shauna swam on without a word was answer enough. "All your officers, agents—"

"They know nothing about N. His story is the concern of only a few people in Washington—Stackhouse and his group. And that circle has completely dismissed the idea of Mary. All the others, my officers and agents, as you call them, they haven't even asked the question. For them there is no fifth person, no woman."

"Then here's to Vladislav staying at large, and never getting interrogated."

"Let's hope so." Shauna pulled through her strokes, brushed against the tile, and turned under the statue. She glanced in Grip's direction and stopped in the middle of the pool.

"You want me to try some guesses?" said Grip.

"No, that won't be necessary. Mary was mine, she's mine. She was there, and now she has been sent underground. She made herself unusable. It was Adderloy she was supposed to get—and now that has finally been accomplished, but she made herself a criminal in the process. Meant well, but pushed too far. Fortunately, I was her contact, the only one."

"Everyone has a boss. What about your superiors?"

"They knew I had a source, but not who, not where. Adderloy is a sensitive subject. You remember I sent two agents after him, who then lay bloated in a morgue in Bangkok. It was impossible to move forward after that, to work with foreign police, to build trust among my own agents. Everything went at a snail's pace. We had no chance of success, only kept up appearances. Mary was the opportunity that emerged. She didn't belong to the agency, but she had what was necessary to do this. She moved freely like no other. So we put up lots of smokescreens for her sake, and so no one would know we'd gotten someone so close to Adderloy. My bosses got only short reports that didn't disclose the source."

"No small stuff she got mixed up in—people killed at the bank, and then Turnbull's death sentence."

"Funny how the military always gets away with these things— bombs a wedding party, excuses itself, and that's the end of it. Why can't the same go for someone sent out by law enforcement? Mary was far behind the front lines, and alone. For obvious reasons, she and I couldn't often be in touch. She always had to consider whether to quit or keep going, constantly weigh profit against loss. They shot Turnbull in the leg, sure, she was in on it. But they would have shot him even if she hadn't been there. And as for the bank victims, Mary couldn't possibly have predicted how diabolical Adderloy actually was."

"Insanity."

"Don't pretend you're upset. You don't exactly play dollhouse with the world yourself. Yes, a terrible mistake. But she thought . . . and I thought . . . there was more going on. That it would be possible to get more than just Adderloy. This thing with his rebel movements and the question of who was funding them. I imagined there was more, told myself there was, let everything go on too long. Thought he'd lead us to bigger and uglier fish. But there was no one. They'd turned their backs on him. That's precisely why Adderloy was in Topeka. I understand that now, but now it's too late."

Grip continued to swim in slow circles around Shauna while she floated on her back.

"Mary found Adderloy in Asia," she continued, "when he was

323

looking for someone to rob the bank with, to plunge Turnbull and his Baptists into ruin."

"And then later they snared the other three."

"They chose themselves. Their lives, and especially N.'s life, were a lost cause. He became an easily manipulated victim."

"So she reported to you and slept with N."

"Do you find it strange? She lived under pressure, that's what this stuff does to people. Haven't you ever had your own fantasies?"

"There are limits."

Shauna raised her head slightly and looked at him, then turned on her stomach and took a few strokes again. The light from below turned her shadow into several figures who swam across the walls. "Adderloy had arranged the factory hall," she explained, "everything that was in it, paid the rent. But in order not to reveal how well planned everything was, he convinced Mary to let the others believe that she had done it, and that she knew Turnbull was a blood donor. This gave the impression that the whole thing was a 'lucky' coincidence, and not in fact a small part of a much larger mission that only Adderloy himself knew about. Mary went along with it, as a way to gain his trust."

"But it was he who called the police?"

"Of course. It was Adderloy's plan all along that Reza would take the fall. But Mary didn't know that."

Shauna and Grip were back under the marble woman. He tried to find a foothold at the edge of the pool, but the tile wall was completely smooth. He glided out again to Shauna, who was quietly treading water.

"And Mary," he said, "stayed with Vladislav and N. until it was useless to try to get Adderloy again."

"She tried a little later, at the motel. But Adderloy never appeared, or rather: Vladislav came at her, and then the police came between them again." Shauna glided on her back, looking up at the statue. "But Mary succeeded in one thing. Before Vladislav made them throw their mobile phones in the ditch, she'd sent a text with the car's license plate. The information was called in, but they didn't find the car until it pulled into that motel down in Florida. Not the police, and not the FBI. Everything points to it being Stackhouse's wolf pack that came. I don't know for certain, because Mary got away and went underground. She never saw N. get arrested, couldn't confirm if they actually got him and took him away. So I never knew. And frankly, I didn't care. I was busy getting Mary out of there, sweeping the tracks." Shauna took water in her hand and splashed it over her face. "I swept like hell."

"And the years went by," said Grip.

"Yes, the years went by. But as you know, it was a thing that couldn't be set right again."

"Turnbull?"

"The bungling that left him on death row can't be blamed on anyone else. Mary and I, we should have put a stop to it. However unpleasant he is, he didn't deserve that. Not to die."

"But eventually, with a little help."

"You want me to say thank you?"

Grip ignored that, asked instead, "And where is Mary now?"

"Oh, you can live a lifetime in New York without having people know who you really are. She's doing fine."

"And the FBI agents and Kansas police—"

"They still think that there were only four men who robbed a bank in Topeka. That's how many they have in the videos, and that's how many drinks there were on the receipt."

"There are many stones that cannot be turned, if this is to last."

"Not at all."

"Take the Lebanese," he said. "If anyone questioned the two brothers at the restaurant, they'd talk about her. Maybe other things too."

"The Lebanese," repeated Shauna, "are surely decent people, but running a restaurant with only a student visa. That's illegal. They were deported. Disappeared. I believe you could trace them on a flight to Ankara."

"You do sweep."

"I master the details," Shauna corrected.

"You can't ensure against everything. Pelicans, for example."

"No, you know about them. But you, on the other hand, have your own pelicans: the trip to Gettysburg, and a night long before that went out of control in Central Park, perhaps at the top of Ninety-Sixth Street."

"How was it," said Grip softly. "N. said he was arrested at the motel, but Stackhouse argued that it happened later. And N. said that Mary was there, and you're telling Stackhouse she wasn't." He drew a long, deep breath. "Maybe it suits more than one of us that N. is dead?"

The pool water lay still as a mirror.

"As long as you know where you have each other," added Shauna, "that means everything," and took a first stroke toward the ladder.

# CHAPTER 39

O
H, DO WE HAVE AN apology?" said Ben, taking the bottle Grip held out to him. Champagne, a Bollinger '96. Ben used to point it out in the locked glass cabinet of the neighborhood Polish liquor store often, saying it was absolutely wonderful, and something of an excuse for why his wallet was too thin. "Or are we celebrating?"

Grip was already sitting at the kitchen table in the cramped kitchen. He'd walked all the way from the bathhouse in Gramercy to the apartment in Chelsea. His hair had dried along the way. It was a half hour he'd never be able to describe—how he'd gotten there, what he'd been thinking. It was a leap between worlds. An airlock had closed behind him, and he hadn't looked back over his shoulder, not even once.

It was only when he passed the Pole's shop window with its sun-bleached labels that he'd felt empty-handed. Once inside the store, at first he had no idea, then recognized the bottle. Grip wasn't in the habit of showing up with gifts.

"I know," said Ben with his back to him, "I won't say a word."

"It's been more than three weeks since you heard from me," Grip filled in. His hand moved absently through a stack of magazines and art catalogs on the table.

"Four." Ben set down the champagne. The Pole had dusted it off and bowed when he sold it. "No phone, not even Internet?"

"Sure, there was."

"I'm not the jealous queen. But tell me it was necessary." Ben was standing with his back to Grip, fiddling with something on the kitchen counter. It was after ten. Ben always ate late if he ate at home, said he was too restless early in the evening. At his shoulders, his white shirt still showed traces of having been ironed, but over the hips it hung wrinkled and untucked. He put down his knife and leaned on his hands, waiting.

"I didn't want to risk anything," said Grip finally.

"Risk, it's always——"

"Especially not this time," interrupted Grip, raising his voice.

Ben didn't listen. "If something had happened to me, it would have been impossible to get hold of you." His forearms stuck out of the upturned cuffs; they looked thinner than ever. "It's not enough that you *think* of me."

"I was hardly thinking of you at all, I . . . it doesn't work that way. There was no time for that, but unlike those fucking doctors, at least I have tried to save your life."

Ben turned around, looked uncertainly at Grip, who shook his head. A kind of apology.

"No more art stuff now," said Grip then, "okay?" He tried to smile, but it was strained. "Nothing like that, not even appraisals on the side. Nothing."

Ben stroked his temple. "You look tan."

"Yes."

"You've been traveling, the sorts of tasks you do . . . for Sweden . . . somewhere." He squinted uncomfortably. "Or was it about the jobs you did here, Arp and that other thing?"

"Drop it."

But Ben went on. "My appraisals, they've never hurt anyone."

"Ben, the door. I don't want you leaving the door open." An attempt to change the subject. When Grip got there, the door had been unlocked, he'd simply walked in. It was an old quarrel.

Deaf ears.

"What you helped with, Ernst, those aren't exactly things that people have had to die for."

"Ben . . ."

But Ben just laughed and said, "You haven't had to kill anyone, right?"

The look.

For a moment, the airlock opened that would forever be kept closed, and something appeared in the gap. A ghost. As when a soul leaves a deathbed.

"We exist, Ben—we exist again," said Grip, then looked somewhere to the side. "We don't have to worry."

A consensus. The gap was closed. Maybe a minute passed.

"Vegetable soup, yes, with a few small pieces of meat." It was only Ben, he of anyone, who could shake off death when it hovered in the room. Not his own, but always that of others. He looked at the bottle. "And Bollinger Grande Année '96. How long are you staying?"

"I'm just here overnight."

"That's perfect."

# CHAPTER 40

T HE LONG, LONESOME CORRIDORS OF the security police.
Grip was in Stockholm, inside with the Boss. Not the highest-
ranking one, not his direct superior either, but the old man. His
room had always been smaller than the other managers', but he at
least had a rug and leather chairs. There were standards.

"Okay, so it all boiled down to nothing," said the Boss. "Just a
case of unsolved identity?"

"Yes," said Grip.

"They figure it out?"

"No, he died."

"And it took you almost four weeks?"

"American bureaucracy, their usual incompetence."

"You questioned him?"

"A few times."

"He spoke Swedish?"

Grip didn't answer directly. He leaned back and forth.

"With an accent maybe?" suggested the Boss.

Grip shrugged. The Boss nodded.

Four weeks had disappeared. Not a single paper filing on the
matter, not even an ink dot at the end. All that existed was a hand-
written note on the Boss's desk with Grip's estimates of his own
expenses. No locations, no dates, no receipts, just: "Food," "Lodg-
ing," and the vague item "Other." The Boss had glanced at the

paper and then set it aside. The amounts would be added as tax-free expenses on his next month's pay slip. Nothing about Diego Garcia, nothing about New York, nothing about the security police reimbursing him for two bottles of tear gas and a very sharp awl.

The Boss sat. Grip stood with his hands in his pockets and looked out the window.

"I'd like to have you back," said the Boss, "full-time. I need—"

"I don't want anything to do with Americans for a while."

The Boss laughed, like a cough. "It's true. The world is about the Americans, you run into them."

"Exactly.

"But you like this—the travel, the independence. Being able to disappear. I need people who can do that."

"Forget it."

"Back to the bodyguards, then?"

Grip nodded.

"What a damned dead end." Some squeaky metal part resisted when the Boss leaned back in his chair. "Overtime, earphone, and practicing two-shot series down at the shooting range, year in and year out?"

"It suits me."

"For now?"

Grip said nothing, continued looking out.

The Boss threw himself farther back in his chair. "So where are you packing your suits off to next?"

"One of the girls is going down to the Riviera."

"Babysitting for a princess. And why always the Riviera? What do they do down there?"

"You already know."

"You laugh at royal attendants' bad jokes, order a taxi for them in the evenings, and shove intrusive photographers in the chest."

"It suits me."

"My ass. You hate it, but it's about the vacation time. I get it—you can come and go."

Grip stood silent for a moment. "I can avoid the Americans," he said then.

"Yes, I guess that's true. When do you leave?"

"Tomorrow. The state jet from Bromma."

"Shit, for a princess to get a tan."

"There's also the opening of an exhibition." Grip watched a bird outside the window.

"And then two weeks on water skis."

"Sure."

"Water-skiing, for Christ's sake, Grip."

"I'm just a bodyguard." The bird disappeared. Grip turned around. "As I said"—he made an apologetic gesture with his hand—"I went where they wanted, but the man in the cell died."

"Died, yes," said the Boss, giving up, letting his cheeks collapse, like a dog's.

Grip nodded and disappeared into the hallway.

# CHAPTER 41

E ARLY SUMMER SUN. THE SKY as intensely blue as a gas flame. Grip walked back home, after a detour to Södermalm at the southern end of town. Went to the Stockholm City Library at Medborgarplatsen, where a librarian had helped him track down a newspaper. He'd called a few days before; she was an old acquaintance. Once he was standing there, she said he might as well keep it, so now he carried it with him, the *Kansas City Star*—she'd ordered all the past week's issues, but there was just one day that Grip wanted. He walked up Götgatspuckeln, came out at Slussen for the view of the water, the green copper church spires, the medieval facades. Along Stadsgårdskajen sat the season's first cruise ship. The white giant was anchored some distance out, and harbor boats shuttled back and forth, ferrying the masses to Old Town. Grip paused, then decided to take the same path, following the walkway down the stairs to Kornhamnstorg square. Once the Slussen traffic was behind him, he opened the paper and folded it in half so he could hold it one-handed.

Then walked and read.

Shortly after midnight on Tuesday, Reza Khan was led into the execution chamber at Lansing Correctional Facility. The condemned prisoner initially wore the same absent expression that reporters observed during his trial. It should be noted that

Khan's emotions were very difficult to read, given that his face bore scars from the severe gunshot wound he suffered in connection with his arrest. He always maintained that his head injuries were responsible for his controversial loss of memory.

Khan was transferred three days ago from death row in El Dorado prison to a secluded cell at Lansing. Authorities having failed to locate any family members, in recent days Khan met only with his lawyer. His last meal consisted of fried chicken.

When the curtain between Khan and the witnesses was drawn, Khan was already strapped to the table, with a needle and tubes attached to both inner arms. The table had been raised, and Khan seemed unprepared to see the assembled faces. Warden Richard Hickock read out the judgment, and only then did Khan become more alert. After Hickock read the judgment, Khan replied sarcastically: "It is hardly a surprise to anyone here that I am going to die." The warden, maintaining his composure, asked if Khan had any last words. Khan replied coolly: "What would you like me to do, cry 'Allah akbar'? No, you must find something original."

There followed a few moments of confusion, when the warden's assistants tried to lower the bunk again but had problems with a latch. While they tried to remove the pin, Khan squinted out at the witnesses on their chairs and focused on one face. Someone described him as smiling, others argued that it was more an expression of surprise, when Reza Khan said: "Now I recognize you," whereupon the pin came out, and the table dropped down.

Grip turned onto Västerlånggatan. An outdoor spectacle he usually avoided in summer: kids with ice cream, Japanese guides,

Viking horns, cameras, and dense flocks that were a pickpocket's paradise. He was heading for the corner at Storkyrkobrinken, dodged two American cruise ladies in broad hats whose sneakers inched along, found a new path through the crowd, and looked down at the paper again.

The first syringe lulls the condemned man, the second and third paralyze the lungs and stop the heart. Khan was anesthetized quickly, but before lapsing into unconsciousness, he mumbled something heard as "Fairy" by a few witnesses. This he repeated a few times. Khan was declared dead by the prison physician ten minutes later. No movement or sign of discomfort could be discerned in the process. One of those present claimed to see some twitching in one hand, another described it as "killing a dog." Reza Khan's remains will be cremated within the next few days and spread to the winds in an unknown location.

Outside the prison, the execution was celebrated by Christian groups formerly accused of the acts for which Khan was convicted. With the release of Charles-Ray Turnbull and tonight's execution, it appears that these congregations' reputations have been restored. "Wrath of God, Wrath of God," chanted a group calling itself the Southern Baptist Conference, when the hearse left the prison.

As previously reported by this newspaper, several analysts believe that the arcane acts of Reza Khan and his group indicate that religious war is now a permanent fixture of American life. When Kansas Republican senator Barbara Freeman heard the news of Khan's execution, she stated: "This is the first terrorist who has received his just punishment since September 11."

Grip stopped. In the corner at Storkyrkobrinken, people gathered around a small table. Four Lithuanians, but only the one in the dirty black hat and neck bandanna caught your attention. He stood behind the table, he with the nimble movements. Already last summer, the police had intervened after someone called, even taken them into the station. But they'd had been obliged to release all four again. "People give us their money, we do not take it, never. We are not thieves."

Three cups on a table—which one hid the ball? *Tchuff, tchuff, tchuff*, the cups shuffled around with the lightning movements of his hands.

Grip had heard they were back this summer. Had to go see them. Stood at the corner opposite, a few steps away from the crowd.

"Put down a tventy, double back if you get right," the man said with an accent in several languages to the audience. The guy in the hat behind the table, and three of his own in the crowd. A note on the table—*tchuff, tchuff, tchuff*. A slight push from behind, or a loud comment at the right moment, enough to distract the bettor's attention: small movements here, bigger gestures there, they even invented little arguments. When the bidding was slow, the three played themselves—*tchuff, tchuff, tchuff*. At those times, it was possible to keep up. Then you thought you could see.

"Amazing," said an American voice when the ball rolled out of the cup in the middle. A short Japanese man raised a hundred in the air and put it down. A real bidder. The tempo changed. *Tchuff, tchuff, tchuff*.

At the baths. In Gramercy. Grip had remained for a moment beneath the steps after Shauna left. By the time he'd climbed up and was heading for the locker room, he'd already put it all behind him. Topeka,

Mary, N., everything had fallen away. Or so he believed. He came to a halt when the thought struck him, and Shauna had already disappeared. He mumbled as he took a few hesitant steps, then turned and walked back. Out to the pool and past the colonnade.

The women's locker room. A little profile of a naked woman on the door. He assumed that they were alone, went inside.

An empty corridor. Farther down he heard water running, moved closer, saw no one but realized she was showering. A door stood wide open in the aisle in front of him, a linen closet. He would just make sure it was her, didn't want to scare anyone, risk making someone upset. One step inside, only to see without being seen through the gap, so he could call out—then put on a towel and come back out again.

The idea that struck him came from his last meeting with N. inside the cell, when N. was so tired and absent, almost confused. That was what he wanted to ask her about.

Grip looked straight into the women's shower room. She was only a few yards away, standing alone with her back to him, her bathing suit lying on a marble bench behind. Nude and almost on tiptoe, she reached around and rinsed out the hair that lay slicked down like a tail at her neck and along her back. White tile and marble, her dark hair. Strong and beautiful.

Like a goddess.

The water streamed, and Grip was hidden, her whole figure framed by the gap.

The nightly interrogations of N. at the end, the FBI's questions about Adderloy, New York, whatever else—it wasn't Shauna who asked the questions. She had people who did it for her, Grip realized that even then. The last time he sat opposite N., he'd murmured, "She came in," but Grip thought it had something to do with traumatic memories from the tsunami. But of course: at the last moment Shauna herself went in, and after that N. had given up. What had they talked about? That was what Grip wanted to ask.

But.

Naturally. She hadn't said anything at all, she had simply appeared in his cell.

N.'s exhausted gaze, like a prayer to die. And Grip had seen his chance, the powdered malaria pills that filled the pen.

The images flowed by, like movie clips. One of N.'s small figures drawn in the newspaper: a cat's narrow eyes. The water poured down in the shower. "Who was it that told us to shoot the pelicans?"

It wasn't only her dark hair that broke up the white of the shower room. The swimsuit was gone; everything about her was exposed. Everything. She was facing away from him, but a pair of eyes looked straight at Grip behind the door. Precisely above her lower back. It was as if the water trickling down her body made it arch. The tail was black and raised to lash, the eyes narrow and gleaming.

The door to the linen closet shut again with a bang. The woman in the shower looked hastily over her shoulder, smiled when she met the maid's gaze, and then turned up the flow again.

A new stack of towels was being brought out to the pool. The maid carried them under one arm, and when she came out the door to the colonnade, she saw the back of a man walking away from her.

"We're closing now."

He didn't answer. A towel around his hips, a toned back.

"Is everything all right?" There was something about his step.

He didn't answer. A moment of light in the gloom, when the door to the men's locker room opened. And the man disappeared.

The feeling of malaise lingered. The maid stood for a moment before she continued away with her stack.


Amazing." The Japanese man at the corner at Storkyrkobrinken was five hundred Swedish crowns poorer. The American woman's husband had lost that and then some. A nudge, a well-timed sneeze, a round of bets in between that someone else had won.

"Just because you've exposed the trick doesn't mean they've committed a crime," said the lawyers who appeared when the Lithuanians were in custody the summer before. "Magic always has an explanation." *Tchuff, tchuff, tchuff.* "People love to be fooled."


A puzzled curse, the ball that rolled from under the wrong cup. The Americans walked away.

Grip looked down at the newspaper. Read again: "Someone described him as smiling when Reza Khan said: 'Now I recognize you.'" At the end of the article, the names of all those present were listed. Grip seethed: Topeka's chief of police, a judge, Khan's lawyer, a few family members of the bank victims, some journalists, and then from the FBI—Grip nodded—Shauna Friedman.

*Tchuff, tchuff, tchuff.*

Grip read again: " . . . he mumbled something heard as 'Fairy.'"

The cups stopped on the table; a hand from the audience about to point hesitated. Grip reeled off quietly: "Fairy, fairy, fairy."

The cup was lifted. Grip stretched and corrected himself. "Mary . . . Mary . . . Mary."